STEALING THE ALPHA'S MATE

ZOE RAY

Stealing the Alpha's Mate by Zoe Ray

Copyright © 2020 by Zoe Ray.

Six Months Ago

"Do I look like a bank to you?"

"Of course not, Jackson. I'm asking for a favor."

"A favor? Jackson, can you drive me to the airport? That's a favor. Friends do favors. I do business, and I'm not in the business of personal loans."

"I understand that, but I was hoping that you'd make an exception."

You have the whole city at your disposal. You have rich and powerful friends. Why come to me?"

"Can you help me or not?"

"I wouldn't be so rude if I were asking for that much money."

"I've done a lot for you, Jackson. You have me to thank for this empire you've built. Things don't have to be as easy as they've been. That can all change."

"What the fuck did you just say to me?"

"I'm sorry Jackson. I didn't mean it. I'm just—"

"Desperate. I think that's the word you're looking for."

"Yeah."

"Don't hang your head friend. Hold it high. That's what you do in the streets. You pretend you have everything together. You're the big man out here. Isn't that right?"

"I do what I have to do, just like you."

"You're nothing like me. You think I don't know that you talk about me with your friends. You tell them what a low-life I am. You condemn me for the things I've done, and then when you're down and out you ask me, the low-life to bail you out."

"I would never say those things about you."

"Don't insult my intelligence."

"I would never."

"My problem with you is that you're a liar. You lie about what you have. You lie about what you do. You lie about who you are, and then you lie about me. I'm the big bad wolf. There's nothing I hate more than a liar. You came to me because you can't stop lying. You want to maintain an image. You don't want your so-called friends to know the truth."

"We all lie. Yourself included. That's why you need me."

"I thought you were smarter than that. I don't need you for anything. I allow you to be the important man you think you are. Don't you ever forget that, and don't you ever forget who the fuck you're talking to."

"Look I didn't mean it like that."

"What's my name?"

"Jackson. I'm sorry."

"What's my name?"

"Jackson Redding."

"Who am I?"

"Red Paw, Alpha of the Bayou City Pack."

"You knew my father well. I'm not him. Your problem is you think we're equals. We're not, and despite my entertaining this ridiculous conversation I won't hesitate to rip out your throat with my bare hands."

"Please forgive me. I understand you're a busy man. Look, Jackson, I know I'm responsible for the mess I'm in, and I would appreciate the loan. Everything you said about me is true, and I'm sorry. If you do this for me, I'll owe you."

"And the truth shall make you free."

"Can you help me?"

"I can."

"I promise I'll pay you back in six months with interest. You have my word."

"There you go lying again. If you were smart you'd walk away."

"I've got it under control."

"I want you to remember how pathetic you are right now. I'm supposed to take the word of a broke, begging, gambling, lying-ass, idiot. Your word doesn't mean shit. I'm giving you a chance to walk away here. I never do that."

"I'm not worried."

"Alright, but we're talking about a seven-figure loan. There's a reason I don't loan money. It's an ugly business that makes me do ugly things. I try to get along with you people, but there's one thing I don't play about, and that's my money."

"Of course. I'd expect nothing less."

"If I loan you money, and you don't pay it back I'll be forced to do some things that you won't like. You need to think long and hard about what you're asking for and what you're willing to lose. Ask yourself if it's worth it, because if I don't get my money back, friend, there will be consequences."

"I understand."

"You don't understand, but you will. Get out of my face. I'll wire the money. You have six months to pay me back. Interest is thirty percent, and I will come to collect."

"Thank you, Jackson. I won't forget this."

"No, you won't."

"Olivia," Jackson calls once he's alone.

"Yes."

"You have the information I asked for."

"Yes, right here. You know you're never going to see that money again."

"I know, but what I'm going to gain will be much more valuable."

"What does this have to do with that?" Olivia points to the folders.

"That'll be all."

"Don't you want to celebrate?"

"Not tonight. I have some things to take care of."

"I'll see you later then."

"Goodnight."

As Olivia closes the door Jackson opens the first folder. "Houston's about to have a problem."

Chapter 1

"Celeste, you're doing such an amazing job." Denise sidles next to Celeste and gives her a side hug.

"Thanks, I'm just having a lucky night," Celeste replies politely patting Denise's hand. Denise isn't fooling anyone. The last thing she wants to do is congratulate Celeste.

So far Celeste made it through her performance with no hiccups. This was one of those rare nights where everything seemed to go perfectly. Her technique was on point during the first act, and it felt like she was flying.

"It's not luck. You've worked hard for this. It's great to see someone like you in the lead role. It's great for the company image."

Celeste looks at the top corner of her dressing room vanity mirror. Underneath the photo of her and her parents, there's a photo of her idol, Misty Copeland. Looking at Denise through the mirror, she's the perfect image of a principal dancer, tall, thin, pale skin, blonde hair, and bright blue eyes. Not only is Denise beautiful, but she's also a gifted dancer. In a perfect world, they could be friends, but Denise is obsessed with competition, and the two women always seem to compete for the same roles.

Celeste doesn't see herself as a threat. She loves ballet and she's worked hard on her technique. Years of extra practice, private lessons, and watching her figure, all to obtain what every dancer wants but none can achieve, perfection. Celeste longs to be a principal dancer at the Houston Ballet. She loves her city and wants to express that love through dance, and while her execution has been described as enchanting, her technique is often criticized. What she lacks, Denise has to offer, perfect technique, but she's criticized for lack of expression.

"What do you mean by someone like me?" Celeste asks Denise.

"I was just thinking what an inspiration you are, women like you and Misty Copeland." Denise points to the photo on the mirror.

"Women like us. What kind of women do you mean? We're both women, just like you, Denise."

"I know that."

"Are you saying I didn't get the role based on my talent?"

"No, I'm always saying how talented you are, and your presence can draw a diverse audience. It's what the company needs."

"I'm sure you know exactly what the company needs."

"The company needs donations. Donations are important, but you already know that."

"Of course they are."

"Your father's donations do a lot to help the company. Some people think that's the reason you got the role, but that's ridiculous."

"My father?"

"You know how people talk. I mean he's one of the company's biggest supporters. It's easy for people to think the company will want to keep him happy, but we all know they wouldn't have given you the lead if you couldn't handle it. Don't pay attention to idle gossip. I don't."

"I need to prepare," Celeste says to Denise.

"See you out there," Denise says.

"I probably won't see you. I'll be busy dancing center stage.

You know how it is when you're dancing the lead. Oh, wait." Celeste gives Denise a sympathetic frown. "Anyway, there's nothing wrong with dancing in the corps, no matter what people say," Celeste says.

As Denise storms out in a huff, Celeste looks into the mirror almost blinded by the bright bulbs meant to highlight imperfections. "Bitch," she says under her breath. It's time for the bun to come undone. The virtuous Marian is about to become a woman. Celeste takes the bobby pins out of her hair and shakes her hair out. Her normally curly locks have been straightened for tonight's performance. She runs her fingers through her silky, tresses and adds some loose waves with a curling iron. Her full lips are coated with a sultry red lipstick and she touches up her flawless brown skin with a bit of powder.

Marcel Creshnov choreographed a breathtaking ballet called Fate. An innocent young princess named Marian falls in love with a commoner named Jared. Their love is forbidden so they must sneak around. Marian is happy with Jared until her birthday arrives she is introduced to her betrothed, a prince from a foreign land whom she detests. Her fate is out of her hands. There's nothing she can do, and she falls into a deep depression. To cheer her up, her handmaiden sneaks her out to meet with her love one last time. They make love for the first time, and something awakens in Marian. She decides she can't live without the man she loves. Her only option is to rebel and leave her kingdom. Unfortunately, she's captured by the prince's guard and forced to return home and marry the prince. With all hope lost Marian decides that she won't be forced to live a life she doesn't want. In a bold protest, she walks down the aisle to her prince and slits her throat with the kingdom watching. Marian decides that her fate is not to marry the prince but to be the one who controls her own life.

The lead, Laura, had gotten injured right before the start of the production which meant one of the understudies would dance the lead role, and as fate would have it, the role went to Celeste. It's the final performance, and Celeste is obsessed with ending the season perfectly. Her family is in the audience, and she wants to make her parents and her city proud.

"Did I just see Denise walking out of here?" her friend Kierra asks poking her head through the dressing room door. Her long black hair is pulled into a tight bun, and she's dressed in a handmaiden costume. Kierra is a dancer in the corps de ballet and was given a solo in tonight's performance.

"What did she want?" Their friend Chase, principal dancer, stands next to Kierra in the doorway flashing his perfect smile. He runs his fingers through his thick dark locks as he waits for an answer.

"Nothing. I have a performance to get through."

Kierra sighs. "Don't let her get in your head. She's just jealous."

"I know. I'm not phased by her." Celeste says.

"Good, because you're killing it," Chase says.

"You're not so bad yourself, for a commoner," Celeste jokes.

"Thank you, princess," Chase says.

"No thank you for making me look good. You're the perfect pas de deux partner." Celeste says.

"Don't give him all the credit," Kierra says.

"Let the lady speak her truth," Chase says.

"You look sexy," Kierra says to Celeste.

"I hope so. I'm about to become a woman."

"Are you trying to look good for the guy that's been eye-fucking you all night?" Chase asks.

"What guy?"

"The one on the first row," Kierra says.

"I try not to look at the audience like that. It's distracting."

"Well, he's fine as hell, and he can't take his eyes off you," Kierra says.

"I'm the lead. He's supposed to be looking at me."

"Not like this," Kierra says.

"Trust me. He wants you," Chase says.

"Y'all are crazy."

"Wait until you see him," Kierra says.

"I'm not looking at some random guy. I have Charles," Celeste says.

"One look at this man, and you'll be saying Charles who."

"Whatever, Kierra. I have to concentrate."

A female voice announces over the backstage speaker. *Celeste and Chase five minute call.*

"It's time. Are you ready?" Chase asks.

The three of them head backstage. Celeste had almost forgotten about Denise's comments until the one-minute call comes over the speaker. Was her presence merely for diversity? Did she get the role because of her father? "I got this," Celeste says to herself.

She squeezes Chase's hand as they run onto the stage. The audience applauds and whistles as they begin their dance. First happy to see one another, but then Marian pulls away, saddened that she won't see Jared again. Chase dances with such power. As Jared, he spins around Marian trying to cheer her up. Marian realizes that she'll never love like this again as she stops Jared and brushes his cheek. They share a kiss and he sways with her to the music. The music slows and their bodies move in perfect harmony. Chase lifts Celeste and she extends her arms and legs as he spins her. The audience applauds as he lowers her into a backbend.

With her head upside down Celeste glances into the audience. A flash of red catches her attention. Were those eyes? Celeste is distracted and misses the beat. She's too slow rising from her dip but quickly recovers. Like a brilliant pas de deux partner Chase instinctively brings Celeste back to the rhythm. Her face turns red. Hopefully, no one noticed. She continues seducing Jared. The music moved through her, and when she faces the audience she looks for the red eyes. There's a man staring at her. His gaze pulls her in, and she's unable to turn away. He licks his lips. He's every bit of sexy that Kierra said. He steals her breath, but Celeste has to force herself to turn away. She concentrates on the music, and on her technique.

Marian is ripped away from the arms of her lover. Celeste uses the anger she feels toward Denise and releases it into her fouettés. Ten enraged turns, but she loses her spot after eight and has to improvise. Landing before the beat, she knows that if she had tried to continue she would've fallen. She recovers like a pro, but she's disappointed. The audience won't know, but she knows, her instructors know, the other dancers know, and Marcel Creshnov knows. She manages to finish the ballet strong. Her death scene is flawless and she hears sniffles in the crowd. She's done her job. She moved them.

The curtain falls, and Celeste takes a deep breath. The dancers in the corps quickly congratulate her before the curtain rises again. Celeste bows to a standing ovation. She smiles graciously, unable to fully enjoy the moment because she can't let go of the mistakes she made.

She looks into the front row. The man with the eyes is gone. She takes the hands of Chase and the prince and walks with them to the front of the stage. She stands back as they bow to applause. After their moment they stand back and Celeste bows. The prince walks offstage and returns with a beautiful arrangement of red roses. They all turn to the corps who takes their bows, and the curtain closes. Everyone gathers around Celeste with praises for her moving performance. They celebrate and hug. The season is over, and they've all done an amazing job. Everyone goes to their dressing rooms to change. As Celeste walks backstage she runs into Denise. They stop but don't speak. Denise looks over Celeste from head to toe and walks away.

Celeste can finally breathe when she closes the door to her dressing room. Her feet hurt and her body aches, but it's a good pain. She leans her head against the door and replays her performance in her mind wondering if she maintained her turnout in the second act. The audience loved her performance, but she can't stop thinking about the fouettés. After banging her head against the wall she changes into a classic, sleeveless black mini dress and slips into a pair of black flats. Kierra and Chase knock on her door.

Celeste walks out of the room and the three of them hug.

"You were amazing," Kierra says.

"You don't have to be nice," Celeste says.

"You were amazing," Chase reiterates.

"I messed up."

"It wasn't a big deal. No one noticed," Kierra says.

"I lost focus during the fouettés. I'm such a klutz."

"I'm not going to let you ruin this," Chase says. "You do this after every performance."

"Enjoy the moment. You killed it."

"Maybe Denise was right. Maybe I got the role because of my father. I clearly don't deserve it."

"Bitch said what?" Kierra asks. "That's it. I'm going to have a word with her."

"Let's go," Chase says.

"No, you're not. I don't need anyone to fight my battles. I was trying so hard to prove her wrong that I messed it up."

"You did not. The audience was moved to tears. Tears," Kierra emphasizes. "Denise couldn't do that in a million years, and she knows it. She's threatened. Everyone knows you're going to be the next principal."

"Now put a smile on that pretty face. You're going to enjoy your moment tonight, or there's going to be some smoke in the city. You hear me?"

Celeste smiles. "I hear you, Chase."

"Now come my dear, your fans await."

They head backstage to say goodnight to the cast and crew. As she hugs one of the dancers, Celeste feels a tap on her shoulder.

She turns around. "Marcel, I'm sorry."

"No, no, you dance beautifully tonight," the older gentleman says. He stands just below Celeste in height, dressed in all black, and his short, salt and pepper hair is freshly cut.

"Thank you," Celeste blushes.

"No, no, thank you. You bring my ballet to life." He kisses her hand and walks off with a wave. Before his exit, he calls out to Celeste. "You come to visit me in Paris sometime, yes?"

"Um, okay," Celeste says.

"See, he wants you to dance for him again." Kierra jumps up and down tugging Celeste's arm.

"Now do you see how great you were? Can you imagine dancing with the Paris Opera Ballet?" Charles asks.

"I like dancing here," Celeste says.

"Well, if Marcel invites you to Paris, your ass needs to go to Paris," Kierra says.

"You're right," Celeste says.

"You were amazing." A pair of strong hands grip Celeste's hips.

"Charles," she beams. She looks into the eyes of the man she loves. "What are you doing here?" She throws her arms around his neck.

"I missed opening night, but I had to see you on stage dancing the lead at least once. I know how much this meant to you." He hands her a bouquet of roses. He wore a black and red striped tie with a black shirt and black slacks. His smooth, dark skin is illuminated by the lights backstage, and he has the most beautiful smile that he reserves for Celeste.

"You should've told me," Celeste says.

"That would've ruined the surprise."

She hugs him again. "I'm so glad you came." She gives him a peck on the lips. "Did you really like it?" Celeste asks.

"I loved it. You were beautiful on stage."

Chase clears his throat prompting Celeste to turn around. "I'm being rude. You remember Kierra, and this is Chase."

Charles shakes Kierra's hand. It's not lost on him that Kierra is less than thrilled to see him. "I'm Charles. It's nice to meet you." He and Chase shake hands.

"I've heard a lot about you," Chase says.

"You too," Charles says.

"As long as Celeste is happy we're happy," Chase gives Charles his most threatening look.

Charles wants to laugh at the thought of being threatened by a male ballerina, but he doesn't want to offend Celeste's friend.

"There's nothing to worry about. Charles is a good man," Celeste says as she grabs his hand.

Kierra rolls her eyes.

"Celeste," her mother shouts.

Celeste freezes and quickly drops Charles's hand. "Mom, dad," she says as her parents approach. She walks toward them, and they open their arms to embrace her.

"Honey, you did such a good job. My baby is so beautiful, and the audience loved you. They loved you." Her mother smoothes Celeste's hair with her hand.

"Thanks, mom."

"That was my baby on that stage. I told everyone on my way back here, everyone."

"She did," my father says.

"Did you like the show, daddy?"

"You did a fine job. We're so proud of you."

"Mr. Emerson, Mrs. Emerson, I'm Charles." Charles extends his hand.

Celeste's parents stare at Charles. They look at his clothes and then at Celeste.

Charles takes his hand back and nods politely.

"Have we met?" Celeste's father Douglas Emerson asks. Douglas is the definition of tall, dark, and handsome in his designer tux.

"Not yet, but it's nice to meet you both," Charles says.

"Who are you, dear?" Celeste's mother, Regina, asks.

It becomes clear that Celeste has never mentioned him to her parents, and Charles has to hide his anger behind a smile. He's not surprised to see that Celeste's parents are as stuck-up as he imagined, but he's determined to gain their trust which is going to be harder than he imagined.

"Charles is a friend," Celeste blurts before Charles can reply. "He came to see the performance tonight."

"That's nice dear," Regina replies. "Did you enjoy the show, Charles?"

"Yes ma'am," Charles answers.

13

There's an awkward silence, and Charles begins to address Celeste's father, but Douglas speaks over him. "Kierra, Chase, wonderful tonight. I hope to see you two at the gala next week."

"Yes sir," Kierra says.

"Wouldn't miss it," Chase says.

Douglas stares at Charles without saying a word.

Charles clears his throat. "Well—"

"Well," Celeste says, but she has no words.

"Why don't we let you all enjoy yourselves? We're going to go," Regina says.

"Thanks so much for coming. Goodnight." Celeste hugs both her parents thankful that they didn't ask any questions.

"That was awkward," Kierra says.

"You didn't want to introduce me to your parents," Charles says to Celeste.

"Of course I did, but this wasn't the time."

"When is the time?"

"Celeste, we'll meet you at the bar," Chase says.

"We can stay if you want?" Kierra says.

"Go ahead. I'll catch up with you."

"Where are y'all going?" Charles asks.

"Celeste, I need to talk to you."

"What is it now?" Celeste asks under her breathe. She turns around. "Madame Sinclair, hi," Celeste greets her instructor.

"Celeste, I have wonderful news. Your performance tonight caught the attention of a donor."

"That's wonderful," Celeste gushes.

"I need to borrow you for a few minutes," Madame Sinclair says.

"Guys, go ahead. I'll catch up."

"Do you want to come with us?" Chase asks Charles.

"No, I'll catch you later." Charles walks away.

Madame Sinclair smiles from ear to ear. She never smiles. "This donor must be something. You're happy."

"This donation will do so much for the company. Do you think you can have a word with the donor just to say thank you?"

"Of course."

Madame Sinclair leads Celeste to the stage. "In here."

Meeting a donor on the stage after a performance seems unorthodox. Madame Sinclair walks off with a wave and no intention of making an introduction. Celeste peeks into the void, wondering if she should take a step forward or walk away.

Chapter 2

The lights are low as Celeste steps onto the stage. There's a click and she's surrounded by a spotlight. "Hello," she says, squinting. "Is anyone here?" The theatre looks intimidating when it's empty. Music swells over the speakers and when Celeste turns around, a man appears in front of her. Celeste gasps as she takes him in.

"I didn't see you there?"

Six feet, five inches of pure sexiness. His thick, muscular body is clothed in a well-tailored blue suit with no tie. The jacket he's wearing can't contain his bulging biceps, and the top button of his crisp, white shirt is undone. He smells like heaven and has the face of an angel, or is it the devil? He clasps his hands and rubs his palms together.

Celeste watches, holding her breath as he circles her, stalking her while holding her gaze. He's a shifter. Celeste can tell by the way his hazel eyes sparkle. He towers over her with light brown skin and brown curly hair. His lips look delectable, his hands are humongous, and Celeste wonders what he can do with those hands as a warm sensation spreads through her body. Her palms sweat and her heart races. Something tells her not to turn her back on him. The sexy stranger isn't coy in the least. He takes in every inch of her body.

His essence is so powerful that Celeste is tempted to cover herself. "Excuse me," she says.

"Celeste," he says. The depth of his voice penetrates her soul.

"That's right," Celeste says. His presence is intimidating, to say the least, and Celeste determines that she should end their peculiar encounter. "On behalf of the Houston Ballet Company, I'd like to thank you for your generous donation. You're helping keep one of the great arts alive, and we appreciate you." Celeste holds out her hand.

"Celeste," he says again. His eyes flash red.

The sound of her name on his lips makes her body shiver. Moisture pools between her legs. Her eyes widen. She clears her throat. "I'm sorry. I didn't get your name."

He shakes her hand, but when Celeste tries to let go he holds on, staring into her eyes.

"Excuse me, I have to go." She turns to walk away, but he gently holds her hand until she's forced to face him again.

"You dance beautifully," he says.

"Thank you. Do you like ballet?"

"No," he says.

"That's odd. Madame Sinclair said you made a rather large donation. What prompted you to do so?"

"Your body is a work of art. I appreciate fine art."

"As I said, thank you. Have a good evening." Celeste removes her hand from his grasp and walks away.

"What are you afraid of?" He stands behind Celeste, inhaling her scent, resisting the urge to move her hair and sink his teeth into her neck.

Celeste can feel his body dangerously close to hers. With each breath, his chest moves up and down against her back, and his manhood is stiff against her backside. Celeste takes a micro-step forward.

"I'm sorry. What was that?"

"What are you afraid of?"

Celeste turns around. "Sir, I don't know you."

"That's going to change. You and I will get to know one another very well."

"That's not possible. I'm a busy woman."

He runs a finger down her arm. "And I'm a busy man."

Celeste jerks her arm. "Who are you?"

"I'll answer your question when you answer mine, but you have to be honest."

"You have the sexy, mysterious stranger act down. I'll give you that," Celeste says.

"I'm pleased that you find me sexy."

"I'm afraid of falling." Celeste changes the subject.

"That makes sense. That's why you don't take risks."

"I take plenty of risks."

"I only know what I saw on stage, and what I see before me. Fear won't allow you to reach your full potential. That's why you hold back."

"I don't appreciate your assumptions. You know nothing about me or about ballet."

"You're afraid of greatness. There's something here, but it scares you." He points between himself and Celeste. "This can be the greatest thing you or I have ever known, but it scares you. You hold back when you dance, because you're afraid of how great you will become, and it cripples you."

"That's absurd."

"What's your dream, Celeste?"

"My dream is to be a principal dancer for the Houston Ballet Company."

"Why?"

"I love ballet, and I love my city."

"Where is the best ballet company in the world? Is it in Houston?"

"No. It's in Paris, The Royal Opera Ballet Company."

"You don't want to dance there?"

"No."

"The city of love, beauty, and culture. You don't want to be the best dancer at the best company? You're not afraid, are you?"

"No. It's just not what I want."

"Interesting."

"It's your turn to answer my question."

"My name is Jackson."

Celeste freezes. A chill runs down her spine. "Jackson who?" She's heard of a wolf shifter named Jackson. Everyone knows of him.

"Jackson Redding."

"Red Paw," Celeste whispers.

"My friends call me Red," he says.

"I can't imagine you have any friends, and I have no desire to be your friend."

He leans his head close to Celeste and growls in her ear. "Being my friend wouldn't be so bad, but you Celeste, are so much more than a friend."

"Why don't you tell me what you're afraid of, Red Paw?"

"I'm afraid we don't have more time." He kisses her soft lips and walks away.

"Hey," Celeste shouts.

Red pauses, but he doesn't turn around.

"You can't do that," Celeste yells.

He resumes his long, confident strides, and Celeste watches until he's out of view. She touches her tingling lips. She's never been so turned on and so furious.

"Who does he think he is?"

On the surface, Houston is like every other city. The rest of the world looks at a map and see's a spot in the state of Texas. The fourth-largest city in the United States with a population of almost 6.5 million is known for opportunities in business, southern charm, and its culture, but in reality, Houston is a world of its own. The maps and facts mean nothing here. Native Houstonians know the city is divided into four territories, the four corners that are governed by their own rules. The mayor and government officials have no power here. They answer to the territory chiefs, the people who actually run the city.

Hate it or love it the city of Houston is dominated by wolf

shifters. That's the way it is, and that's the way it's always been. Wolf shifters run in packs, stake their claim, and take whatever they want. Their weapon of choice is fear. With power and unmatched strength, they terrorize, destroy, and steal, and none is more notorious than Jackson Redding, also known as Red Paw, Chief of the Northwest Territory. The sound of his name strikes fear in the hearts of those who have heard of his ruthlessness. Legend has it he's the only red wolf in the world, and he has special powers. He has the largest pack in the city, and with numbers steadily increasing, so does his control.

Three of the four territories are controlled by shifters, and the fourth is controlled by Douglas Emerson, the most beloved and respected man in Houston. He's a realtor, philanthropist, and Chief of the Southwest Territory. The Southeast is controlled by shifter Jason Blaze, and the Northeast is controlled by shifter, Tate Washington.

There's so much Red wants to say to Celeste, so much he wants to know about her, but he has business to tend to.

CELESTE EMERSON IS MARIAN IN MARCEL CRESHNOV'S FATE.

An oversized banner hangs from the top of the Wortham Theatre. One week prior as Red drove through the bustling streets of Downtown Houston he was captivated by the beautiful face and body displayed on the ad. Celeste had an elegant, almost innocent look about her and he couldn't get the image out of his mind. Determined to see the woman in the photo, he purchased a ticket to his first ballet that day, and when she graced the stage it became overwhelmingly clear why.

First, it was her eyes that appealed to him, then her scent. Her body moved like water. Her passion was addictive, and when she graced the stage for the second act, he was hooked. The timing couldn't be worse, but he had to meet her. The beautiful woman who danced like an angel was his fated mate.

Unfortunately, Red has to put Celeste out of his mind for

the time being. He has a meeting to attend. His pack awaits his arrival outside an old office building in Missouri City. Jason Blaze, Chief of the Southeast Territory uses the building for secret pack meetings, but Red knows all of Jason's secrets. He steps out of his black SUV. His pack is dressed in all black. His leaders walk behind him followed by his warriors in a triangle formation.

As soon as Red steps into the dimly lit room, Jason, alpha of the Southside Pack stands. His pale skin turns red. His wolf is enraged. He slams his hand on the table with a growl. "What the fuck are you doing here, Red? I told you no. We have nothing to discuss."

Pop, pop. With swift hand movements and without warning Red kills Jason with two shots to the head. Jason's body hits the ground with a thud before anyone knows what happened, and Red's nine-millimeter is securely tucked in the back of his pants.

As beta of the Southside Pack, Jason's brother Johnny has to take over immediately. Dread, anger, and heartache hit him all at once, but he can't let Red's actions go unanswered.

Johnny growls. "You can't do that. There are rules. There's a code. Territory Chiefs are off-limits."

Red looks over his shoulder to his left and nods at Olivia, the tall blue-eyed brunette who is his beta.

"Red will only talk to the alpha."

"Thanks to Red our alpha is dead. That means I'm alpha now." Jason turns to Red. "You won't get away with this."

"You're in no position to make threats, alpha," Red says.

Jason knows there's no way he can take Red. With his hands trembling and his heart racing, he observes Red and his men. Red's pack is ready to pounce. "What's this about?" he asks.

"I always thought you were smarter than your brother. I hope I'm not wrong about that. Now that your brother is no longer with us we have business to discuss."

"What business is that?"

"Your brother kept secrets from you. He and I had a deal,

and he couldn't keep up his end of the bargain. Your brother owes me a great deal of money, and when the time came to collect, he couldn't pay."

"You're lying."

"Watch your mouth," Olivia says.

"What do you want?" Johnny asks.

"I made your brother an offer, and he refused. I hope that I'm right, and you're smarter than he is… or was, may he rest in peace."

Olivia pulls out a stack of papers and sits it on the desk in front of Johnny.

"What's this?"

"A contract transferring ownership of your properties and businesses to me. You're an attorney, aren't you? And unbeknownst to your brother, all the family holdings are in the name of a corporation controlled by you. Seems like neither of you can be trusted. You will sign them over to me in exchange for erasing your debt. You will also hand over control of the Southwest Territory to me, and your pack belongs to me. None of you makes a move in this city without my permission."

"I can't do that."

"You can either sign or you can see what happens when you don't. The choice is yours."

Red's pack growls behind him, baring their canines to the remaining six leaders of the Southside Pack.

"I'll sign." Johnny hangs his head knowing he has no choice. They're outnumbered and outmatched.

"Yes, you will," Red says.

"Don't do this. Are you crazy?" one of the leaders asks.

Olivia leaps across the room and pulls the man from his chair placing him in a chokehold. He struggles to break free, but Olivia has the strength of an alpha male.

"Tell your pups to learn their places. Show your alpha some respect." Red says.

Olivia throws a pen on the table in front of Johnny.

Johnny signs the contract, losing his dignity as the pen

leaves the page. Everything his family worked for is gone. Olivia releases the man from her hold and hands the contract to Red.

"You've made a wise decision," Red says as his pack clears a path allowing him to exit. He pauses before leaving the room with the contract in his hands, still facing the door. "Kill them," he says.

"You can't do this," Johnny shouts. His words fall on deaf ears as Red exits the room.

Olivia snaps the neck of the man next to her. His lifeless body drops to the floor. The remaining Southside Pack leaders rise from their seats. The table is pushed over and flipped upside down. The man next to Olivia punches her in the jaw. She laughs, picks him up, and slams his body onto a table leg. The warriors jump into action taking out the remaining members of the Southside Pack, ripping off limbs, breaking bones, and tearing them apart. Blood splatter covers the room and seven bodies lay lifeless and broken on the floor. The Southside Pack is no more.

Olivia howls along with the Bayou City Pack. They celebrate the dismantling of their rivals as Red drives away.

Celeste leaves the Wortham Theatre with that encounter with Red on her mind. She's forced to remind herself that she's happy with Charles, but the spark that she felt from that kiss with Red won't disappear. To her surprise, Charles waits impatiently by her car. His arms are folded over his chest and his legs are crossed as he leans against the driver's side of her blue sedan. He's furious, and guilt eats away at Celeste.

The glaring differences between Charles and Celeste usually go unaddressed, but on nights like this, they can't be ignored. Charles has tried to tell Celeste that she's privileged. Her father protects her and his rich friends from the dark side of Houston. There's a great divide between classes. The rich are untouchable. Shifters don't bother them because they have money and power while the poor are fair game, left to fend for themselves, forced to bend to the mercy of shifters. They're expendable.

According to Charles, Celeste's father is instrumental in the destruction of the lower class, but Celeste won't hear it. She's convinced that her father is some sort of saint who saved the city. The way Douglas Emerson looked at Charles like he wasn't even worth acknowledgment reaffirmed everything he believed to be true about the man.

Celeste wraps her arms around Charles, hoping he'd forgotten about what happened backstage as she ignores the stiffness of his body. "Baby, I'm so glad you came," she says.

Charles steps back.

"What's wrong?" Celeste asks.

"Don't you ever do me like that again."

Celeste is stunned. She expected Charles to be a little agitated, but he's angry.

"I spent money on a fucking ballet ticket for you. Do I look like I watch ballet?"

"I know. I really appreciate it. I could've gotten you some comp tickets."

"This is not about the tickets."

"You're overreacting."

"I don't need this shit."

"What are you talking about?"

Charles paces in front of the car. "You don't do that to me after everything I've done for you. I got another job."

"You quit Mick's?"

"No, I got a second job."

"Why? I already don't see you enough."

"Mick said he'd sell me the auto shop."

"Charles, that's great." Celeste gushes, though she couldn't help but wonder why he'd want that old shop.

"If I save and buckle down, I think I can do it in less than two years."

"Two years?"

"I know it'll be an adjustment, but I thought I could own my own business. Here I am trying to make moves so I can marry you, and you play me like this."

"How much do you think you'll make there?"

24

"Mick has a pretty decent clientele. I know the people of the community, and I know the ins and outs of the business. I'll do well."

"Okay baby I think that's great."

"But that's beside the point. I wanted to do all this shit so I could impress you, and you're embarrassed by me."

"That's not true."

"Why haven't you told your parents about us?"

"I told you it wasn't the right time."

"You're too old to be scared of them, Celeste."

"They'll forbid it."

"Why do you care?"

"My father is Chief of this territory. He has an image to maintain. I can't just embarrass my family. I want to have my parents' blessing when I get married, and I want them to be happy for me."

Charles shakes his head. "So, I'm an embarrassment."

"You know that's not what I mean. I just don't want to fight with them."

"I'm out of here." Charles walks.

Celeste grabs his arm. "Charles, no. I love you."

"Well, tell your father that," he yells.

"Don't be like that."

"I'm not afraid of your father. I welcome the opportunity to speak with the great Chief Emerson."

"If you despise my father so much, what makes you think meeting him is a good idea? Look, I want you to get to know him, the real him, but I can't just spring you on him. I know my father. I have to handle him my way."

Douglas and Regina would be horrified if Celeste brought Charles home. A mechanic from Acres Homes was not the kind of man they wanted their daughter with. For years Celeste dodged their attempts to match her with their idea of a suitable man. Her mother constantly reminded her that she should've been married with kids by now, but Celeste has always been determined to find love on her terms.

"I love you too, but I'm not going to be your secret,"

Charles says.

"You're not a secret."

Charles looks unconvinced.

Celeste takes his hands. "Baby, you're not. I'll tell my parents about us. I promise." Celeste's hands move up Charles's arms.

"Don't do that," he says.

"Baby," she purrs. "I mean it. I'm sorry." She stands on the tips of her toes and nibbles his ear. "I'm going to make it up to you. Can you please forgive me?"

The bulge in his pants pokes her hip. Charles takes Celeste by the waist and pushes her against the car.

Celeste's body tenses with excitement. "I like that," she says.

Charles kisses her neck and chest before kissing her lips with a fiery passion.

They pull apart panting. "Why don't we go hang out with Kierra and Chase? You can get to know my friends better."

"Hang out with the ballet boy and your stuck-up friend. Nah. That's alright."

"Isn't it a step in the right direction? I want you to get to know them."

"What I want is—," Charles slips his hands underneath Celeste's dress heating her skin.

Celeste gasps as he parts her thighs. He kisses her neck as he spreads her lower lips and presses his fingers inside her.

"Do you want to go to my place?" Celeste asks.

"I'm not going to make it to your place. Your pussy is so wet. Did you get that wet for me?"

"Only for you." Celeste takes her car remote from her purse and unlocks the doors. "Get in."

Charles slips into the back seat and pulls his pants below his waist. His throbbing dick shoots straight up. Celeste is excited as he pulls her onto his lap and closes the door. He slides his hips forward and Celeste hikes her dress up as she sinks onto his lap, moaning as their bodies connect.

"Damn baby, you feel so good." Charles's eyes roll back as

Celeste moves her hips and he palms her ass.

Celeste pauses.

"What's wrong baby?"

"Nothing," she lies. Red's face pops into her mind. She tries to fight it, but images of his sexy gaze replaces Charles's face. His hands grabbing her intrigues her, and what a big dick he must have, occupies her mind.

Charles lifts his hips, thrusting into her from underneath.

Celeste cries out as she imagines Red's face again. She holds Charles's face between her palms, staring into his eyes, biting her lip so she can concentrate on him. She wants this moment to be all about him. She moves her hips in circles, squeezing and clenching him. "I love you," she says.

"I love you," Charles says. He lowers the top of her dress and squeezes her breast before taking her nipple into his mouth.

Celeste moans as he sucks and teases her skin. Before she knows it Red is on her mind again. His hazel eyes staring at her before they flash red. She imagines running her fingers through his curly hair and burning desire encompasses her. She alternates bouncing up and down on Charles and sinking onto his lap with eager thrusts. She bites his neck and sucks as she furiously rides him.

Charles's eyes widen. Celeste seems to be possessed. She's never been so wild. "Shit Celeste. What's, oh, what—" Charles can't form words.

She takes his tongue into her mouth, sucking. Her kisses are as wild as her hips. Charles grips the roof of the car and leans his head back thinking he could get used to this.

He tries to stifle his moans, but Celeste is in overdrive.

Celeste can't contain her cries of ecstasy. She had a burst of energy as she comes.

Charles grabs both her breasts holding on, squeezing, and grunting as he explodes. He lifts Celeste off his hips and sits her next to him as creamy white liquid oozes from his dick. Celeste takes his dick in her mouth and sucks the cum from his head. Charles tries to stop his body from convulsing, but as Celeste swallows his cum he loses his mind, grabbing her hair, guiding her head down his shaft.

"That was good," Charles says as they adjust their clothes.

"It was," Celeste agrees thinking that should be enough to make Charles forget why he's angry.

"What got into you tonight?"

"You have that effect on me." She hopes she's not lying. She hopes that this particular performance was all about Charles. She detests Red, and she convinces herself that she only thought about Charles during their encounter. "You want to go to my place?" Celeste asks.

"Why don't we go meet up with your friends?" Charles replies.

"Are you joking?"

"No, let's go before I change my mind."

"Really. Thank you. Thank you. You're going to love them." Celeste smiles from ear to ear.

"I love to see you smile," Charles says.

Charles seems to get along well with her friends. One of the things Celeste loves about him is his ability to connect with people. Chase doesn't have a problem with Charles, and Kierra manages to keep her snarky comments to a minimum. She even laughs at his jokes. As Celeste watches Charles entertain her friends, she thinks about his desire to buy Mick's. She likes that he has goals, but Mick's won't be enough to impress her parents. Their desire is for her to marry a man with family connections. Still, owning Mick's is a step in the right direction.

Celeste tells herself that if Charles buys Mick's that'll be good enough for her, and she'll marry him no matter what her parents or anyone else thinks.

Chapter 3

A grassy hill sits in Hermann Park overlooking a grand outdoor stage with a 1705 seat auditorium. Whether she's performing with the Houston Ballet or watching a classic film while sitting on the hill, Celeste, like many Houstonians, loves to visit Miller Outdoor Theatre. Her parents call it Hippie Hill and wouldn't dare entertain themselves by sitting outdoors in the heat, but they're top donors of the theatre that exposes the city to culture and entertainment free of charge.

Celeste and Charles sit front and center on a red and black checkered blanket at the top of the hill, giving them the best view of the stage. Thankfully they arrived early for Motown Revue Night. The hill is packed and the crowd is eager to hear some good music. Charles plays with her hair, running his fingers through her silky strands as Celeste lays on his lap.

Chase and Kierra find Celeste and Charles in the crowd. They hug and dig into some pizza and wine as the show begins. Celeste sits between Charles's legs with his arms wrapped around her from behind.

The crowd sings along to The Jackson 5, The Supremes, Boyz II Men, Patti LaBelle, Gladys Knight, and more.

"Are you having a good time?" Celeste asks Charles.

"It's cool," Charles says.

"I knew you'd love it."

The show is good, but Charles loves the price more than anything, free. Dating Celeste is expensive, and his wallet is happy to have the night off.

"I'm going to go to the concession stand. Do you guys want anything?" Celeste asks during intermission.

"No," Charles says.

"I'm going to go to the bathroom," Kierra says.

"I'm good," Chase says.

Celeste and Kierra head down the hill together.

"Charles is not so bad when you give him a chance. Admit it," Celeste says to Kierra.

"He's okay, but you two seem to be getting close. You're not supposed to get serious with a guy like that. Have a fling and move on."

"I'm not going to do that. I love him."

"The mechanic? What can he do for you? He's broke."

"He treats me well. That's all that matters."

"That's cute, but there's no way it can work. What will your parents say?"

"I don't care what they say."

"Then why didn't you introduce him to them last week. The tension in the air was thick."

"Who I'm with is none of their business."

"You're Houston royalty. The whole damn city cares who you're with, and you need to think about how Charles fits into that. There's no way it can work, and the sooner you cut him loose, the more heartache you'll save you both."

Celeste tries to ignore Kierra's comments, but she's visibly upset. Kierra hadn't said anything she hadn't thought about before, and that's what was most frustrating.

"I'm sorry Celeste. You know I love you. I'm just looking out for you."

"He's hardworking and loyal. I don't care how much he has. I thought my friends would want me to be happy."

"I do, and if Charles makes you happy, then don't listen to me. I'm sorry okay."

"Whatever."

"I'm going to go to the bathroom. I'll see you back over there."

The line is long which gives Celeste time to think about her relationship with Charles.

"You see that girl over there?" Chase asks Charles breaking an awkward silence. He points to a petite blonde on their right.

"Yeah," Charles replies.

"She's cute, right?" Chase asks.

"Not my type, but yeah." Charles can't help but wonder if Chase wants to know who does her makeup or something.

"She's been flirting with me."

"How?"

"Winking at me, motioning for me to slip away with her."

"Does that bother you?"

"Hell no. She's sexy."

"What?" Charles has a coughing fit.

Chase pats him on the back. "You okay, buddy?"

"Yeah, it just went down the wrong pipe. So you're, you are… into women."

"I'm straight."

"Oh, my bad."

"Don't worry about it. I'm used to people making assumptions about male dancers."

"It's all good."

"Do you think I should try to talk to her?" Chase asks.

"She's with somebody, man. Do you want to be that guy?"

Chase shrugs.

"There's plenty of single women out here. You don't want to get involved in a messy situation."

"You're probably right." Charles doesn't know it, but he's passed Chase's test. He seems to be a decent guy. "Look, I know Celeste cares about you," Chase says.

"I care about her too."

"Good. Don't fuck it up. She's one of the good ones, and if you break her heart I'll have to kick your ass."

"Is that right?"

"It is, and you don't want to be the guy that gets your ass kicked by a ballerina."

Charles laughs. "I got you," he says. "I just want you to know that I know how special Celeste is and I have no intention of fucking it up."

"That's what I want to hear," Chase says.

Though Charles isn't threatened by Chase in the least, he's glad that Celeste has a good friend to look out for her.

"I've been thinking about you."

Celeste freezes. It's Red Paw. His voice is ingrained in her memory and replays in her mind since the night they met. He places his hand on her hip. An electric pulse spreads through her body.

"I know you've been thinking about me," he says.

Celeste turns around and backs away from Red's grip on her waist. She extends her hand.

"Mr. Redding, it's nice to see you again."

"Why so formal?"

"I want to make it clear that our relationship is strictly professional, and you need to keep your hands and your lips to yourself."

"I'm not going to lie to you. I can't do that."

"You'll have to. I have no interest in anything else."

"Your body tells me otherwise."

"My body is over here minding its own business," Celeste says.

"Dilated pupils, rapid heartbeat, hardened nipples. The scent of your arousal is strong. Why do you think that is, Celeste?"

"Mr. Redding the things you're saying are—"

"True," he finishes her sentence.

Celeste looks around. She notices shifters are in their midst dressed in all black. They stand throughout the crowd, but many of them have their eyes on Red. "Friends of yours?" she asks.

"I brought some associates to ensure the safety of the

patrons tonight."

"Is that what you do? Protect the people of the city, because that's not what you're known for."

"That's what I try to do. I am responsible for a territory."

"You're not responsible for this territory. This is my father's territory."

"We have to help one another out when we can. Besides I wouldn't want anything to happen to you."

"There are police here."

"I don't fuck with police. You have me. I'll protect you."

"How can you talk about protection when you're responsible for so much destruction? People fear you more than anything. When people talk about Red Paw no one mentions protection."

"I'm hurt that you think so little of me," Red says. "Be honest, Celeste. Tell me exactly how much destruction I'm responsible for."

Celeste is at a loss for words.

"That's what I thought. You don't know shit about me. I thought we had something special. Have I given you a reason to believe those things?"

"We don't have anything." Celeste makes it to the window of the concession stand. "Can I have some fries?"

The woman behind the window prepares Celeste's order. Red pulls out a big wad of cash and puts a twenty-dollar bill on the counter.

"I can get it," Celeste says.

"Not while I'm around."

"You've already been generous to the company. I can't accept anything else from you."

"It's not a problem. I have plenty of money. What I need is you?"

"I have to go."

"Don't run from this."

"From what? There's nothing to run from."

His finger brushes her cheek.

Celeste closes her eyes as his touch ignites her. She grabs

his hand with the intent of pushing it away, but she can't resist the way her body awakens at the touch of his skin against hers. She thinks about the moment his lips touched hers and fantasizing about him while she was with Charles. "What's happening to me?" she says.

They step away from the concession stand. "Come with me," Red says. His velvety voice is music to Celeste's ears.

"Where?" she asks.

"Let's get out of here." He walks with her. They're close to the crowd but far enough to give them a little privacy.

He presses her back against a tree.

She looks into his intense eyes. "What do you want from me?"

He leans in. His face is an inch from hers. She inhales his masculine scent and feels his power surrounding her, pulling her in. Her lips are drawn to his. First a peck, then undeniable desire. His tongue slips into her mouth. He's been dying to touch her since he saw her laying out her blanket on the hill in those khaki shorts and white tank top. Her skin feels like satin, her thighs are supple. Her breasts are firm. His fingers graze her hardened nipple. Passion pours from his lips. His wolf growls as Celeste kisses him with equal passion, using her free hand to feel his chest and grab his shirt. When she realizes what she's doing she pulls away breathless.

"No. I can't. I can't do this."

Red is unmoved by her panicked behavior.

"Why did you do that? I have a boyfriend. He's here," Celeste says.

"Come with me," Red says.

"Did you hear what I said? I can't do that. Charles is waiting for me. I have to go."

"You don't," Red whispers in her ear. "Don't you want to stay with me?"

"Red," Celeste pleads.

He kisses her neck right above her collarbone, taking his time, teasing the sensitive skin with his tongue. "I'm going to claim you," he whispers.

Celeste drops her fries and grabs the back of his head as his lips work down her chest.

"Red," she whispers.

He kisses her lips.

Her body attaches to his like a magnet. Everything and everyone fades as she slips her hands underneath his shirt. His skin is warm and his body is solid. She sinks her fingers into his back and waist.

"Is that a gun?" she asks pulling away.

"Yes."

"I knew you were trouble."

"You love that shit." Red's desire and his dick swells as his hands roam beneath Celeste's shirt. He unbuttons her shorts in a swift motion and slips his hand inside her panties.

"You're dangerous."

"Come with me," he says in between kisses.

"Where?"

"Home."

Celeste looks at the fire in his eyes. "O—"

The music begins to play. Performers run onto the stage. Kierra has returned from the restroom, and Charles wonders where Celeste is. He calls her cellphone.

Celeste feels her phone vibrate. "Shit," she shouts pushing Red away. "It's Charles." Celeste is horrified. "What am I doing?" she reprimands herself. The phone continues to vibrate. What is she supposed to say to Charles? Dread overcomes her when the phone stops. She fixes her clothes. "I can't," she says to Red. "I have to go." She's angry with him but angrier with herself for the attraction she feels.

"No," Red commands.

"I'm here with Charles. I can't do this. What were you thinking?"

Red begins to speak, but her phone vibrates again.

Celeste dismisses Red as she walks off, answering the call with one hand in her ear to block out the noise as she walks. "Hello."

"Baby, the show started back up. Where are you?"

"I'm coming. The line was long."

Red follows Celeste.

She struggles to hear Charles on the other end. "I came looking for you. I don't see you," Charles says.

"I'm down here."

Red grabs her hand, and she yanks her arm, looking at him with disgust.

"Where?" Charles asks looking around. "Oh, I see you." Charles almost drops his phone when he sees who's standing behind her. "Celeste, let's go," he says. His voice is stern like a parent reprimanding a child. He hurries to her side and grabs her hand.

"Charles," she says.

"What happened?" Charles asks Celeste as Red watches them with intensity.

"I, I—"

Red interrupts her. "She dropped her fries. It was my fault. I made her lose focus. Then my body collided with hers and they fell."

Heat flares on Celeste's cheeks and her ears burn. Her heart races and her throat dries. "I was going to get some more fries," she says.

"I insist on paying. Why don't you go back to where you came from? I'll take care of the lady," Red says to Charles.

"I got it. We don't need your help." Charles grips Celeste and kisses her on the cheek to send Red a message.

Red's wolf growls. "It's not a problem. She'll be in good hands. Isn't that right, Celeste?" Red asks.

Celeste's neck snaps back, looking at Red, pleading with him with her eyes not to say anything.

"She's good. Trust," Charles says.

"Is that right, Celeste? Do you want me to leave you in the hands of this man? I'm not sure his hands are as capable as mine."

"With all due respect, she's taken care of. Thanks for looking out, but I got it from here."

Red touches a lock of hair that hangs in Celeste's face and

36

tucks it behind her ear. She flinches. "Goodnight, Celeste," he says.

Charles watches as Red walks away. "What were you doing talking to him?"

"What do you mean?" Celeste asks.

"That's Red Paw," Charles says. "Don't take anything from him."

"That's Red Paw," Celeste fakes surprise.

"What did he want?" Charles asks.

"He wanted to get me some more fries. That's all."

"This is what I try to tell you. You have no idea what goes on in this city. Stay away from him. Stay away from shifters. Do you understand me?"

"Charles, calm down. It's not like I'm ever going to see him again. You're overreacting."

"Forget the fries. Let's go back." He leads Celeste back up the hill by her hand. Kierra and Chase are waiting. Charles can't fight the feeling that something isn't right, but he convinces himself not to worry. He wanted to punch Red's smug face, but that would've gotten him killed.

"What did you get?" Kierra asks Celeste noticing her hands are empty.

"I had some fries, but I dropped them."

"French fries. What would Madame Sinclair say?"

Celeste tries to act normal. "Neither you nor Madame Sinclair will deprive me of my cheat day," she laughs uncomfortably.

Red stands at the bottom of the hill, listening to Celeste laugh and talk with her friends. He almost had her, but he wouldn't be deterred.

Chapter 4

The music swells into the summer night underneath the elegant tent erected in the heart of downtown Houston. Purple lights can be seen from the distance highlighting the tent for onlookers to admire. Surrounding streets are blocked off and traffic is rerouted. The night's event is invite-only. The annual Emerson Foundation Charity Gala is a splendid affair. No one would expect anything less from Douglas and Regina Emerson.

Celeste looks like a princess in a flowing, lilac gown, a color that compliments her skin tone. Her shoulders are bare, and her hair is pulled back into a neat bun, showcasing her long neck. The dress makes her feel beautiful, the way it moves against her skin held together only by a matching lace belt. The gentle breeze of night air blows the slit open as she walks exposing her long legs.

She and Kierra sip on champagne as they watch partygoers dance and converse. Kierra's long locks are swept up and held together at the top of her head. The stretchy fabric of her black gown hugs her body. She stands a few inches shorter than Celeste with flawless brown skin.

"Have you heard of Red Paw?" Celeste casually asks her friend.

"Of course, I have. Who hasn't?"

"Have you ever met him?"

"No, thankfully."

"What do you think he's like?"

"He's probably the type of man you never want to meet because knowing him means he owns you."

"That sounds a little ridiculous, don't you think?"

"I don't know. Just be glad we don't have to worry about him."

"I met him," Celeste says.

"Really? What does he look like?"

"He's tall and light-skinned. He has curly hair and hazel eyes that turn red."

"I heard he's sexy as hell. I guess it's true."

Celeste shrugs. "He's okay."

"Just okay."

"Yes." Celeste turns her head.

"Don't lie to me, Celeste. You can't even look at me. He must be really fine."

"You saw him too."

"I did?"

"He was at the final performance of the season."

"He was at the ballet?"

"In the front row. We talked."

"Shut up." Kierra's eyes widen with recognition. "He was the guy? What did he want?"

"Honestly, I'm not entirely sure. He donated a lot of money to the company, but something tells me there's more to it."

"Did your boyfriend have a problem with you lusting after a sexy shifter?"

"I wasn't lusting, but Charles did get territorial when he saw me talking to Red. It was very sexy."

"Red? You call him Red?"

"I don't call him anything. He told me to call him Red."

"What else did you two talk about?"

"Nothing."

Kierra gets in Celeste's face.

"What are you doing?" Celeste asks.

"Girl, do you want him?"

"You're being ridiculous."

"Just calling it like I see it. He's a step up from the mechanic."

"Kierra, that's disrespectful."

"Isn't he a mechanic?" Kierra rolls her eyes.

"Charles was raised by a single mother in the hood. He's beating the odds. Mick wanted to keep him out of trouble. He took him under his wing and taught him a trade. You don't know what his life was like, trying to stay out of trouble when that's all that was around him. Plus, he had to take care of his family at a young age."

"I don't need his life story."

"Not everyone grew up like us, Kierra. Charles is a manager. He's a businessman. He's going to buy Mick's."

"Have you ever had sex with a shifter?" Kierra asks changing the subject.

It was clear Kierra didn't care about what Celeste was saying. "No, and keep your voice down. Have you had sex with a shifter?" Celeste asks.

"Yes, where have you been?"

"What do you mean?"

"Everyone knows the sex is amazing."

"How does everyone know that?"

"You think these bored housewives are satisfied by their husbands? Girl please."

"How did I miss that?"

"You were busy turning your nose up at everybody until you met Charles."

"Girl, please. I've had my fair share. I just got tired of these boring, uptight, superficial, know-it-alls."

"So you wanted a thug."

"He's not a thug. Far from it. That's not my type."

"All you had to do was get a shifter side piece, or at least a fuck buddy," Kierra says.

"Well, damn. I guess I didn't get the shifter memo. What's

it like?"

"Unbelievable, I promise you. They're animals."

"Technically they are."

"The growling, the man-handling, the stamina, and the size." Kierra fans herself. "Shit, I need to find me a shifter tonight."

"If it's that good why haven't I ever seen you with one. You've never introduced me to a shifter boyfriend."

"Have you been hiding under a rock? It's not that simple."

"No, I've been dancing. What do you mean?"

"Shifters mate for life. They're good to hook up with, but unless you're their mate, that's all it'll be."

Celeste smiles and nods at partygoers, hoping that no one wants to talk to them. She has no desire to be pulled into a pointless conversation. There are some high tables along the wall. Celeste motions to Kierra to move to one of them.

"I don't spend my time worrying about shifters. I have Charles."

"How many times can Charles make you cum?"

"He gets the job done."

"Sure he does."

"I wonder where my parents are."

"They have guests to tend to, and so do you."

"I'm not in the mood tonight."

"What's wrong?" Kierra asks.

"Leave us."

That voice. Celeste knows Red is behind her. She takes a deep breath as he steps around the table.

"Hello, there," Kierra says.

"Leave us," Red says to Kierra. He's wearing a tailored black suit with a white t-shirt, and now, thanks to Kierra's revelation, all Celeste can think about is what he'd be like in bed.

"Excuse me. I can't leave my friend with someone I don't know," Kierra says.

"Red, do you want me to remove her for you?" A man dressed in all black says. He's standing next to another big man in black. They're both shifters. They must work for Red.

"No, you can remove yourselves," Celeste says. "Let's go, Kierra." She grabs Kierra's arm and they walk away.

"What was that?" Kierra asks.

"That was Red Paw," Celeste says.

"Why is he here?"

"I don't think I want to know."

"I want to know," Kierra says. "He's everything they said and more."

"I didn't get to tell you something."

"Tell me what?"

Celeste looks around. "He kissed me."

"Who? Red Paw?"

Celeste nods.

"How could you not tell me that?"

"You were going on and on about shifter dick and I didn't get a chance to."

"When did this happen?"

"After the show."

"Oh, shit."

"And last night."

"When?" Kierra asks.

"He was at the Motown Revue."

"Does Charles know?"

"Hell no. He knows he was there, but not that we kissed. Could you imagine?"

"How was it?"

"It was rude."

"And."

"There's my baby girl," Celeste and Kierra are interrupted by Douglas and Regina. Douglas is wearing a designer tux and Regina is radiant as usual in a glamorous red gown with a train. Her smile lights up the room, her hair is flowing, and she looks like the queen that she is.

"Hi, daddy. Hi, mom." Celeste gives her parents kisses and hugs.

"You look absolutely beautiful," Regina says as she

smoothes Celeste's hair. She couldn't be prouder of her daughter's good looks and poise.

"Thank you. So do you," Celeste says.

"Good evening, Chief Emerson, Mrs. Emerson," Kierra greets the Emerson's with air kisses.

"Kierra, lovely to see you," Regina says.

"You as well. Your event is amazing, but I'd expect nothing less. The orchestra is spectacular."

"My wife has a gift for planning these things. I'm a blessed man," Douglas says.

Celeste looks at her mother with a loving smile on her face. Her smile fades when she notices Red Paw approaching over her parents' shoulders. "What's he doing here?" Celeste asks.

"Who?" Her father asks.

"Red Paw."

"You mean Jackson Redding. He's a friend," her father says.

"Why are you friends with him?" Celeste asks.

"Chief Emerson, I need to speak with you." Red's expression is serious.

Celeste notices that her father is uncomfortable but he tries to cover it with a smile.

"Jackson, glad you could join us," her father says.

Regina's smile fades, and she clutches her husband's arm.

"Honey, why don't you and Kierra go try the salmon puffs," Douglas says to Celeste.

"Hello Celeste," Red says.

"Do you two know one another?" Douglas asks.

"Nice to see you again," Red says. He takes Celeste's hand and pulls her close. She's once again entranced by his scent as he kisses her cheek. "I don't chase pussy," he says in her ear.

"We don't know one another," Celeste says to her father. "Excuse us." Celeste motions Kierra with her eyes to walk away with her, but Red's grip on her hand is firm, not at all as gentle as he was with her previously. Celeste tries not to make a spectacle as she attempts to snatch her hand from his. She looks at the people around her. Kierra's mouth hangs open.

Her mother's eyes widen with horror, and her father pretends not to notice, but Celeste notices that he won't make eye contact with her or with Red.

"Let go of my hand," Celeste shouts.

"Celeste, dear," her mother says. "Don't cause a scene."

"I can't believe this is happening," Celeste says. She realizes that she can't be too surprised. Shifters get their way, and she can't expect anyone to challenge Red Paw, not even her father, not even on behalf of his daughter. She can't help but wonder why her father calls Red Paw a friend. *Did my father make a deal with Red Paw? Is he the reason we're protected? Why have our paths never crossed before?*

"Jackson, why don't you mingle, and I'll catch up with you in a moment?" Douglas says.

"I'm not here to mingle. We'll talk right now." He releases Celeste's hand.

Celeste has never heard anyone speak to her father this way. "You can't come into my father's event and behave like this," she says.

"I'm not going to repeat myself," Red says.

"Ladies, Jackson and I need to talk. Will you excuse us?" Douglas says.

"Mom, what's going on?" Celeste asks.

"Baby, I don't know," Regina replies. Regina is terrified. Red Paw showing up at their event can't be good. She tries to keep a smile on her face to keep Celeste from worrying, certain that her husband will handle the situation like he always does and everything will be fine.

"Are you okay?" Kierra asks Celeste.

"I'm fine." Celeste keeps her eyes trained on her father and Red as they walk out of the tent. Something doesn't feel right.

"Has that man threatened you?" Celeste asks Regina.

Regina looks at Kierra, then at Celeste. "Of course not, dear. Don't be silly." She plasters a fake smile on her face.

"Mom," Celeste shouts. Regina's not acting like herself, and she's distracted.

"Everything's fine, dear," Regina says.

"Celeste, do you have any idea what's going on?" Kierra asks.

"I need some air," Celeste says.

"I'll come with you," Kierra says.

"Alone," Celeste says. She goes to the bar gets a shot of whiskey, hoping it will calm her, but her leg jumps up and down. She can't stop her fingers from tapping on the bar top. She needs answers.

She heads in the direction of her father and Red. They're standing just outside the tent. Their conversation looks intense. Her father is adamant about something. His hands move in outrage and Red just stands there. They talk calmly. It looks like they're working something out. Her father bows his head. Celeste walks closer, not sure of what she'll do or say. She catches the tail end of their conversation.

Her father looks defeated. "I don't have a choice," he says.

He hands Douglas some papers and a pen, and Douglas signs. Red then hands the papers to a woman dressed in all black. She's tall and serious. She has long brown hair and blue eyes. She's kind of pretty. Celeste can't help but wonder who she is to Red.

They shake hands, and Red pats Douglas on the back like he's a lap dog.

"Is everything okay here?" Celeste asks her father, ignoring Red. Douglas can't look his daughter in the eyes.

"Yes, sweetheart."

"Are you sure? What's going on?" Celeste asks.

"Your father and I were just taking care of some business," Red says.

"What kind of business do you two have?" Celeste asks her father.

"You're about to find out." Red nods at Douglas.

"Come with me, Celeste." Douglas has the most pathetic look on his face.

Celeste's stomach tightens. "Daddy, tell me what's wrong."

"Nothing's wrong. I'm going to make sure you're taken care of, baby girl."

"And so will I," Red says.

"What does that mean?" Celeste asks.

"I need you to trust me." Douglas takes his daughter's hand and leads her to the front of the tent to the stage. Red walks beside her.

Douglas takes the microphone. "Good evening. Can I have your attention please?"

The voices and the noise in the room cease as guests face the stage.

"Can my beautiful wife join us on stage please?"

Regina makes her way to the stage as gracefully as she can and stands beside her husband.

"I want to thank you all for coming to The Emerson Foundation Charity Gala."

Guests applaud.

"I want to thank my beautiful wife for her hard work and the dedication she put into planning this lovely event."

Guests applaud. Regina smiles and waves at the crowd.

"I," Douglas pauses and clears his throat, then nods at Red. "We have an announcement to make. Since our friends, loved ones, and community leaders are here, now is the perfect time to let you all know about some changes."

"What changes?" Celeste asks under her breath. She tries to keep a straight face for the onlookers. She jumps when Red puts his arm around her waist. There are whispers among the crowd.

Red clutches Celeste's side and whispers in her ear. "You will not embarrass me. Do you understand?"

Celeste freezes.

He tightens his grip on her side. "Put your arm around my waist and smile."

She does as Red says.

"Effective immediately, I will no longer hold the title of Chief of the Southwest Territory."

Everyone in the room gasps.

Celeste wants to yell, but Red reminds her of his warning with his grip.

"Please settle down," Douglas urges the confused crowd. "I have wonderful news." He faces Celeste and Red. "Mr. Jackson Redding has proposed to our daughter, Celeste, and they are engaged to be married. Effective immediately, Mr. Redding will take my place as Territory Chief. I know you all have a lot of questions. Please understand that my son-in-law is now the man in charge and I am stepping down to focus on our philanthropic efforts. It's been my honor to serve as your Chief. Thank you."

"Kiss me," Red says.

Celeste pleads with her eyes.

Red looks at her lovingly and caresses her cheek. His touch is surprisingly gentle. Celeste gasps. Her eyes widen in horror as their lips touch. His hands tease the back of her neck as he pries her mouth open with his lips. He takes his time and studies her tongue with his. When Celeste doesn't respond he takes her tongue in his teeth and sucks. He wraps her body in the warmth of his strong arms. A moan escapes her throat as his hands move to her hips, and for a brief moment, Celeste returns his kiss. She's forced to pull away when she remembers what he's done.

The crowd is outraged. Celeste's knees grow weak. She can't breathe. Tears threaten to fall from her eyes. A feeling of dread overcomes her. Her eyes can't focus, and all sound is muted. *What has my father done?*

The Southwest Territory was the last to not be controlled by shifters, now no one knows the fate of the Southwest or the city of Houston. Shouts and cries of disbelief come from the crowd. Red raises his hand. Men wearing all black invade the tent and stand amongst the unsuspecting crowd. Celeste hones in on the brunette with blue eyes standing directly in front of the stage. Who is she? She glares at Celeste with the same look Denise always has. Celeste knows that look well. This woman does not like Celeste. Things become quiet when the guests realize they're surrounded by wolf shifters. Women clutch the arms of their partners and friends. Men struggle to pretend they're not afraid, but fear is all over their faces.

Red grabs the microphone. "Say hello to my pack."

His pack howls and he howls back.

"Thank you, Douglas. You've done well as Territory Chief. Needless to say, things are about to change, but on behalf of myself and my fiancé, I hope these changes will be beneficial for everyone. I'll be reaching out to the community leaders who will keep you all abreast of anything you need to know. For now, the party is over. You may all go home."

Everyone stands still.

"Now," Red says with an eerily calm voice.

His pack ushers the guests out of the tent as they howl and bark and Celeste can see everyone else is just as confused as she is. Kierra is in the crowd with Chase. They call Celeste's name, and Celeste wants to run to them, but Red is holding her. All she can do is wave. She puts on a smile hoping it will stop her friends from worrying about her. She only wants them to get out of the tent safely. Kierra looks over her shoulder as one of Red's men pushes her out of the tent. "I'm okay," Celeste mouths to Kierra with a nod.

"Leave us," Red says. His pack exits the room behind the guests.

"Doug, do something," Regina cries.

"It'll be okay, dear. I need you to come with me," Douglas says. He takes Regina's hand and guides her off the stage while he comforts her.

"Daddy," Celeste cries. "You can't leave me here. Daddy!"

"Celeste," her mother yells. She tries to go to her daughter, but Douglas urges his wife to keep walking. Tortured by shame, he can't bring himself to turn around.

Celeste can hear her mother's sobs as her father ushers her out of the tent.

Chapter 5

This grand ballroom setup now feels like a prison. Celeste and Red are alone. Music plays over the speakers, and Red presses his body against hers.

"I don't know who you think you are, but what you've done is insane," Celeste says.

"Is that so?"

"My father can't make me marry you. No one can."

"Fate has made that choice for you. You'll not only be my wife but my mate."

"Do you think what you did here tonight is okay? Everyone may be afraid of you but I'm not, Red Paw."

"I don't want you to be afraid of me."

She pushes him and backs away. "What do you want?"

"I thought it was clear that I want you."

"You can't have me. I'm not a bargaining tool."

"You're not a bargaining tool. My interest in the territory has nothing to do with you, and my interest in you has nothing to do with the territory."

"You can't just steal my father's territory."

"You are to be my mate, not my mother."

"I will not be your mate. Stop saying that. I don't even know what that means."

"Dance with me, and I'll tell you."

Celeste scowls at him.

"Your curiosity outweighs your temporary dislike for me." He holds his arms open. "Come to Red," he says.

"Hell no," Celeste shouts.

"I don't bite unless you beg me to."

"That's not what I heard."

"What have you heard?"

"That you'll do anything and step over anyone to get your way. You're dangerous and heartless, and cruel. I can't marry a man like that."

"You should know better than anyone not to believe gossip. What if I believed everything I heard about you?"

"What have you heard about me?"

"You're a spoiled brat whose daddy takes care of her. Your parents make all your decisions. You've never had to worry about anything, and can't be bothered to think for yourself."

"Are you calling me stupid?"

"I would never say such a thing about my mate, and I wouldn't believe what people said."

"That's what people think of me? I have a college degree. I'm in dancer. I worked my ass off. I've created a life for myself, one that I wanted. I'm way beyond the point of my parents taking care of me. I take care of myself."

"Fuck what people think. I don't care what anyone thinks, and you shouldn't either. I looked into you. You volunteer in your spare time, and not for attention. You're involved in organizations that have nothing to do with your parents. You love to dance, and pursued it despite your father's objection. He wanted you to take over his business, but you had other dreams, and he eventually came around. I formed my own opinion. I think you're kind and caring, and I suspect you want to start a nonprofit organization. If I had to guess I'd say something for underprivileged children."

"How did you know that? I've never spoken about that to anyone."

"People lie, facts don't. I just paid attention to what was

there."

"The facts couldn't possibly tell you that much."

"They do when you're interested in the subject at hand."

"I don't even know why I'm talking to you right now."

"You want to know if what they say about me is true, and you want a taste of this shifter dick."

"Go fuck yourself."

Red raises an eyebrow. "You find it hard to resist me, but you desperately want to. You're drawn to me whether you like it or not."

Damnit, he's right. "What makes you say that?" Celeste asks.

"I wouldn't be here with you at this moment if the connection we share isn't real. You felt it when our lips touched, didn't you?"

"I felt nothing."

"Don't lie to me, Celeste. I don't like that. What you're feeling, it's powerful, it's consuming, and you want to fight it, but it's not going to go away no matter how you try, because you're my mate, and there's no escaping that."

"What are you talking about?"

"Dance with me, and I'll tell you."

"There's nothing you can say to persuade me."

Red holds his arms open. "I just want to dance."

Celeste is reluctant as she moves closer to him. "One dance, and you'll see there's nothing between us. I understand you think we had a moment, but it was an accident."

Red positions Celeste's hand on his shoulder and her other hand in his palm.

His touch excites her skin, and Celeste is terrified of his magnetic pull and her desire. "Watch your hands," she says.

"Yes, ma'am," he says.

The song playing over the speakers ends and a classic tango instrumental begins.

Celeste is stiff as she makes minimal effort to move.

Red subtlety leads her to the rhythm of the music. "Don't you love the tango?" he asks.

"Explain yourself," Celeste says.

"It's so sensual, so primal." He growls knowing he's tempting her.

Celeste studies him. His posture and frame are perfect. His steps are accurate. He leads the dance like an expert.

"I don't need you to explain tango. Explain what you meant by I'm your mate."

"Dance first."

Celeste slowly relaxes, telling herself that one dance can't hurt and means nothing. Their bodies move together in step and when the beat halts Red dips Celeste with his body pressed to hers. They rise slowly in time with the music, looking into one another's eyes, and glide across the stage floor. Celeste's dress moves along with her body. She moves away from Red and dances to the music as he follows holding out his hand until she takes it and twirls back into his arms. He grabs her neck and trails his palm down her body as she leans back and lifts her leg behind his. She comes back up and he slides her across the floor cheek to cheek holding her thigh. When the beat halts he caresses her leg from ankle to thigh and surprises her with a kiss on her neck. He releases her with another spin and she returns with her back to him. Their arms are spread and he leads from behind. He takes her hand underneath his and explores her body as his hips move against hers. He lifts her by her waist, and she extends her leg into an arabesque as he spins her. They end their dance with Celeste sliding down Red's body, nestled in his arms.

It takes a few moments for her to speak. "How did you do that?" she asks quietly.

"You don't know anything about me," he says.

"I believe you owe me an explanation. I'm listening," she says.

"I'm claiming you tonight," he says.

Celeste laughs.

"I didn't say anything funny. You are the one for me, my mate, my future, the mother of my children."

"That's not how it works."

"That's how it works for wolves. When we find that special someone we mate for life."

"You can't make those decisions on your own. I will be all of those things, but not for you. I have a man, and his name is Charles."

Red growls. "I'm being very patient with you. I've put up with your mouth, your attitude, and your disrespect, but you will never mention him to me again, Celeste. Once you're mine, you're mine."

"He's my reality. I can't be your mate."

"Fate has made that decision for you, and for me as well."

"What does fate have to do with anything?" Celeste asks.

"Fate is why your heartbeat responds to my touch, why you want me so desperately that you're afraid, and why you think you should resist me, but you won't. Our connection is beyond basic comprehension. My kind knows this. We understand what it means to find a mate, the person who completes you, and for me, that's you, Celeste."

"That's not possible. You don't know me."

"Humans need to rationalize everything with your timelines and courtships. You think there's a plan laid out that tells you how things are supposed to happen and when. You need to understand that I'm more than human. I don't need to rationalize the way I feel about you. My wolf knows, and I know. That's all I need."

"Your wolf?"

"He keeps pushing me to take my mate. He urges me when I see you or think of you. I feel it when I touch you. As you can imagine. It's hard to concentrate on anything else. I've waited patiently. Now I need to mate, and I need to do it tonight. There's a full moon, and I can't fight it any longer. I don't want to. I want to take you, feel all of you, mark you, claim you."

"That's your problem. I don't have those feelings, and I can't be your mate or your wife."

"What's fated can't be denied. You want me." He reaches into Celeste's dress and cups her breast. Her heartbeat responds to his touch. "What will I find when I untie your belt, and I will untie your belt. What will I find when your dress falls open? Huh? When my hands explore your pussy, will I find you dripping wet for me?"

Celeste tries to fight the intoxication caused by his voice. "How dare you say that to me?"

"You can't lie to me. I can scent desire, and it seeps from your pores and your pussy."

"That's not desire, it's disgust."

He growls. "Are you sure about that?"

Celeste's knees buckle. "Yes," she whispers as his heavenly scent pulls her in. She tries to stop her desire, but there's something there that she can't fight.

"Say yes again."

"Yes," she says.

He sinks his hands into her ass and kneads. His dick is ready to take off like a rocket. Celeste loses herself in his touch. She didn't realize he was kissing her neck, but when she does every touch of his lips causes her skin to tingle. Red is right about one thing. Celeste is dripping wet. She tells herself it can't be because of him. It must be his kisses, teasing the most sensitive spot on her neck. It must be because his hands are so big and powerful. It's not because she wants him.

Red knows the truth. He knows Celeste wants him as much as he wants her.

"You can't control me," Celeste says.

"I don't have to. Don't listen to me. Listen to your body. You want me to be in control, don't you Celeste?" He sucks her neck. "Have you ever had a man take control, fuck you like an animal, fulfill every carnal desire your body could want?"

"Mmmm."

"You'll beg me to take you over and over again. You'll beg me to take control of your body, and I'm going to write my name on that pussy, because you're mine." He unties the lace belt of the lilac gown. She's lost in the sound of his voice and the touch of his lips on her skin. Her whole body tightens. Her dress falls open, exposing her naked body. Red slides the fabric from her arms and lets the dress drop to the floor.

His eyes flash red as he licks his lips and circles Celeste. Her body is beautiful, and she's everything he imagined.

She covers herself with her hands.

"I want to see you," Red says.

He guides her away from her dress pooled on the floor. His touch is gentle and kind as he peels her hands from her body with no resistance.

Celeste tells herself she wants him to see her. She wants to see his face when he realizes that she's not his.

"Red," she whispers.

"Yes, baby."

"Is it true what they say about the full moon?"

"What do they say?"

"That it makes you feel things, do things."

"You tell me," he says.

"Red," she whispers.

"Close your eyes," Red says.

Celeste closes her eyes.

"Tell me what you want."

"I can't."

"You can. You know exactly what you want. Don't you? You're a woman who knows herself. Tell Red what you want, now."

"Touch me."

"Nothing would give me more pleasure." Red runs his thumb over Celeste's nipple. Her head rolls back, her eyes still closed. He squeezes the nub between his thumb and index finger and twists.

Celeste sucks in air as fire courses through her body. She moans her enjoyment. She grabs his hands and places them palms open at her sides. His hands are so big and warm. They feel so strong. "I want to feel your hands and your lips."

"I want you to look at me," he says.

Celeste opens her eyes as his hands and lips roam her body and neck.

He unzips his pants and pulls out his dick. Celeste can't tear her eyes away. Its beautiful color matches his skin. His length and girth are more than impressive. Celeste's eyes hone in on a throbbing vein that leads to the smooth head. All she can think about is that head pressed against her pussy, paving the way for him to fill her with every inch of his manhood.

"Touch me," he says.

Celeste stares.

He places her hand on his shaft and watches her reaction. "Do you want this alpha dick?"

Celeste can't resist any longer. She wants to feel him. She moves her hand down his length. His skin feels like silk sliding down a steel rod.

He freezes, and then she freezes.

"Don't stop," he whispers. His dick jumps in her hand.

"I shouldn't do this," she says.

Moisture drips from his tip and Celeste's mouth waters. She uses it to coat his head and slides it up and down his shaft as it pours.

"Touch yourself," Red commands.

Celeste obeys, reaching between her legs as she looks into Red's eyes, shocked by how wet she is as she presses two fingers into her pussy. "Mmmm," she moans.

He grabs her hand and sucks her fingers. "I can't wait to feast." He growls as he removes his jacket. His arms are covered in tattoos.

Celeste can't resist helping him remove his shirt. His chest is covered in tattoos. He looks dangerous, and Celeste had no idea she could be so turned on by ink. Her hands roam his chest and arms.

"I'm your fated mate. Do you desire your mate?" he asks.

"I do," she says, and his lips crash into hers. She succumbs fully to her desire, no longer willing to fight this feeling that she's never felt before. Other than dance, she's never wanted anything so desperately, and at this moment she feels compelled to explore it.

"Look at me," he says.

She stares into his hungry eyes.

"My mate calls me Jackson." He slips his finger inside her and Celeste holds on to his shoulders as he presses her g spot over and over. "Whose pussy is this?" he asks. He presses again.

She doesn't want to say it, but it feels so good. "Jackson's," she moans.

"That's a good girl."

After a series of rapid thrusts, her head is spinning.

"Whose pussy is this?" he asks louder.

"Jackson's," she says.

He adds another finger and another series of rapid thrusts. "I can't hear you."

Celeste leans her head back as she cries out, "Jackson."

He squeezes her breast with his free hand and sucks her neck.

"Louder."

"Jackson," she shouts.

"Give yourself to me," he commands.

"I— I—," Celeste doesn't know what to say.

"Give yourself to me," he says.

"How?" she asks.

"Submit your body and your soul to your mate," he says.

Another finger slips inside her. "Oh," she moans biting her lip, digging her nails into Red's skin.

"Will you submit to me?" he asks.

"Yes," Celeste says.

"Who do you belong to?" he asks.

Her breaths are ragged, "Jackson," she shouts.

Red picks her up and her legs wrap around his waist. His pants fall and his gun hits the floor with a loud thud. "Mine," he says as her body attaches to his like metal to a magnet. His dick breaches her lower lips and he pleases himself lapping his tip in her juices. He pauses at her entrance and lowers her as he grunts through gritted teeth. Celeste looks so beautiful, so innocent in his eyes as she holds on to his shoulders.

She closes her eyes and braces herself to take all of Red. "Fuck me," she whispers.

Red howls so loud Celeste swears the whole city can hear. It's the sexiest sound she'd ever heard.

Red sinks Celeste onto his dick. Finally, he feels her warmth, her pussy grips him as he nestles himself deep inside her. Nothing compares to the connection he has with Celeste. It's clear that her body was made for him. He holds her tight and slides her up and down his pole, savoring every second and every nerve-tingling sensation.

"Jackson," she yells digging her fingers into his back.

"Who do you belong to?" he asks.

"I belong to you."

"Tell me you love this dick, Celeste. Let me hear you, Celeste."

Hearing her name on his lips over and over adds to her pleasure. She moves her hips to meet his thrusts.

"Tell me," he says.

"I love this dick," she moans.

"Tell me you're mine."

"I'm yours," she says.

"I couldn't hear you.

"I'm yours," she shouts.

Jackson thrusts his hips and arms driving himself deeper into Celeste "Tell me to mate you," he says as he pounds relentlessly.

Celeste claws at his back never wanting the feeling to end. "Mate me," she screams. "Mate me, Jackson."

"Say it again."

"Mate me."

"Again."

"Mate me."

Red howls as he lowers Celeste to the floor. He lifts her leg over his shoulder and makes her eyes roll back with long, deep, strokes as he kisses her leg. Celeste reaches for him, wanting to feel his body on top of hers. She places her arms around his neck and her legs wrap around his waist as he tortures her with agonizing pleasure. "Is this how you mate?"

"You feel so good to me, Celeste."

"You feel good too."

"I'm about to own this pussy, and once I unleash there's no stopping. There's no turning back."

Celeste lifts her hips and grinds against Red feeling the fulness of his girth.

"Shit, you love this alpha dick, don't you baby?"

Celeste responds with her moans and her body, squeezing her walls as she lifts her hips, gripping Red's dick as she latches onto his neck with her teeth, sucking and biting.

Red moves his neck away from her lips and thrusts into her with fury.

Celeste screams, cursing, moaning, and calling his name. Howling invades her ears, but this time it's not Red howling. His pack responded to his mating call and entered the tent unbeknownst to Celeste. She looks up and sees them watching, dressed in all black, growling and howling. The woman from earlier front and center, her angry blue eyes glaring at Celeste. Celeste instinctively jumps. She wants to flee, but Red holds her in place. He never loses rhythm. He's not at all phased that they're being watched by a room full of people.

Celeste can barely speak, the way he's pounding her, but she can't focus. She panics. "Red," she manages to say. She hits his shoulder trying to get his attention.

"It's okay, Celeste. This is how we mate. They have to witness, so they know that you're mine, baby. It's our way."

"Red," Celeste shouts.

"You feel so good, Celeste. I know you want to cum. Cum for me. Let go. Forget about them, and look into my eyes."

She looks into his beautiful hazel eyes and gets lost in a trance. Euphoric pressure takes over her body. She can't contain her cries. The howling seems distant. All sound fades, and his body is all that matters. Celeste concentrates on his breathing.

He bites his lip. "That's right baby. You feel so good. This pussy is mine and only mine. I won't let anyone get to you. Nobody touches you but me."

She wraps her arms around his head and kisses his lips. Everything feels exciting, dangerous, and at this moment she feels a freedom that she's never felt. She's not worried about anyone's opinion or what she should be or what she should do. She concentrates on Red.

"Tell them whose pussy this is," he shouts. This is the loudest she's heard him speak.

The authority in his voice makes her quake, as she tells them. "Jackson's."

His hand wraps around her neck. Before fear can creep in, Celeste sees the pleasure on his face as he chokes her. He moans, and that excites her. The thought of this big, sexy beast enjoying her body, responding to her body in front of his pack excites her. She tries to catch her breath as she cums again.

"Get on your knees," he says as he flips her around.

She obeys.

She's looking directly into his pack. All eyes are on her. She can't form words as he lowers her head to the ground. She lifts her ass and arches her back as he enters her from behind. He growls as he grabs her hair and jerks her bun until it unravels and her curls pop out. Her hair is wild she throws her ass back at him as he loses control inside her. One hand grabs her hair and the other holding her waist as he thrashes into her, showing no mercy. She screams in delight. Red growls and his pack howls. Celeste tries to steady her hands on the floor. She closes her eyes and blocks out his pack. He releases her hair and grabs both hips as her body begs for more.

He pushes her flat against the ground. His body pressed against hers. His leg is lifted at her side and he slowly moves against her.

"Say it," he says in her ear.

He's told her to say so many things Celeste doesn't know what he's asking for. She just knows this shit feels good as fuck.

He scratches her back, digging into her skin, marking her. The pain only adds to her arousal. "Say it," he commands.

Celeste says the first thing that comes to mind. "Mate me, Jackson."

Every primal instinct Red has unleashed. He's proud. His pack is there to witness his mate enjoying him, begging for him, wanting him. His canines descend. The wolf is ready. He sinks his teeth into Celeste's neck and sucks.

Celeste's head spins. It feels like she's outside her body, watching, unable to speak, unable to do anything other than feel. She's never craved anyone like this. Their bodies become one.

She cums so hard, she thinks she's going to pass out. It feels like fireworks are going off inside her, and Red howls. She feels every bit of his strength when he thrusts into her, claiming her body for himself, making his mark on her pussy.

His growl sounds more like a roar as he circles his hips. He's going to explode. Celeste can feel his pleasure blended with her own. The pressure is too much. He grabs Celeste's hair and pulls her head back. She's afraid he's going to rip her hair off the scalp as he releases into her. Warmth spreads inside her and gushes out of her body as he pounds her. Celeste concentrates on the sound of their bodies slapping together. She can feel his cum sticking to their bodies as she grips the ground.

Red pulls Celeste to his chest and covers her body. "Leave us," he commands. He holds Celeste in his arms.

Celeste molds her body into his. The pack has left the room, and Celeste closes her eyes briefly. When she comes to she's rested in Red's arms. He kisses her lips, and she doesn't resist. She feels him. His touch ignites her in every way. She clings to him, desiring to touch him, feel him, get lost in him.

"What happened?" she asks as they pull apart. Her neck stings. She touches the sensitive spot. When she looks at her fingers and she sees blood, she panics. "What did you do?" she asks.

"I claimed you as my mate."

"What are you saying?"

Red picks up his t-shirt and wipes off his dick. "You begged me to mate you over and over, and that's what I've done."

"Bullshit," Celeste shouts. She can barely move her legs as she tries to stand.

"It's done." Red stands.

"You tricked me."

Red grabs Celeste by the arm as anger rises. "Don't insult me. I won't tolerate it."

"Let me go. I didn't agree to any of this. You're crazy."

"Put your clothes on. Let's go."

"I'm not going anywhere with you." Her head starts spinning. "I can't breathe." She places her hand over her heart and heaves as she tries to catch her breath. "What have I done? Oh, no. What have I done? No, no, no."

"That's not what you were saying earlier."

"You disgust me. How could you do this to me? I don't know you." Celeste feels dizzy. "What have I done? I couldn't have done this. I wouldn't do this to Charles. This isn't happening."

Red grabs her throat and squeezes as rage courses through his body. "Do not mention him again. Am I clear?"

Celeste is terrified of the enraged look in his eyes. She tries to escape his hold, but he's too strong. She scratches at his fingers and tries to pry them off of her neck, but nothing works. She nods as she struggles to breathe.

"As alpha of the Bayou City Pack, chief of this territory, and as your mate, you will not disrespect me again, will you Celeste?"

Celeste shakes her head.

"I can't hear you." He loosens his grip.

"No," she says as tears fall from her eyes.

He releases his hold.

Celeste holds her neck coughing and trying to catch her breath.

"Let's go."

"Go where?"

"Home," he says.

"I can't."

"It's not up for debate. You're my mate. You will move into our home."

Celeste finds a towel near the stage and hesitantly uses it to wipe herself while she tries to think. *I can't go with him. I won't.* "Jackson, I need to get my things. I'm not prepared to go to your home."

"Your things are being packed and moved."

"I need to talk to my parents."

"Your parents can't do anything for you."

"Can I just go to my parents' house? I'd like to spend some time with them."

"It's not like you'll never see them again."

"But this is different. This is a big change for me. I need to speak to them."

"Your parents understand what must happen. Let's go."

"I don't understand," Celeste shouts. "Please, Jackson. Can I talk to my mom? I'm worried about her. I need to make sure my mom is okay? Please."

"No."

Celeste gathers her dress from the floor and wraps it around her body. She looks at the lilac lace belt that lies on the ground. Her eyes are stuck there. She can't move. As her head hangs, tears fall from her eyes and she watches the drops as they splatter against the stage floor. She sobs, covering her eyes with her palms.

"Stop crying," Red commands.

Celeste manages to straighten her body. She tries to be strong, but can't stop the flood of tears. "I'm sorry," she manages to say. "I can't hold it in."

He zips his pants and throws his jacket on over his bare chest, leaving his t-shirt on the ground. He picks up her belt and holds Celeste's dress in place as he secures it.

"Stop crying," he says.

"I can't help it."

"Celeste, that's enough," he says frustrated. Tears don't normally affect Red, but Celeste is his mate and he can't stand to see her cry.

Celeste buries her head in her hands afraid that he'll hit her.

"Get yourself together. You can't behave this way."

Her knees get weak.

Before she can hit the ground, Red catches her and holds her close. Warmth radiates from him, comforting her. He sighs. "I'll take you to your parents. I'll give you a few hours to get your shit together, and I'll pick you up at dawn. Look at me," he says. He tilts her head so they're eye to eye. "I'm not stupid, and you're not going to make a fool out of me. If you try to cross me there will be consequences."

Celeste nods.

Red grabs her hand and leads her to his black SUV. There are two matching vehicles behind his. A man stands next to the door of Red's car. Celeste tries to ignore him as they pass. She's disgusted by the sinister grin on his face.

"Celeste," he says licking his lips.

Celeste's head snaps, but before she can say anything Red stops. Celeste can feel his rage as he releases her hand.

The man shakes his head and takes a few steps back, holding out his arms. Fear paralyzes him as he realizes what he's done. He pleads with Red. "I was just fucking around," he says. "I'm sorry ma'am. I'm sorry, Red."

Celeste feels sorry for him. It looks like he's going to cry. Red's chest moves up and down. His fists are clenched at his sides as he stalks toward the fool.

"Red," Celeste shouts. She doesn't know what he's going to do, but she knows she needs to stop him.

Red hits the man in the throat with the bottom of his fist while everyone watches. There's a loud crack, and the man clutches his throat. He can't talk. A high-pitched whistle is the only sound that escapes his throat. Red watches him struggle before he grabs the man's head and snaps his neck.

Celeste screams as Red walks away, unbothered by the

lifeless body that drops to the floor behind him. She'll never forget the terror in the man's eyes as his body falls. She's never seen a man killed before, and the fact that it happened so close to her shakes her to her core.

"What are you doing?" Celeste shouts.

"Nobody even thinks about fucking my mate. Is that understood?" Red says.

"Yes, alpha," his pack shouts. They sound like an army.

Red opens the car door. "Get in the fucking car," he says.

A shaken Celeste does exactly what he says while she struggles to breathe.

Another man is holding his door open for him as he positions himself in his seat. Celeste's hands shake as she puts on her seatbelt.

Red drives off, and the two cars ride behind them.

"Why did you do that?" Celeste asks. "You didn't have to kill him."

He stares at the road.

"You're a monster just like they say." She rocks in her seat.

His eyes turn to slits.

"Don't ignore me." Celeste gets angry. "Maybe he wouldn't have done that if you hadn't fucked me in front of him. Everybody's not trying to disrespect you. What the fuck is wrong with you?"

"Shut the fuck up," Red says clenching the wheel.

"Jackson, what do you want from me?"

"Don't ask me no more stupid-ass questions."

"I'm just trying to understand."

He doesn't respond.

"It doesn't make sense. You want me to be with you, have your kids. You can have anyone you want."

"I can, and I want you."

"Does this have something to do with my father?"

"No."

They ride in silence. Celeste tries to calm herself and get through to Red.

"How do you know my father?"

"Your father and I had a contract that he broke."

"Tell me about this contract."

He doesn't say anything.

"Jackson," Celeste pleads. "I need to know what's happening. Our territory was supposed to remain under my father's control. People are going to be upset. They'll want answers."

He ignores her pleas and turns the radio up, drowning out Celeste's voice.

"Fuck you," she says under her breath.

The truck comes to a screeching halt. Celeste's body jerks and the seatbelt jerks her back into place. She clutches her chest.

"What the fuck did you say?"

Celeste is speechless.

"What did you just say?"

She didn't think he could hear her. "Nothing," She shakes her head. "Nothing."

"Don't get fucked up in these streets. Watch your fucking mouth."

"I'm sorry."

He resumes driving.

Celeste doesn't attempt to say another word. Soon, they arrive at her parents' house.

"Give me a kiss," Red says.

When their lips touch, the spark is undeniable, but it doesn't outweigh Celeste's hatred. "Thank you," she says.

Red opens Celeste's door and walks her to the front door. "I'll see you in the morning," he says as he rings the bell.

"Celeste," Regina shouts with tears in her eyes. She holds her only child close. "My baby," she cries.

"I'll be back to pick her up," Red says.

When he's gone Regina pulls Celeste inside and cups her face in her palms. "Are you okay? Did he hurt you?" Regina is shaking Celeste, inspecting her as her father stands by. Celeste isn't sure what her mother is looking for, and neither is her mother. She touches her neck where Red bit her. The spot is still sensitive.

Celeste flinches.

"Douglas," Regina cries. "Douglas, look." She shows her husband Celeste's neck.

Celeste isn't sure what the big deal is, but her parents know she's marked and mated to Red Paw, and there's nothing they can do.

Celeste has never seen her father cry. This is the closest he's ever gotten to doing so in her presence. He holds his tears back and pretends that nothing is wrong.

Celeste is unmoved by her parents' weary looks. She has questions but can't bring herself to speak to them. What they feel can't compare to what she's going through at this moment. She removes herself from her mother's grasp and walks across the foyer to the grand staircase and climbs the steps without looking back as her mother calls her name.

Chapter 6

Celeste steps into her old bedroom and slams the door shut. Her old bathroom has a luxurious tub, and it's calling her name. Her movements feel foreign like there's another force propelling her forward. She's on autopilot as she steps into the scalding hot bathwater and settles in. The heat doesn't affect her. She sits with her knees to her chest and stares at the wall.

Things are happening to her and around her, and Celeste feels like she's the only one who doesn't know what's going on. Maybe no one can help her, but she can't help but wish someone would've tried. She realizes how selfish that sounds. She honestly wouldn't want anyone endangering their life for her. She's never felt so lonely in her life.

"Fuck everybody else. I can't count on anybody but myself. Lesson learned."

Celeste grabs a loofa and furiously scrubs her body. "Who am I? I betrayed Charles, and I fucked myself by fucking with that fucking Red." She'd be lying if she said she didn't want him. She was desperate to feel him. She said whatever he wanted her to say, and used her body to please him. It was so stupid, but it felt so good. Her mind is at war with itself. Charles, bless his heart, is a good man and a good lover, and Celeste loves him, but Red penetrates her mind, body, and soul. "I can't believe I fucked him in front of his pack. That's some stupid shit. I would never do something like that."

Thinking about him now, if she wasn't sitting in a tub full of water, she'd be wet all on her own. Her mind replays every thrust, every touch, every kiss. Despite her disdain for the man she wants more, and she wants it now. She drops her loofah and touches her neck. Her body craves Red's touch. She runs her finger softly down her chest until she reaches her breasts. Her hips swirl against the floor of the tub. She grabs both of her breasts and squeezes them together. Electricity spreads throughout her body as she plays with her hardened nipples, moaning as she remembers Red's hands on her body. She lifts her breast to her mouth and flicks her tongue over her nipple, imagining it's Red's tongue as she sucks. Her arousal spikes and she bites. Her hips circle and grind as she imagines she's sitting on his dick, so long, hard, and thick. She opens her legs and massages her clit.

"Jackson," she whispers as she penetrates her flower with her fingers. "Oh shit," she whispers. "Fuck me, Jackson."

The water sloshes as she lifts her hips, pushing her fingers deeper, harder and faster. She doesn't attempt to hide her cries of ecstasy. She no longer cares what anyone thinks. She holds sides of the tub as she cums, living in the glorious feeling until it fades, and she has to catch her breath. Once the moment passes she immediately hates herself. She picks up the loofah and scrubs and scrubs wondering if she'll ever be clean again.

"What's wrong with me?" Tears fall from her eyes. She has to do something, and she doesn't have a lot of time. Red says he's coming for her. He also told her not to try anything, but Celeste is determined not to go home with him.

"I need to hurry. I can't sit here and feel sorry for myself." Celeste puts on a t-shirt and sweatpants with a matching zip-up jacket. She ditches her clutch for a purse that she can carry on her shoulders. She goes into her father's office. His office has the appearance of perfection just like her father. Not a book or a piece of paper out of place. There's a hidden safe behind his mahogany desk hidden by a family portrait, and the code is her birthday.

She opens the door to find some passports, jewelry, and cash. Something looks odd. She thought there was more money in the safe. It doesn't matter. She just needs enough to start over somewhere. She takes some stacks and puts them in her purse. The house phone has been ringing nonstop. Word has gotten around and everyone in the territory wants to know what the fuck is going on, just like Celeste. Someone has some explaining to do, and the time is now.

Celeste heads downstairs with her purse and a duffel bag filled with casual clothes and some toiletries. Her parents wait on a couch downstairs. Celeste is calm as she sits across from them and clasps her hands together looking into their eyes.

"Celeste," her mother begins.

Celeste holds up her hand and Regina closes her mouth. "I don't want to hear your lies. I don't want to hear about your concerns. I want to know what the fuck is going on, and I want to know right now. What is your business with Red Paw?"

"Baby," Douglas starts.

"Don't baby me. I want answers. What happened to our territory?"

"It belongs to Jackson."

"Why?"

"The Southwest Territory has been protected by the Bayou City Pack. Red decided he no longer wants to honor our agreement. He wants control."

"Why?"

"He doesn't like to explain himself," Douglas says.

"So he protects the territory. What do you offer him in return?" Celeste asks.

"I pay him very well," Douglas says.

"Lot's of people pay shifters, but they don't control their territories. You do, or you did, so what was different about your arrangement?" Celeste asks.

"Don't concern yourself with this Celeste."

"How can I not concern myself with it? I'm in the middle of it. Tell me the truth right now."

"The truth is you're not ready for the truth. You think you want to know, but it's best if you don't."

"That doesn't fly anymore. I ignored accusations about you. I thought you were an honorable man. I defended you. You owe me the truth."

"I don't owe you anything. I raised you. I protected you. I took care of you. I gave you the world."

"Then you gave me to that man. I'm not fooled by you anymore. Who are you?"

"Alright, Celeste. Let's get into it. The city had a problem. Shifters were powerful and growing in numbers. The human population felt threatened as both shifters and humans flocked to Houston. They were hated and hunted, and they fought back. Something had to be done. I formed an organization that governed and regulated shifter activity in the city. The shifters had to be given something for their compliance. For there to be order, the city was divided into two territories. One was controlled by shifters and one by humans. As the population continued to grow, shifters became more powerful and more threatening. As the leader of this organization, I had to do something. I had the human connections they needed and if I wanted my organization to maintain order I had to offer them something."

"What did you do?"

"We allowed shifters to conduct their business, their way, and since members of the organization were already in positions of power we used our resources to protect them."

"Who are these people?"

"A network of judges, police, politicians, and business owners, people in high places. This organization covers up their dirt and their crimes, ignores their illegal activities, and helps them move in the shadows as long as they agreed that certain people were off-limits. That's why the world doesn't know what goes on in Houston. We do what we have to do to protect and preserve this city."

"Did you know about this?" Celeste asks her mother.

"She didn't," Douglas says.

"What is this organization called?" Celeste asks.

"The Guardians," Douglas replies.

"So it's true. You and your rich friends are protected. And you let the shifters do what they want to everyone else. How could you do something like that?"

"I did what needed to be done. Someone had to step in. I could either watch the city be destroyed or create a system that worked for everyone. I saved us."

"You profited from people's misfortune. You allowed shifters to terrorize the city. Charles was right about you. This system doesn't work for everyone. It works for you. You betrayed this city. You didn't save it."

"I had two choices. I could watch the city go up in flames, or I could join the winning team. Houston is a thriving city thanks to me. Shifters are the future. I decided to make them my friends, and not my enemies."

"You're a monster."

"This is adulthood, Celeste. Hard choices have to be made, but you wouldn't know anything about that. I made choices so you wouldn't have a care in the world. If you thought about anything other than dancing around in a tutu you'd know all of this."

Regina is ashamed of her husband's confession. She can't even look at her daughter.

"Look at what your choices did, Douglas," Celeste shouts. "Do you think you made things better? Your shifter friends turned on you. What are you going to do now?" Celeste is so disgusted she doesn't even want to call him dad.

"This is just a minor setback," he says.

Celeste is outraged. "A minor setback? What about me? This isn't minor, Douglas. Did you promise me to him? Did you trade your own daughter to that man, for what?"

"Celeste I would never do that? You're my daughter, and I love you. I wouldn't do that."

A single tear falls from Celeste's eye. "What happened

then? You walked away from me. You left me with him," she cries. "You didn't protect me."

"I don't know honey."

"You're going to have to do better than that. I saw your face when you saw him."

"Jackson already controls the Northwest. I made some calls. He recently acquired the Southeast Territory as well. Jason Blaze is dead along with all his advisors. His pack has been dismantled. It's Red Paw. No one knew what he was up to. I guess he wants more. Money and power make people do terrible things. He no longer cares about our agreement. I'm just as surprised as you."

"He now controls three of the four territories? How did your guardian friends allow this to happen? Shouldn't you have seen this coming?"

"Believe me, if there was something I could've done, I would have. He informed me that he was taking over my territory. He told me that if I didn't make the announcement and hand over control he would kill you and your mother. He told me that he'd take over the territory whether I handed it over or not, and he threatened to destroy the gala. If I didn't give up control you can't imagine the kind of destruction he'd cause."

"Did he want to kill me or marry me?"

"What?"

"He told you he wanted to kill me, and he told you he wanted to marry me. Why would he do that?"

"I don't know why he does what he does."

"Why me?"

"I don't know. I guess to keep me under his thumb. He just sprang this on me tonight. I didn't know that you knew him."

"And you just let him do it."

"I didn't have a choice."

"You had two choices, Douglas. You could've said no, or you could've given me to Red. You made your choice, and I didn't have one."

"Would you rather be dead along with everyone we

know?"

"I'd rather you fought for me, your daughter. I'd rather you not be a coward."

"Watch how you talk to me. I'm still your father."

"You're not my father."

"Would you rather he killed me right then? You would've been mourning my death right now instead of yelling at me."

"You said he threatened me and mom."

"He's a threat to us all."

Regina sobs.

"Mom, are you just going to stand by and let this happen?"

"I'm sorry baby," Regina cries.

"Celeste, you are not a victim here. I did what needed to be done, and now you'll have to make a sacrifice. I'm sorry it has to be this way. All our lives are at stake, and you're going to have to suck it up and do what you have to do for the territory and the city. Make Jackson happy. It might not be so bad," Douglas says.

"You're a disappointment," Celeste says.

"I'm being honest with you. We don't have any cards to play here, and being with him is better than sneaking around with that mechanic."

Celeste gasps.

"You thought I didn't know about your little boyfriend. I know everything that happens in this city."

"You didn't know Red was coming for you."

"I did not work my ass off so you could throw your life away. You need to see this through."

"You want me to go back to him?" Celeste asks.

"You have to," Douglas says.

"I don't have to do anything. Your buddy Red Paw fucked me tonight in front of his pack. He had his way with me."

Douglas turns his head and holds up his palm like he doesn't want to hear anymore. "Please," he says.

"Is that hard for you to hear, Douglas? You left me alone with that man. You gave me to him, so you'll listen. He fucked me so good he had me begging for more. When it was over I

74

said something he didn't like and he choked me. I watched him kill a man with his bare hands just moments later. That's who you want me to go back to daddy."

"He promised me he wouldn't hurt you."

"And he's such an honorable man that you believe whatever he says. Is that right?"

"You're smart. I believe you'll be okay. That bite on your neck tells me you're his mate now."

"What do you know about it?"

"He couldn't do it without your permission. Did he force you to say yes?"

Celeste looks at the ground.

"You agreed, so don't come in here yelling at me. You made a choice too. You have to live with it. He won't hurt you. I believe him."

"No, you don't. You believe that if you don't think about it, you won't have to deal with it. I'll just have to live it, and you'll be sitting here in your big house while the city you betrayed suffers." Celeste stands.

"Where are you going?"

"I'm out of here."

"You can't leave."

"Adulthood means I can decide as you said. The way I see it I have two choices. I can stay here and be controlled by Red, or I can leave and take control of my own life. You should try taking control of yours."

"What do you expect us to do?"

"I expect you to do what you've done all these years. Take care of yourself."

"Celeste," Douglas approaches and puts his hand on her shoulder. "I would never do anything to hurt you. I'm trying to protect you."

Celeste kisses her father on the cheek and gives her mother a hug and kiss. "I love you mom," Celeste says.

Her mom squeezes her tight. She holds her face in her hands. "I love you, baby."

"I love you, Celeste," Douglas says.

Celeste grabs a set of keys off the wall rack.

"I love you too," she says as she slams the door shut.

As she drives her father's car with the music turned loud, Celeste doesn't want to think. She just wants to drive. She's leaving Houston and these people behind, but before she does, she has one stop to make.

She knocks, and the door opens.

"Hey, what are you doing here?"

"I'm leaving, and I want you to come with me."

"What are you talking about? Come inside," Charles says.

"I'm leaving this God-forsaken city behind," Celeste says as she crosses the threshold into Charles's apartment.

"Why?"

"I've been living a lie. This whole city is seriously fucked up. No one can save it. I want to go somewhere else, somewhere where I can build a life with you. We can be together. We can get married. I can get a job, and you can open a business. Fuck what my parents think. Let's just go, now."

"What changed your mind?" he asks.

"I found out who my father is. You were right about him all along. He's a liar and a criminal, and I don't want anything to do with him or that life."

Charles is confused by Celeste's urgent desperation. "Okay, calm down. Tell me what happened."

"We don't have time. I can tell you in the car. Are you coming or not?"

"This is not a spur-of-the-moment decision. I have to think about my family and my job. I can't just move to who knows where on a whim."

"You can. You have to," Celeste pleads.

"Why? Tell me what's going on right now."

"My parents promised me to Red Paw. He wants to marry me, and he won't take no for an answer. I want to marry you, and we need to leave. We need to leave now. I love you, and if you love me, let's go."

Charles sits at his tiny dining room table and rests his

forehead in his palms. "You've got to be fucking kidding me," he says.

"I wish I was." Tears fall from Celeste's eyes. "I have to get out of here."

Charles rushes to Celeste and holds her in his arms. "It'll be okay," he says as he kisses her forehead. "Let's go."

Joy and relief overcome Celeste. "Really?"

"Of course, I just want to be with you. I'll keep you safe."

Celeste jumps up and hugs his neck. "Thank you, Charles. Thank you."

He pulls her in for a kiss. Celeste feels like shit hoping that he doesn't notice her hesitation. A few pecks help her return his affection. She betrayed Charles tonight. She knows she shouldn't be there, but she couldn't leave without seeing him, and she can't tell him what I did. The guilt eats away at her, but she's convinced she can get past it, and she will be the best wife Charles could ever hope for.

"Go pack," she says.

Charles goes into his room and comes back minutes later with a backpack and a bag.

"You got everything you need?" Celeste asks.

He looks into her eyes. "I got everything."

Celeste smiles. "I don't deserve you."

"I'm the lucky one," he says.

"Let me get my bags. We'll take your car," Celeste says.

"Where are we going?" he asks.

"I don't care. Anywhere else. You can pick if you want to. Let's just drive."

Charles holds her shaking hand as he drives. "It's going to be okay Celeste. Can we make a quick stop?" he asks.

"I guess, but it has to be quick."

Celeste notices he's driving around downtown Houston. The tent from the gala still sits there. She can't bring herself to look at it with the purple lights still moving across its surface like there's something to celebrate. They stop at Hermann Park. Celeste smiles big. "We were just here yesterday."

"I know, but it's a special place," Charles says.

"You brought me here on our first date."

"That's right. I wanted to do something different, show you something special."

They hold hands and walk thinking about all the moments they shared. "All you showed me was bugs, dirt, and how much my feet could hurt." Celeste laughs.

"Nobody told you to wear those high heels."

"I was trying to look good for you."

"You always look good, Celeste."

"Thank you."

They stop at the lake and sit on the grass looking at the water and the full moon. He holds her close, and she lays her head on his shoulder as they watch the ripples of the water in silence.

"Celeste, I need to ask you something."

Her heart pounds. "Sure."

Charles stands. "When I first met you, I thought there's no way this beautiful girl will give me the time of day. When I got to know you I saw your good heart, and how much you care about people. You're an amazing woman and I saw that the day I brought you here, the day I fell in love, the day I knew you were the woman I wanted to marry." He gets down on one knee.

"Charles," Celeste says.

He pulls a box out of his pocket and opens it. There's a beautiful diamond ring inside. "I'm a lucky man. I don't deserve your love, but I'd be luckier if you'd accept my proposal. Will you marry me, Celeste?"

"Charles, I don't know what to say."

"You said you wanted to get married. Say yes."

Celeste plasters a huge smile on her face. "Yes," she says.

Charles leans in for a kiss. "I love you," he says.

"I love you too."

"What are you going to do about ballet?" he asks.

"I'll figure something out, but we have to go."

"I just wanted to say goodbye to Houston in a special way." He slips the ring on her finger.

"This is special. Let's get out of here."

"Wait." Charles climbs on top of Celeste, kissing her while he rubs her body.

Celeste moves her head to the side. "What are you doing?" she asks.

"I'm celebrating. Why don't you join me?"

"We can celebrate after we leave."

"We can spare a few minutes." Charles kisses her neck. Thankfully it's not the side with the bite mark.

Celeste feels uneasy and downright dirty. She wonders if she made a mistake by going to Charles.

He grips her pants and pulls them over her hips.

"Charles," Celeste tries to form a sentence.

"Yeah, baby."

He lifts her shirt and kisses her stomach.

Celeste struggles to say anything as he works his way down her body. His lips approach her lower lips, and Celeste can't take it. "Charles," she shouts. "Get off me."

Charles is confused. "What's wrong?"

"Nothing, nothing's wrong. Come here."

They kiss, and Charles unbuckles his pants. Celeste moans out of obligation. It's not that it doesn't feel good. She just doesn't feel good about herself. Her body is still sensitive from her encounter with Red. Charles's dick throbs as he positions himself between her legs, oblivious to her hesitation. He rubs his head against her pussy. Celeste is dry. He licks his hand and massages his dick.

"Stop," she yells as he approaches her entrance.

The look in his eyes is determined. He wants Celeste as much as she doesn't want anyone right now.

She pushes his shoulders before he can penetrate her. "Stop, stop, stop," she yells over and over until he realizes what's happening.

"What's wrong? Is everything okay?" He panics looking over her body.

"I can't. I don't want to, not right now."

"Why not?"

"I've been through a lot today. I just need to get out of here. Please," she cries.

"Okay. I'm sorry baby. I didn't think." He kisses her ring. "We can go."

"I love you," she says looking into his eyes. She gives him one last kiss before they leave. This time her heart is in it. She closes her eyes and gives her all because that's what Charles deserves.

"Hello, mate."

A chill runs down Celeste's spine.

Chapter 7

Calm and always controlled, Red exudes dominance. What Celeste doesn't know is how he found her. Her body darts upright, and she struggles to fix her clothes.

"I thought we had an understanding," Red says.

"Excuse me, if you have something to say, you can address me," Charles says.

"You think you can fuck my mate, and I'm going to let you live?" Red asks.

"With all due respect. We're engaged. Celeste is going to be my wife. You need to leave her alone."

"Is that right Celeste?" Red asks.

Celeste hangs her head.

"You're engaged?" Red asks.

"That's right," Charles says.

"Does your fiancé know that you fucked me hours ago? Huh? Look at me," he says.

Celeste struggles to hold her head up, but she looks at Charles.

"Don't lie. It's pathetic," Charles says.

"I don't have to lie. Celeste belongs to me. Did you tell him that I made you cum, made your legs shake? Did you tell him you rode my dick and screamed my name while you begged me to mate you?"

"Stop it," Celeste shouts.

"I mean, you told your father. Why didn't you tell your boyfriend?"

"Charles, let's just get out of here." She grabs his arm.

"Yeah, let's go," Charles says.

"You're not going anywhere with my mate."

"We don't want any trouble," Charles says.

"I tried to do something nice for you, and this is how you repay me," Red says. "This is why I don't do favors. People always fuck over you. Bring your ass here," he says.

Celeste walks toward Red. She can feel his rage, and it's uncontrollable.

Charles grabs her arm. "What are you doing? You're not going anywhere with him."

"I have to," Celeste says in tears.

"He doesn't own you. I'll take care of you," Charles says.

"You can barely take care of yourself. Get the fuck out of here," Red says.

Charles pulls Celeste's arm and walks.

Red growls and Celeste stops in her tracks. The look on his face is savage.

"Charles, get out of here. I'm going with Red." Celeste struggles to break free of Charles's grip.

"The hell you are," Charles says.

"He's right. We fucked. I'm his. I belong to him, and I have to go. It was a mistake coming to you."

"Celeste, what are you saying?"

She looks at Red, then back at Charles. "It's over." She takes off the ring and hands it to Charles. I shouldn't have accepted this. "Jackson, I'm sorry." She heads toward Red.

Charles holds her arm. "I'm not letting you go with him."

Red growls.

Celeste pleads with her eyes. She needs him to understand she's only doing this for his good. "You have to let me go," she says, her voice shaking.

"No," Charles shouts. "Put this fucking ring back on."

Red approaches like a raging bull. He grabs Charles by the neck and throws him to the ground. Celeste winces. Charles struggles to get up. He jumps to his feet and charges at Red, pushing him. Red doesn't budge. He punches Charles in the stomach, then in the face. Blood and spit fly out of his mouth. His head whips around and his body follows.

"Jackson, stop," Celeste yells and pleads but Red is unfazed by her cries. "Charles walk away, please."

Both men square up. Charles refuses to allow Celeste to leave with Red. He swings at Red and misses. "Celeste, run. Get out of here," he shouts.

"No," she shouts.

Charles punches Red in the jaw.

Red punches him in the eye. Charles can barely stand and Red unleashes in a jealous rage, punching him until he falls to the ground, then kicking him repeatedly. Charles looks like a rag doll, bloody and bruised.

"Stop," Celeste pleads, but Red lifts Charles by his shirt and keeps swinging. "Jackson, stop!"

Celeste jumps on Red's back and hits him. "Stop. I'm coming home. Stop, please," she cries.

Red's fury can't be contained. His wolf wants blood. One thing you don't do is mess with a shifter's mate, especially an alpha. He pries Celeste off his back and she falls to the ground.

"Ahhh," she screams.

Red whips around to make sure Celeste isn't hurt.

Charles isn't moving, and he doesn't make a sound.

Celeste picks herself up and runs to Charles, but Red catches her by the hood of her jacket. She removes the jacket from her arms and lunges for Charles.

"Charles, Charles. Can you hear me?" She pushes his body and listens for a sound.

Charles doesn't move.

"Let's go," Red says.

"Charles, please say something."

"Let's go," Red says.

"You killed him," Celeste screams. She unleashes. She runs to Red and jumps on his back, her fists are balled and she hits him as hard as she can. "You killed him," she screams. "I hate you." She continues to hit him. Her arms grow weary, and she realizes she's not doing any damage. Red twists his body to pull her off of him. She smacks him in his head. He stands still with his arms folded over his chest showing Celeste that her efforts are futile. Celeste doesn't care. If she could kill Red, she would. She wants to hurt him. She wants to make him suffer the way he does others. She wishes she had something to stab him in the neck. "Fuck you," she shouts as she pushes the back of his head. She digs her fingers into his eyes. Red finally grabs her hands and flips her body over his head.

"You finished?" he asks once she's planted on the ground.

"No," Celeste shouts. With all her might she strikes him across the face. There's some satisfaction at the sight of his head turning to the side on impact. She braces herself and holds her knuckles to her face unsure of what to expect.

"Let's go," he says.

"You may as well kill me too because I'm not going anywhere with you." Celeste bounces from side to side, ready to fight. She swings when he reaches for her.

He reaches again, and Celeste knocks his hand away. He grabs her hair.

"Ahhh," Celeste yells.

"I'm getting tired of this shit," he says.

"Let me go," she shouts. "I'm not going with you. I hate you."

Red ignores her protests as he drags her through the park by her hair. He releases her with a shove. "Get in the car," he says opening the door.

Celeste takes a deep breath and takes off running in the opposite direction as fast as she can. Determined to get away from him, she runs and doesn't look back. She doesn't know where she's going. She doesn't know what's ahead. She doesn't care if she runs out of breath. She has no plans to stop running. Red doesn't seem to be after her. She feels relieved.

Maybe she can escape him. She finally turns around and her heart sinks. She screams and almost trips but manages to steady herself and keep running. Red is on her heels. A gust of air whips past her. Before she knows it Red is in front of her. He doesn't say anything. He's showing her that she can't get away. Celeste doesn't care. She keeps running.

Red is amused, and Celeste is determined. Suddenly he speeds ahead and disappears into the woods so Celeste can see exactly what his body is capable of.

Celeste stops running once Red disappears from her line of sight. She puts her hands on her knees and attempts to catch her breath. She looks around wondering if she should take off in another direction. Her eyes focus on something moving in the dark. Something heads directly toward her. He growls. Celeste screams. It's a wolf. He stops an inch from her body. His sharp canines are exposed as he growls. His fur is a deep, dark red. His body is more than twice the size of a wolf in the wild. He's a magnificent creature, but Celeste hates him, and it hits her that there's nothing she can do. "Ahhhhh," she yells in frustration. She falls to the ground, pounding her fists into the dirt, tears streaming from her eyes.

The wolf stops growling and whimpers. His fur and his snout brush against Celeste's skin. He licks the side of her face. Celeste holds on to the wolf's neck and buries her face in his fur. Maybe Red is a ruthless bastard, but the wolf cares. Are they two different beings? Celeste feels comfort from the wolf, and she can feel how much he cares for her.

Red shifts and cradles Celeste in his arms. He's naked and he's calm. His dick is erect. *This motherfucker.* Celeste is annoyed. You'd swear he was delicate and innocent the way he comforts her. He eventually rests his head in Celeste's lap and stares up at her.

"I don't understand you," Celeste says defeated, running her fingers through his soft, curly hair.

"No one does," he says.

"I want to. I need to," she says.

"Just hold me," Red says.

Celeste stares into the distance, void of emotion, holding him as he requested, stroking his hair because there's nowhere for her to go, no one who's going to save her, and like it or not he's all she has.

It occurs to Celeste that she's no better than Red. She blames herself for getting Charles killed. She blames herself for getting that man outside the gala killed. She blames herself for sleeping with a monster, and she concludes that she's a monster too. She doesn't know what her fate is after tonight, but she makes a vow to herself that someway, somehow, she'll get away from Red Paw.

Red breaks a long silence and interrupts Celeste's thoughts. "If fate hadn't chosen you as my mate, I would've chosen you myself," he says.

"I'm honored," Celeste says.

"You're beautiful, Celeste. You're smart and feisty. I love that shit."

"I'm also a liar and a cheater. I'm a real catch."

"You fucked up tonight," he says.

"What did you expect? That I'd happily follow you? Did you think I'd thank you for tearing me away from everything I love? Did you think I'd jump into your arms and declare my love? Did you expect me to fall?"

"You think you can get away from me? You can't. I know things are complicated right now. I didn't expect to find you at this point in my life, but here you are."

"I didn't expect to be ripped from everything I know. You did that too."

"One day you'll understand."

"I don't see that happening."

"I heard you call my name," he says.

"When? While you killed my fiancé?"

"When you were at your parent's house. Maybe you were alone. I assume you were." His voice is so deep and sexy. "What were you doing Celeste?" Red asks. "I smelled rosemary. What were you doing? Were you taking a bath? Were you trying to wash away what we shared? But you couldn't, could you?"

"That's enough," Celeste says.

"I could scent your desire. I heard your moans. I felt your body calling mine. That's how strong what we have is. I wanted to burst in the house and take care of your need." His dick twitches. "I heard you whisper my name. What did you say?" He grabs his dick and strokes himself.

Celeste looks at the stars.

"What did you say, Celeste?"

"I said —"

"What did you say?"

"I said fuck me, Jackson."

"You said fuck me, Jackson."

"How do you know that?"

"Shifters can hear very well."

"That explains a lot."

"Did you enjoy fucking me, Celeste?"

"I think you know the answer to that."

"Did you enjoy fucking me, Celeste?"

The floodgates open again. Celeste refuses to answer.

"You want me right now. Don't you? Can you feel how much I want you? I know you feel it."

Celeste realizes that she's felt what he was feeling more than once tonight. "Does that happen when you're a shifter?" she asks.

"Yes, we can sense emotion. We can scent pheromones. We can also detect deception. You can sense what I'm feeling because we're mates. We're connected, love, whether you like it or not, and I wanted to believe you even though I knew you were lying. I wanted desperately to trust you, my mate, but I can't, and that hurts. Didn't I tell you there'd be consequences?"

"You did."

"You'll come home with me. You'll stay on the grounds, and you won't be allowed to leave."

"That's so romantic. So far, you've been a superb mate. Thank you for this experience."

"What should I do? You betrayed me," he says.

"And you're punishing me?"

"Well, that's because of your choices, Celeste."

"What did you expect me to do?"

"I expect you to be a loyal mate, and if you can do that, maybe things will be different."

"What about you?"

"What about me?"

"What's your punishment Red?"

"What?" he asks.

"You could've said something to me. You could've talked to me. You could've given me a choice, but you imposed your will on me. You betrayed me and my family. You should be punished. What's your punishment?"

"I tried to talk to you. You walked away from me."

"You didn't try hard enough. You ambushed my family and friends with your demands. Why would I listen to anything you said? Why wouldn't I try to get away? You weren't loyal to your mate. What's your punishment, Red?"

"My punishment? Ha," he says. He pulls Celeste's face to his. "I've been a bad wolf. I get no head tonight."

He gets off the ground and runs off, returning seconds later with his clothes. Once he's dressed in his jeans and t-shirt he carries Celeste to the car. They ride in silence to his home.

Red resides in a palatial estate with everything one can imagine. He has swimming pools, a gym, tennis and basketball courts, a sauna, a theatre, and much more.

"How much money do you have, mate?" Celeste asks.

Strolling the grounds, walking beneath the moonlight, someone on the outside looking in would think it's romantic.

"Enough," he replies.

"How did you get it?"

"Hard work and dedication," he says.

"I'm exhausted. Can I see the rest later?" Celeste asks.

"Let me take you to your room."

"My room? Won't we both be in your room?"

They walk into the house in silence greeted by the staff.

After a trying day, Celeste can barely keep her eyes open. Red carries her over his broad shoulders up the stairs to the bedroom.

"This is our room," he says as he stands her on the floor. "I haven't had time to get it completely ready for you, but your clothes are in the closet. Let me or the staff know whatever you need. I'll make it happen."

"Am I supposed to be impressed?"

"You're supposed to show me some respect. Watch your fucking mouth."

"Could you not talk to me like that please?"

"Your mouth is reckless."

"Fine. I'll do better, and I hope you will too. I don't want this to be any worse than it has to be, and I don't need you cursing me out every day. Can we at least agree to respect one another?" Celeste extends her hand so they can shake on it.

"Take your clothes off," he says.

"No."

He growls.

"Is that how you respond to everything?"

Red picks Celeste up and lays her on the bed. He's surprisingly gentle.

Celeste turns her head to the side as he peels his clothes off and then hers. He removes her shoes and works his way up, removing her pants, shirt, and jacket. The warmth of a blanket covers her. The lights go out, and Red lays next to Celeste, looking at the ceiling. Though Celeste is exhausted she can't seem to fall asleep.

"Red," she whispers.

"Yes," he replies.

"Can I ask you for something?"

"Yes."

"Can you hold me?"

He gets under the covers and wraps his humongous body around hers, and Celeste settles into his arms. There's so much he wishes he could say to her. Celeste doesn't understand what it's like to be a man, to be a wolf shifter, to be an alpha.

There's no way she can know how much he cares for her or how complicated his life is. He's done irreparable damage to his mate, and that was never his intention. With Celeste finally asleep in the warmth of his arms, he listens to her breathing and he makes her a promise. "You're safe with me."

Celeste awakens after a quick nap to the sound of Red snoring. He squeezes her tight, instinctively holding her close. "Celeste," he says.

"What is it?" she says.

"Celeste," he says.

"Jackson, what?"

"Stop," he says.

Red talks in his sleep.

"Don't go."

"Seriously," she says to herself. The big bad alpha is begging her to stay, holding on to her for dear life. She closes her eyes and breathes with him, allowing herself to feel his feelings, trying to understand her opponent. She picks up on something deeper than the carnal attraction they share. There's a longing, a need, there's something genuine and warm. Celeste opens her eyes in panic as she wonders. *Is that love?*

Chapter 8

Celeste awakens in Red's arms with her head on his chest and traces his tattoos with her finger. His morning wood rises, poking her stomach, and her body lusts for him. She peeks at his face and he's still asleep. Flashbacks of their bodies intertwined play in her mind, she turns her body so her back is against his front and his wood pokes her behind. She wraps his arms around her body. He holds her close and resumes snoring. She backs her body closer to his, leans forward, and pokes her ass out telling herself she's trying to get comfortable but all she gets is frustrated. No matter what movements she makes he won't wake up and stick her with his dick like her body craves. She flips her body and looks at the ceiling.

As Red awakens, Celeste stretches as he stretches, repositioning herself against him once again.

Red rises from bed without a word and walks into the bathroom.

Celeste can hear the water running as he brushes his teeth and washes his face. He emerges some time later showered, shaved, and sexy as sin.

"Are you going somewhere?" Celeste asks.

Red walks into the closet and picks out some clothes, black jeans, and a button-down blue shirt.

"Red," Celeste calls.

He doesn't answer. He grabs some shoes and socks and sits on the edge of the bed.

Celeste sits up. "Where are you going?"

Red doesn't say anything.

"Do you hear me talking to you? Hello? Jackson? You're not talking to me? What the hell?"

"I have shit to do," Red says as he walks out the door.

"Don't leave me," she pleads.

The door closes.

Celeste throws a pillow at the door. She's confused, to say the least. He turned cold. That's not the man that held her last night. She thought she could reason with him. She thought he had affection for her. "Fuck him," Celeste says. Anger courses through her veins as she climbs out of bed and gets dressed in a simple white t-shirt and blue jeans.

For a moment she thinks about Charles. He was the only one who stood up for her. What was he thinking? He must've known he couldn't take on Red. He's the one who told Celeste how dangerous Red was. Charles didn't have to die. He tried to be her hero, but she betrayed him, and now he's gone. The only way to get through this is to be strong, which means letting go and when she gets away she'll find a way to honor Charles and take care of his family. It'll be the least she can do. "I'm sorry Charles," she says quietly knowing that if the roles were reversed he'd never put her out of his mind.

Grief and guilt overcome Celeste. She turns out the light and climbs back into Red's gigantic bed with luxurious sheets, hugging a pillow that curves to her body, unable to fight her tears until she falls asleep. She'll have to be strong tomorrow.

Howls and cheers greet Red as he steps into his warehouse. His pack congratulates him on finding his mate. He says thank you and shakes hands as he walks into his office.

Olivia follows. Her long hair swishes side to side in a slicked-back ponytail as she stomps behind Red. "Why didn't you tell me?" she asks as she closes the door.

"You knew about my plan to take the Southwest."

"I didn't know you planned to take a mate. Something tells me it wasn't a surprise to you."

"You're my oldest friend. Aren't you happy for me?"

"As your friend I'm concerned. What were you thinking?"

"Tread carefully Olivia."

"You mated a fucking ballerina. Seriously? Don't you think you should've discussed that with me?"

"I don't think it has anything to do with you."

"She can't be the right mate for you. What about the pack? She has nothing to offer."

"She'll be good for the pack and with our newly acquired territories, she'll be instrumental in gathering the support of people of the city. It'll be a lot easier to be in charge if I have their beloved princess at my side. They won't perceive my actions as hostile, just a father-in-law passing the torch."

"Are you saying it's a mating of convenience?"

"I don't answer to you, Olivia. Celeste is my mate. Period. You need to respect that."

"Your mate should be an alpha female, someone who understands our ways and can help you lead the pack."

"This is not up for debate. If you can't accept it, you can leave."

"You would choose her over me?"

"I hope I don't have to. I need you now more than ever."

"Exactly." Olivia is happy to hear Red admit that he needs her. "We have to prepare if we're going to take down Tate Washington. You don't need the distraction."

"Trust me. Nothing is going to get in the way of me giving Tate what he deserves. It's been a long time coming."

"I'm glad you haven't lost your edge. What do you need me to do?"

"I need you to keep an eye on Celeste."

"You've got to be kidding me, Red."

"Someone needs to protect her when I'm not there and there's no one I trust more than you."

"I can't babysit the ballerina. I need to be by your side, watching your back. It's my duty."

"Your duty is to do what I tell you. Is that going to be a problem?"

"No, Red."

"You will guard her at all times. She goes nowhere without my permission, and no one gets to her."

Olivia rolls her eyes. "Understood."

There's a knock on the door.

"Come in," Red says.

The door opens. It's Tasha, the short, curvy, thirsty chick that thinks her job in the pack is throwing herself at Red.

"What do you want?" Olivia says.

"Good to see you too, Olivia," Tasha says.

"We're busy," Olivia says.

"I'll be quick." Tasha saunters to Red's desk. "I heard you mated. Congratulations."

"Thank you, Tasha."

"I'd be lying if I said I wasn't disappointed. We had some good times."

"We did."

"Our arrangement doesn't have to end." She touches his hand. "I'm available whenever my alpha needs me."

"I'll keep that in mind," Red says.

Tasha flips her hair and smiles at Red then walks away. She winks at Olivia, and Olivia growls.

"Still got it," Red says when the door closes.

"Ugh," Olivia says. "Why didn't you put her in her place?"

"It's just harmless flirting."

"If you were my mate, I'd want you to shut that shit down immediately."

"Chill, Olivia."

"How long do I have to babysit?"

"Until things settle down. You can get to know Celeste. Maybe you two can be friends."

"That'll never happen."

"Don't be a snob."

"We have nothing in common. I'm a fighter. She only cares about hair and makeup and twirling on a stage."

"There's more to her than dancing just like there's more to you than fighting."

"Why are you even here?" Olivia asks.

"I have work to do."

"It's Sunday. Shouldn't you be enjoying being mated? Is there trouble in paradise already?"

"Celeste lost someone she cares about. She's grieving."

"Shouldn't you be there with her?"

"That'll be all."

Olivia leaves Red's office.

Red stares into the distance thinking about Celeste. Things hadn't exactly gone as planned and instead of enjoying his mate, he struggles internally.

Later Celeste is awakened by a knock on the bedroom door. She doesn't bother to move or respond.

"Miss Celeste."

She hears a man's voice and ignores him.

"Miss Celeste it's Harrison. I'm the chef. I brought you something to eat. Can you open the door?"

Celeste listens to Harrison asking her over and over to open the door until he gives up. When the knocking stops she turns over and covers her head with the blanket until she cries herself to sleep once again.

She doesn't know what time it is when Red comes home, but she knows it's late when the bedroom door creaks open.

Red enters the room quietly. Celeste isn't asleep as evident by her heartbeat. She's holding her breath. He carefully removes his clothes and climbs into bed. He stares at the ceiling until Celeste falls asleep and he can do the same.

The next day before sunrise Red leaves without a word while Celeste is still asleep.

Celeste is awakened by a knock on the door.

"Miss Celeste, I have breakfast for you," Harrison says.

Once again Celeste remains quiet and Harrison leaves.

Harrison makes a few more attempts throughout the day, but Celeste continues to ignore him. She's cried so much her head is pounding and she's weak. She hasn't changed clothes.

She's barely moved and she's alone. All she can do is clutch the pillow that's weighed down with her tears.

The next day is the same, and Harrison knocks on the door again.

Once again Celeste doesn't answer. This time a determined Harrison opens the door and steps inside to find Celeste lying in bed.

He turns on the lights.

Celeste opens her eyes.

"No need to be scared, Miss Celeste. I'm Harrison, the chef." The older gentleman with salt and pepper hair and cinnamon skin wears a black chef coat and pants and smiles at her holding a tray. "I brought you some food."

"I'm not hungry," Celeste says.

"You have to be hungry. You haven't eaten a thing in days."

The heavenly scent of food fills the room and Celeste's stomach growls. "I'm fine. Thank you."

"Now you and I both know that's not true. Why don't you eat something?"

"I don't need anything to eat. Could you please leave me alone?" Celeste asks.

"I can't do that. I've been slaving over a hot stove. You wouldn't want all my hard work to go to waste now would you."

"Does it matter what I say?" Celeste asks.

"No ma'am, it does not. I'm afraid I can't leave your room until I see you eat with my own eyes. Go on now. Sit up."

Celeste sits up with her back against the headboard and Harrison sits a tray on her lap and unfolds the sides. "I can't eat this," Celeste says.

"I won't accept that. Do you have allergies?"

"No."

"Do you have any medical conditions?"

"No, but I have to watch my figure. I'm a ballet dancer."

"I'll create some menus tailored to your needs, Miss Celeste. In the meantime, you're going to eat what I have here for you."

"But—"

"No buts. Eat."

Celeste stares at the southern fried chicken, macaroni and cheese, greens, and potatoes. Her mouth waters.

"Nothing like some good old soul food," Harrison says.

Celeste takes the fork in her hand, stares into the distance, and drops it on the plate.

Harrison picks up the fork and sinks it into the greens. He holds the fork to Celeste's mouth.

She stares at the fork in front of her face before she opens her mouth and takes a bite. The savory flavor bursts into her mouth. "Ummm," she says.

"Ha, ha," Harrison says victorious as he feeds her another bite. "You like that, don't you?"

"This is delicious," Celeste says as she picks up a chicken leg and takes a bite. "Oh my God," she says as she chews. Her appetite kicks in with every bite, and she takes the fork from Harrison and tastes everything on her plate.

"Now you eat up, Miss Celeste. You're going to need your strength. You hear me."

Celeste nods as she eats and her body awakens.

"Thank you," she says.

"No problem."

"How did you learn to cook like this?"

"Growing up in the south and then culinary school."

Celeste coughs.

"Let me get you some water." Harrison leaves and comes back with ice water and hands the glass to Celeste."

She drinks it all at once, realizing that she hasn't had water in days.

"Take your time," Harrison says.

Celeste nods.

"Now Miss Celeste, you're going to have to pull yourself together now, okay. This world ain't going to stop spinning. You hear me?"

"Yes, sir."

Harrison watches Celeste until she finishes the last bite on her plate. "Now your belly is full. It's time to get up out of this here bed and fix yourself up. You can't stay in here forever. Whatever has you down, you can't let it take you out. You hear?" He holds up her chin.

Celeste nods.

"Now I don't want to have to come in here again."

"Okay."

"Alright now. Old Harrison is going to get going."

"Thank you, Harrison."

Celeste stretches once Harrison leaves the room. He's right. She needs to get herself together. She gets out of bed and takes a shower. The warm water soothes her skin and eases her mind as she washes her hair and cleanses her body. Red really did have her things moved to his house. She closes her eyes and inhales the fresh scent of her lotion as she applies it all over her body. She looks at herself in the mirror wondering who's looking back at her.

She applies leave-in conditioner and styling cream to her hair and lets it air dry, and she puts on some leggings and a camisole. Her jewelry box sits on top of Red's dresser. She opens it and pulls out a silver chain with pointe shoes dangling from a diamond. She attaches the necklace to her neck before she walks out of the bedroom for the first time.

The house looks bigger than she remembers. There's a man sitting in one of the rooms playing video games. He doesn't say anything when Celeste walks by. She continues to walk around the house, peeking into the rooms.

"There she is. Finally decided to grace us with your presence, princess?"

"Excuse me," Celeste says as she turns around. She recognizes the woman's face but doesn't know her name. "Who are you?" she asks.

"My name is Olivia."

"Olivia, you have such beautiful eyes," Celeste says.

Olivia is caught off guard by Celeste's compliment. "You've been locked in your room for a while. I thought you

98

were dead."

"Nope. Still kicking. I was just looking around."

"Do me a favor and stay out of my way. Don't do anything stupid, and we won't have a problem."

"Why do you care what I do?"

"I've been tasked with keeping an eye on you."

"Aren't I lucky?"

"Just make sure you stay on the grounds."

"Or what?"

Olivia growls. "Or you'll have to answer to me."

"Who are you exactly?"

"Red and I are as close as two people can be. I'm beta of the Bayou City Pack, and you can't imagine the things I'm capable of." Olivia walks past Celeste pushing her shoulder with her body as she passes. The ponytail in her hair swishes from side to side.

"It was nice meeting you too," Celeste says.

She continues her self-guided tour and finds the gym. The room has mirrors which is great. The floors are not ideal, but they'll do. The only thing she needs is a barre. She clutches her necklace and takes off her tennis shoes. She lays on the floor and stretches. With everything that happened her body is begging to dance. She alternates her legs, bending her knees to her chest and extends, pointing her toes. She twists and bends her body going through her usual warm-up and improvises using the bar on a weight bench to complete her stretches.

Though there's no music she dances one of her favorite contemporary solos, a beautiful piece that's always moved her. The beginning is rough as she has some emotions to work through. She watches herself in the mirror as she moves her body, perfecting her technique. She hears the angelic music in her head as she practices the piece for hours, beginning again and again. Finally, she's there. That place she goes when she dances with passion, when she feels like she's flying, and she's in another place far above the problems of the world, a place where there's only her and the music.

All her emotions pour out through her limbs. This solo is

fluid, sensual, and beautiful, and she performs the piece flawlessly as her body takes her on a journey of love. She leaps in the air. She lands and turns, spinning to the floor bending back and lifting herself, reaching as she stands and glides through the air, flying, and she lands bending her body forward, bowing her head and arms.

She catches her breath as she stands and wipes the sweat from her forehead, and she sees him through the mirror, watching.

"Jackson, how long have you been standing there?"

Without replying he turns and walks away.

"Hello to you too," she says under her breath. She takes her time putting on her shoes. Instead of going to the bedroom she goes to the theatre and falls asleep watching a movie.

Harrison brings Red's dinner to his home office at his request.

"Let me talk to you for a minute," Red says.

"Sure," Harrison says.

"Looks like you got Celeste to eat today. Thank you for that."

"You're welcome, son."

"With that being said, I don't want you talking to her."

"What do you mean?"

"I mean I just need you to do your job. You are not to talk to my mate anymore. Is that understood?"

"Now hold on, Youngblood. Look here. I've been working for you for a long time Mr. Red, and I like you, I do. I would never disrespect you or your home, and I sincerely hope I haven't done anything to offend you."

"You haven't. That'll be all."

"With all due respect, Mr. Red, I'm a grown-ass man. Now I work hard for you, and I like my job, but I don't take too kindly to being told who I can talk to. Now, what's the meaning of this?"

"That'll be all, Mr. Harrison."

"You got yourself a nice young lady, and she's all alone here. She's going to need someone, and that someone should be you, but if you won't step up and be there for her I won't turn my back on her. That's just foolishness. You walk around here. You leave the girl alone, crying. You don't talk to her. You don't spend time with her. She's your mate, ain't she? You picked her."

"You don't understand."

"I understand plenty. You've got to take care of her, physically and emotionally. That's your job as the man. Now, it's up to you to show her how you feel about her. Give her a reason to want to be here. That ain't got nothing to do with me. Do you hear? Old Harrison ain't going to steal your girl. I have been married for over forty years."

Red shakes his head. "What am I going to do with you? Get out of my office, old man."

"You just think about what I said," Harrison says as he leaves Red with his thoughts.

Chapter 9

Celeste wakes up in bed wondering how she got there. The last thing she remembers is falling asleep in the theatre. Red is gone as usual and Celeste decides to get some breakfast.

Olivia is walking out of the kitchen when she arrives.

"Good morning, Olivia."

Olivia rolls her eyes and walks past Celeste.

Celeste ignores Olivia and looks in the fridge. Everything is neatly labeled and dated as Harrison keeps things in order in his kitchen.

"What are you doing in my refrigerator?" Harrison asks.

Celeste closes the door.

"Sorry."

"Well don't you look lovely today," Harrison says.

Celeste smiles. "Thank you."

"That's why I love cooking. A good meal puts a smile on that pretty face. Now get back and let me get you something to eat. You're not going to put me out of work, not today."

"I wouldn't dream of it. You're amazing at what you do."

"Why thank you."

"How long have you been a chef?"

"Almost fifty years."

"And you still got it. Where did you go to culinary school?"

"Le Cordon Bleu." Harrison gathers food from the fridge.

"In Paris?" Celeste asks with excitement.

"The very one."

"I've always wondered what it would be like to live in Paris."

"It's a wonderful city. You're young. What's stopping," he caught himself. "Why haven't you gone?"

"I grew up in Houston. Everything I know and love is in this city. I wanted to be close to my parents so when I got my contract at The Houston Ballet Company I felt like my life was complete."

"How do you take your coffee?" Harrison asks.

"With almond milk."

Harrison sits a mug on the kitchen island with a napkin.

"Thank you," Celeste says as she sits at a barstool.

"I left Houston when I was seventeen years old," he says.

"Seventeen? I would've been terrified."

"I wanted to be a chef and I wanted to learn from the best so when I got my high school diploma I got on a plane and left the city behind. I got a job in a restaurant, and I got accepted at Le Cordon Bleu. I studied there for a year and a half."

"That's amazing."

"Life is too short to ignore your passion. You know what I mean?" Harrison asks.

"I know what you mean," Celeste says.

As Harrison prepares breakfast Celeste thinks about her life. What if this is it? What if being Red's mate is all she has. Did she live the life she wanted? Or was she too afraid? Those thoughts weigh heavily on her as she eats and talks to Harrison about Paris.

At some point, she tunes him out with thoughts of what she should've done with her life and breaks down crying.

"What's wrong with you?"

"What am I going to do, Harrison?" she cries.

"Look at me."

Celeste holds her head up.

"You're going to do what you have to do." He grabs a

napkin and wipes Celeste's eyes.

"I ruined my life," Celeste says.

"It ain't over till it's over. You still got a lot of living to do."

"I don't think that's possible."

"Do you still have breath in you?"

"I may as well be dead."

"Don't you go talking like that. You're going to be just fine. You're feeling low right now, but you're strong, and you're smart. No one can take that from you."

"Can you see the future or something?"

"I just have a little more experience. That's all. Look here. I've known Mr. Red a long time, and I can tell you that he cares about you."

"He doesn't."

"I know what I'm talking about. Now you're going to have to work on him. Show him the sweet, beautiful woman you are. Things will be better if you have him on your side."

"What am I supposed to do?"

"You're going to pull yourself together, or these wolves will eat you alive. They don't respond to tears. You hear me?"

"I hear you."

After breakfast, Celeste heads to the gym. Dance will make her feel better, but when she tries to open the door she realizes it's locked. "You've got to be kidding me," she says as she twists the door handle side to side. She bangs her hand on the door in frustration. "I can't believe this." She storms off and heads to the front door.

"What do you think you're doing?" Olivia stops her.

Celeste jumps, startled. "I'm just going outside, Olivia."

"I don't think so," Olivia says.

"Why not?"

"I can't babysit you right now. You need to stay here."

"Are you seriously trying to keep me from going outside?"

"I don't want to have to chase you."

"Why would you have to chase me?"

"I don't know. Why am I babysitting the pampered princess he chose to mate? There are more important things

I'd rather be doing, but here we are."

"You don't know me, and you can't talk to me like that."

"What are you going to do about it?"

"I'm going outside."

Olivia growls. "I can take you down before you even think about turning the knob."

"Are you threatening me?" Celeste doesn't want Olivia to think she's afraid of her, but Olivia is intimidating, to say the least. Celeste sizes her up. *That's a big bitch.* She's long-legged, fit, and strong. "You can go out back."

"Unbelievable," Celeste walks off.

She goes into the den where a man is sitting on a large leather couch playing a video game. The day before he was in the same spot playing the same game. He's a big man with golden eyes. He's a shifter as well. He hasn't said a word to Celeste, but he seems harmless. Celeste sits on the couch. He gives her a once-over and turns his attention back to the game.

"Hi," Celeste says.

"Sup."

"I'm Celeste."

"Yeah, I know."

"Do you have a name?"

He sighs. "Big Don."

"What are you playing?"

"Soldiers Of Fortune. You wouldn't know nothing about it."

"You'd be surprised."

"Yeah right," Big Don says.

Celeste studies his character on the screen. "I know you need to take cover. You're a sitting duck."

"Yeah, sure."

His character gets shot.

"Oooh," Don shouts. "Alright, you got it." He hands Celeste a controller.

"Really," she says as he ends and restarts the game allowing her to join.

"Just make sure you watch my back," he says.

"I got you." Celeste plays along with Big Don. It turns out they make a good team.

They play in silence until Celeste can't take it anymore.

"Do you work for Red, Big Don?"

"Yeah, he's my cousin. I watch the house for him."

"Can I ask you something?"

"I guess."

"Am I wearing shifter repellant or something?"

"What you mean?" he asks.

"Nobody wants me here."

"It's not like that shorty. Red mating you was a shock to everybody. Just give them time to adjust."

"Even Olivia?"

"Except Olivia. She probably doesn't want you here. She's overprotective of Red. They've been friends for a long time, but if you ask me she wants him for herself."

"And this is what I'm dealing with."

"Plus, cuz snapped that man's neck so everybody has to be careful around you, being his mate and all. You got that man losing his mind."

"And you're not worried?"

"Man, I'll beat Red's ass."

Celeste's jaw drops.

Big Don looks around. "Don't tell him I said that though."

"I won't." Celeste laughs. "So, what's around here to do?"

"I don't know. There are some bars, shit like that. The Woodlands isn't my scene. We hang out further down I-45."

"So why stay here?"

"Our pack meets in the woods behind the house."

"When?"

"Twice a month and special occasions."

"And other than that, is it pretty quiet?"

"Yeah, not too much popping off over here?"

"Do you think Red will let me go to pack meetings?"

"I don't know he's kind of funny about that stuff. Are you telling me you trying to be down?"

"I want to be included."

106

"Good luck with that."

"When's the next meeting? I'm going to see if I can go."

"Saturday."

"So how does everybody find the meeting spot in the middle of the woods?"

"Instincts, but if you get lost there's a trail behind the house. It goes through the woods and leads to one of the main streets."

Celeste turns the conversation to the game. "Watch this. Watch this. Got him," she shouts.

"That was cold," Big Don says admiring Celeste's skills.

When they're done playing Celeste heads to the backyard to look around. There's a giant pool outside the door with a beautiful cabana and matching deck chairs, perfect for entertaining. The backyard is massive in size with a basketball court and tennis court. The yard is surrounded by bushes and beautiful, colorful foliage and there's no gate. Could it be that easy?

Friday comes and with the next pack meeting being Saturday, Celeste determines it's now or never.

Olivia sits in one of Red's guest rooms surfing the internet, simmering as she had been since the moment Red told her to keep an eye on Celeste. He could've gotten anyone to watch Celeste. It was an insult, but Olivia wouldn't dare disobey Red.

While thinking about Celeste, Olivia realizes she hasn't heard her moving around or talking in a while. "Where are you, Princess?" Olivia opens the live feed of the security cameras to pinpoint her location. "She's the most boring person ever. I don't know why he just had to mate her," Olivia says to herself. "Is there something wrong with this thing?" Olivia taps the laptop screen.

"Shit!" she shouts. She calls security. "Hey, are all the cameras working?"

"Yeah."

"Shit! Do you have eyes on Celeste?"

"Let me check. Negative."

"Did she come by the front gates?"

"Negative. Is something wrong?"

"I need you to find the last place she was."

"Alright, give me a minute."

"Now," Olivia shouts.

"I'm looking. Calm down."

"Don't tell me to calm down. Don't forget who you're talking to. Are you going to tell Red to calm down when he finds out you lost his mate?"

"The last place I see her is in the backyard. It looks like she went past the bushes and into the woods."

"Why would she do that? Was she alone?"

"Yes."

"Why would she do that?"

"I don't know. She was walking and just kept going."

"How long ago?"

"About thirty minutes."

"Okay. Thanks."

"Do I need to notify Red?"

"No, don't do that. I'll take care of it." Olivia hangs up the phone. "This dumb bitch. Wait until I find her." She runs into the backyard, sheds her clothes, and shifts into a powerful white wolf with piercing green eyes. She jumps over the bushes and heads into the lush, green forest, tracking Celeste's scent. The sun will be setting soon, and Celeste has no idea what she's doing. It shouldn't be too hard to find her.

She howls hoping to scare Celeste when she notices her footprints in the dirt. She sniffs and follows the scent to a dirt trail. It looks like Celeste found the trail and then strayed from it. If she's trying not to get caught maybe she has some sense after all, but there's no way she'd go too far into the woods. She has to be close to the trail, and she couldn't have gotten far. Olivia howls, sending another message to Celeste as she runs. Celeste's scent is closer, but she must've lost sight of the trail and ventured into the woods. Olivia shifts and goes after her on foot.

"Celeste," she shouts. "I know you're close. Come out." She

howls.

Celeste jumps at the sound of Olivia's voice and howling. She hides behind a tree and stands still.

Olivia shouts. "Celeste. It'll be dark soon. You have to be scared. I can protect you if you come out. I can smell your fear. You don't know these woods."

Celeste is determined not to go with Olivia under any circumstances. She walks away from Olivia's voice on her tiptoes, hoping Olivia can't hear her. Her heart pounds and her eyes dart from side to side careful not to make a sound.

"Celeste, I don't have time for this. I'm not playing with you."

Celeste keeps walking, but she has no idea where the trail is anymore.

There's a growl in the distance.

Celeste thinks it's Olivia so she ignores it. She refuses to let Olivia threaten her.

"Celeste, where are you?" Olivia runs into the woods quickly approaching Celeste's location. She howls.

Celeste keeps walking. Olivia's steps are getting closer. She has to hide. She looks around and sees a patch of bushes. She hides behind them and waits.

"Celeste, you're in danger."

Olivia shifts. Celeste is close. She spots the bushes and hones in on Celeste. "Gotcha," she says to herself when she scents Celeste hiding on the other side of the bushes. What Celeste doesn't know is she's not alone.

Celeste releases the most ear-piercing scream Olivia has ever heard.

Olivia starts to shift, but then she pauses. Her mind starts churning. She could rescue the princess or she could let the mountain lion have her. Red would never know, and Olivia could be the hero when she kills the animal who took Red's mate.

"HELP!" Celeste shouts. Terror paralyzes her. The animal stands twenty feet in front of her growling. He looks hungry. Celeste backs away wondering what happened to Olivia.

"Okay, okay, okay," she speaks calmly as she walks backward, her knees trembling and her voice shaking. "It's okay," she says to the growling animal. Tears stream from her eyes. "Please, please, don't hurt me. Just walk away. Walk away please."

The mountain lion roars and stalks toward Celeste.

She trips and falls into the bushes and the mountain lion charges at her. Celeste screams and covers herself with her hands as he leaps in her direction. There's nothing she can do, and in a split second, she realizes that her life is over.

In the nick of time, Red Paw charges onto the scene, soaring through the air, and knocks the mountain lion out of Celeste's path, pinning him to the ground.

Celeste opens her eyes when she realizes she's alive. "Jackson," she shouts.

With a furious growl, Red unleashes on the animal, sinking his teeth and claws into its flesh as the mountain lion claws at Red and struggles underneath him. The mountain lion uses his hind legs to push Red off, and Red tackles him again while the animal struggles to get off his back. The mountain lion scratches Red across the face, sinking its claws into the wolf. Olivia shifts and her white wolf dives in. She sinks her teeth into the mountain lion's hind leg and tugs. Red sinks his claws into the animal's flanks. Blood gushes as he digs into its flesh. He growls as he thinks about the animal attacking his mate. He sinks his canines into the mountain lion's neck and tugs. The animal is weak. He claws at the air but is unable to put up a fight. Olivia and Red rip the animal apart.

Celeste covers her eyes and turns her head.

Red and Olivia shift.

"We make a good team," Olivia says.

Red has his eyes trained on Celeste.

Chapter 10

Celeste stands and wipes the dirt from her pants. "Thank you," she says to Red.

His wolf is a powerful animal, but the naked man walking toward her is a beast all on his own.

"Have you lost your fucking mind? What are you doing out here?" Red shouts.

Celeste is shaken to the core by Red's tone, but she manages to turn and walk away.

"Where the fuck do you think you're going?" Red asks.

"Away from you," she says.

Olivia stands back and watches. Red and Celeste don't acknowledge her presence. It's as if she's invisible.

"Get back here," Red shouts.

Celeste continues walking in no particular direction. She just wants to get away from Red.

"I'm not going to tell you again. We're going home."

"Home?" Celeste yells as she turns around. "That's not my home."

"Bring your ass here. Do you want to get attacked by another animal? What would you have done if I wasn't here?"

"I don't even know why you care." Celeste resumes

walking away.

"Are you fucking serious? You don't think I care."

"No, and I'm not going back with you. You should've just let it kill me."

"Why the fuck would I do that?" Red shouts.

"You know what I can't figure out?" Celeste turns and points at Red.

"What?"

"Why the fuck did you mate me? Why the fuck did you force me to move to your house? Why couldn't you just leave me alone?"

"What's your problem?" he shouts.

"Seriously? What's my problem? You are! You act like you just had to have me. You take me away from my life. You move me into your house. Why? You don't even want me around. So why did you bring me here? You won't look at me. You won't talk to me. You leave early in the morning and come home late at night. You won't even touch me. You leave me by myself or with that horrible woman."

Red runs full speed toward Celeste. She doesn't have a moment to react before he has her pinned to the ground. Celeste looks terrified as Red hovers over her.

"Where?"

"What?" she asks.

"You want me to touch you. Is that it?"

She hadn't heard his deep, sexy voice in so long. It's music to her ears. "That's not what I said."

"I heard what you said. I have excellent hearing."

"Get off me. I hate you," Celeste shouts.

"You love me."

Olivia watches in disbelief. She and Red were the perfect team, taking down that mountain lion together like the alpha male and female they are. All he can think about is Celeste, and the pheromones in the air indicate they're about to fuck as if Olivia isn't there at all.

"Boy please."

"Girl you know you can't resist all this." Red rolls his body

112

against Celeste like a stripper.

Celeste sucks in her lips.

"Huh," Red says as he puts his hand behind his head and grinds his hips.

Celeste bursts out laughing. She tried to fight it, but the look on Red's face is priceless, and cute if she had to admit it.

"You're laughing," he says looking in her big, beautiful eyes.

She cups his cheek with her free hand. "You're smiling. I didn't know you were capable." Celeste clears her throat and removes her hand. "Anyway, get off of me. I'm going home."

"You are home."

"This is your home. I don't fit in here, and you don't even like me, so why am I here?"

"Who said I didn't like you?"

"You don't have to say anything, and you haven't. You haven't said a word to me since I got here. When we met you wouldn't shut up. You acted like I was special. Now you treat me like shit. So just let me go. I don't have to be here. You have your territories. You don't need me."

Red sits up and pulls Celeste to a seated position. "Look at me." Red takes deep breaths and wrestles with the next words out of his mouth.

"What?" Celeste asks confused.

Red speaks slowly. "I need you."

"For what?"

"My life is complicated, not for the faint of heart. Sometimes it's dangerous, and I'll admit I'm not perfect, but it's my life. This is my pack, my people. I have a lot on my shoulders, but you are my mate, and I need you. I need you with me."

"You can't expect me to believe that, not with the way you've been acting."

"Things don't always happen the way we imagine them. None of this is what I imagined."

"What did you imagine?"

Red stares at the sky before he finally speaks. "I thought

that when I found my fated mate, she'd want to be with me."

Celeste's body stiffens. He's sad, hurt. She can feel it. "I guess you're disappointed."

"You're not a disappointment. I am. I failed."

"You failed at what?"

"This."

"Why did you do the things you did?"

"I had to."

"Maybe you had to take over the territory. Whatever, that's your business, but you killed Charles."

"He stole my mate. I couldn't let him get away with that."

"It was my choice. I asked him to go with me. I loved him."

"Celeste, I don't know if you're lying to me or yourself. I'm sure you care about him, but I didn't force you to fuck me on that stage. Can you honestly tell me that you don't feel this?"

"You didn't have to kill him."

"It's done."

"You hurt me."

"I was hurt too, but I didn't want to hurt you. I didn't want to kill him, but I wasn't myself. Wolves are territorial and we'd just mated. Rage took over. I got caught up, and it happened before I knew it. I don't make a habit of fighting those who are weaker than me. What would I gain from that?"

"Jackson, what do you want from me?"

"Look, you ask too many fucking questions."

"Can you answer that one?"

"Come here."

Celeste reluctantly moves closer to Red.

"I'm not going to hurt you." He lifts her and sits her in front of him, wrapping his legs around her. His head hangs over her shoulder. "I want this?" He places a hand on her chest. Her heart races at his touch.

"My heart? How do you expect to have that?"

"I answered your question."

"I need you to talk to me," Celeste says.

"I need something else from you," he says.

"What, Jackson? What can I do for you?"

"Kiss me."

"You can't be serious."

"I need a kiss from my mate, and I don't want to take it. I want you to give it to me."

Celeste ignores his request. "How did you imagine life with a mate?" She unknowingly snuggles against the warmth of his body.

"She'd be beautiful, like you, and she'd look at me like I was her hero or some shit. I'd take care of her and spoil her because she'd be my queen, and she'd want me and only me. We'd have a family, and she'd be down for me."

"That's surprisingly romantic."

"It's is what it is."

"Were your parents like that?"

"They were."

"And you want to be like them?"

"Something like that. My father was a beast, and my mother was savage. They ran the streets like Bonnie and Clyde. They built an empire together."

"And you inherited the kingdom?"

"I wasn't supposed to. I had an older brother."

"Had?" Celeste asks.

"He died."

"I'm sorry. That must've been hard." Celeste looks back at him.

"I used to look up to him. He should've been next in line, but he was killed when I was young. My father was grooming him to be alpha, and he went into a situation that he wasn't ready for."

Celeste feels his anguish, and he holds on to her.

"I wasn't always this way. I was like the black sheep of the pack. The rest of my family is loud and in-your-face, but that was never my style. Everybody used to call me Lil Red because they thought I wasn't shit, just a light-skinned pretty boy. I didn't try to prove them wrong. I just watched. I watched my parents. I watched their pack. I watched everyone around me. They used to make fun of me, but I didn't care. You can learn a lot about people when they don't see you as a threat. They don't care what they say in front of you. They treat you any kind of way."

"Were you bullied?"

"You could say that. I got to see firsthand how people treat you when they have no respect for you. People prey on the weak with no remorse. I got older and decided that was the end of that. One of my father's men called me Lil Red, and I informed him that I didn't go by that name anymore. He told me to shut up. He said he'd call my punk-ass whatever he wanted. He was respected and high ranking in the pack, and that meant he could do whatever he wanted, and little runts like me had to take it. It's the way our world works so my parents did nothing when I was mistreated. I told him he wasn't going to disrespect me anymore, and he laughed at me. He came at me asking what I was going to do about it, and I showed him. He was twice my size at the time, and I took him out."

"What do you mean by took him out?"

"I killed him with my bare hands. He put up a fight, but he had no idea what I was capable of. No one did. That was the last time anyone called me Lil Red."

"Is that why you're so notorious?"

"The world is not kind, and they will stomp all over you if you let them. No one respects weakness. They may feel sorry for you, but they won't respect you. I made a name for myself, one that was respected. When I finally shifted, and my red wolf emerged, people assumed he was the source of my strength and thought I was special because of it."

"So you just want everyone to be afraid of you?"

"If that's what it takes."

"Have you considered there's something more powerful than fear?"

"What's that?"

"Love."

"Sounds like one of those fairytales you dance to."

"Ouch," Celeste says.

"The world doesn't work that way. Love doesn't conquer all."

"Maybe it does. People will go to great lengths for love, but not so much for fear. They'll only do what's required."

"Maybe in your world."

"What happened to your parents?" Celeste asks.

"What happened to Bonnie and Clyde?"

"They're dead," Celeste says.

"That's what happens when you're not ruthless enough. My parents were betrayed by someone they trusted, someone they loved."

"Are you sure you want to be like that?"

"I won't be like that," he says.

"What's your endgame? Are you trying to take over the whole city?"

"That would be crazy," he says.

"You're kind of crazy."

"What about your parents?" he asks Celeste. "What were they like?"

"I wanted what my parents had. They were always so in love, always affectionate. My dad always doted on my mom. He's kind to her. He always thought about her feelings. Now I wonder if that was real, or if it was part of this image he constructed."

"Do you think love is showing affection like that?"

"I did. Now I'm not so sure."

"It's real."

"If he turned on me so easily, how could he be the man I thought he was? He was supposed to protect me."

"Selfish people fall in love too."

"I don't know anything about love anymore."

"You do, and it's my job to protect you now."

"I did some things I'm not proud of. I'm not going to pretend I didn't. I wanted you desperately the night we mated, but I never thought that I'd be that woman. It was selfish of me to go back to him. He was a good man. I didn't deserve him, and as angry as I am at my father, I don't know

117

if I'm any better than him."

"You're still worthy of love, Celeste."

"That's nice of you to say, but I'm not. I would've pretended nothing happened, and Charles would've never known."

"Everybody fucks up."

"Not like that. I used him to ease my guilt, and I got him killed."

"That wasn't you. That was me. My actions, my fault. I lost control. Don't blame yourself."

Celeste places a hand on his face. "I see so much in you. You're smart. You don't have to be this way."

"I wish I didn't."

"Jackson," Celeste wishes there were words that could get through to him, but she knows he is who he is. "We didn't have to be this way."

"Maybe."

"Why did you open up to me?"

"That's what mates do."

"Do you have any regrets?"

"I regret that I hurt my mate. I hope someday you can forgive me."

Celeste wonders if she can ever forgive him. There are moments when she thinks she could feel something for him, and she wonders if what he says is true, if being mates is that real, and if this is what it does to people. "How would you kiss your mate?" she asks as the sun sets and the sky is a beautiful blend of purple and red.

"Like she was the only woman in the world."

Red doesn't expect it when his mate's lips touch his. First a peck, then a look.

"Don't read anything into this," Celeste says as she turns to face Red.

Red allows Celeste to take the lead. She kisses him slowly, and he can feel her nerves. Her body instinctively moves closer to his and she wraps her arms around his neck. His finger grazes her spine. They savor this kiss, taking their time, losing themselves, embracing the passion between them. The way they hold one another, their desperation for one another, it feels so real.

Celeste pulls away, panting, wanting more. "Have you ever been in love?" she asks.

He kisses her again. This time with more intensity. He loses himself for once in his life and closes his eyes, feeling the kiss, the passion, allowing himself to get caught up as he wraps her in his arms.

Every part of Celeste tingles, down to the tips of her fingers. "Jackson, have you ever been in love?"

He opens his eyes.

"Jackson," Celeste whispers.

"I know what you want. Say it," he says.

"I can't."

"Say it."

"Jackson."

"Say it."

"Make love to me, Jackson."

He growls and in an instant, Celeste is on her back, and Red is on top of her. Their bodies sink into the grass. He bites her lip. "Tell me you'll never leave me."

"I'll never leave you."

He pins her arms to the ground. "I'd kill anyone else for lying to me, Celeste."

"I know."

"Beg for my forgiveness."

"I'm sorry, Jackson. Please forgive me."

"Whose name is on that pussy?"

"This pussy belongs to you, Jackson."

"Don't you ever disrespect me again. Ever," he says.

"I won't."

"You're going to be a good mate, aren't you?" he asks.

"I will."

"I want nothing more than to make love to you, Celeste."

"Please," she pleads.

Red looks at his mate, beautiful, confused, and broken, and

wonders if the damage can be undone. He doesn't know that his fear is the same as hers, falling. Not just falling, but falling so hard he'll never be able to recover. He hesitates. Should he give himself to his mate that way?

Celeste removes her hands from his hold and reaches for him, wrapping her legs around his waist, pulling him in. He knew mating would consume him, but he couldn't have been prepared for this. The soul tie, the unbreakable bond, the longing and desire, caring about her feelings, wanting to trust someone, to rely on someone, things that could be dangerous for a man like him. "You're going to ruin me," he says.

Celeste kisses his lips. "You've already ruined me."

With that, Red rips her clothes from her body and removes her shoes. "What the hell is wrong with your feet?" he asks. Celeste's feet are calloused, blistered, and bruised.

"The price of being a dancer. It's hell on the body."

"I had no idea." He kisses her foot gently.

Her heart pounds with excitement as Red licks his way up her body. He sucks her neck, the tender spot where he claimed her, and her and her body goes limp in his hands. As Celeste moans he swears she's going to cum right then.

"Jackson," she whispers as her legs squirm.

His canines descend, and he teases her skin with their sharp edges. He takes her breast into her mouth. sucking and squeezing with one hand, he grabs her throat with the other. He trails his canines down her stomach.

Celeste moans and runs her fingers through his hair.

He moves between her legs.

Celeste holds his head looking at his canines and shakes her head no.

Red massages her clit and watches her head roll back. "I won't hurt you," he says. "I'll never hurt you." He pries her legs wide open and teases her labia with his canines, barely scratching, just enough to make her quiver as his tongue studies her pussy.

"I'd never ruin something so beautiful," he says. He sucks her clit and alternates lapping her juices while his fingers penetrate her until she cums, crying his name. Still, that's not enough for Red. He lifts her hips off the grass. Every thrust of her hips drives his face deeper into her essence. With every groan he wants more, exploring her with the perfect amount of pressure, flicking and devouring her sweet honey that pours into his mouth, allowing the wolf to taste her. He flicks, sucks, and licks Celeste to ecstasy as she writhes beneath him.

"Jackson, please, Jackson," she whispers. Her legs tremble. An explosion of pleasure washes over her as she cums again. She can't keep her hips on the ground. She presses Jackson's head deeper. "Jackson, I never," she cries.

She doesn't need to tell him. He knows. He holds her hips, locking her in place until he's satisfied. He makes his way up her body and kisses her lips.

Celeste groans as she tastes herself, sucking his tongue, latching on to his body, needing him. "I'm yours," she says.

"And I'm yours," he says filled with pride. His eyes flash red and back to hazel. He's perfectly positioned between her legs.

"Do you mean that?" she asks.

"Yes, mate. Only yours."

He enters her with the longest, deepest strokes, torturing her with agonizing rapture. Her hips meet his in a slow, torturous rhythm. Her nails dig into his back. He lifts her leg and twists his torso, driving himself deeper inside her, kissing and biting her leg. A tear escapes her eye as she cums again. This is more than pleasure. This is perfection, tender, juicy, perfection. He kisses her neck as he takes her body to euphoric heights she's never known. He releases her leg and hovers over her.

"Please don't stop," she cries.

He kisses her lips as she moans into his mouth. She runs her hands down his body, pulling him closer. She opens her legs wider as he sinks deeper. She whimpers his name over and over as her fingers sink into his lower back, digging into his skin, marking his back. Red thrusts into her grunting and growling. He lifts his body and watches his dick slide in and out of her body with her legs in the air. Her body slides in the grass under his force. She wraps her legs around his neck while he smacks her thigh.

"This pussy feels so good. I'm about to cum," he says.

Red's eyes close and his head jerks back. He howls as he releases into his mate. His body convulses, and he can't form words. He grabs her body, digging his claws in wherever he can and Celeste sinks her nails into his back as she cums again. He collapses on top of her, and she holds him between her legs. This feels like heaven to Celeste. She'd never felt a connection like that in her life, and when he said he was hers, she believed him.

Celeste lays on Red's chest and kisses his tattoos. "No one has ever made love to me like that," she says.

"That's what mates do," he says stroking her hair.

Olivia seethes at the sight of Red and Celeste lying in the grass, looking at the stars, holding hands and she wonders what kind of spell the ballerina put on her friend. Red has fucked many women, but he's never been a fool like he is for Celeste and this day has made that glaringly clear. Her hands ball into fists and anger courses through her veins as Celeste mounts Red and rides his dick as he howls at the moon.

"I've seen enough." Olivia shifts and her white wolf flees the woods.

Chapter 11

Celeste opens her eyes to find herself in Red's arms.

"Good morning, mate," he says.

"Good morning, mate."

"I like the sound of that."

"I didn't know what to expect from you this morning."

"You can expect breakfast. Are you hungry?"

"Starving," Celeste says.

"Let's get something to eat." He grabs his phone and calls Harrison to let him know to prepare a special breakfast for him and Celeste.

"I see you, Youngblood," Harrison says.

Celeste is disappointed, but she doesn't want Red to know. He looks at her putting on a pretty pink maxi dress while he puts on his shoes.

"What's wrong?" he asks.

"Nothing's wrong, I'm ready for breakfast."

"Is there something you want to tell me?"

"No."

"Is there something you need?"

"No," Celeste says.

"What did I tell you about lying?"

"I'm not lying. I just want to get breakfast."

"Okay." Red stands as Celeste slips on some sandals. He catches her off guard and pushes her against the wall with her back to him.

"What are you doing?" Celeste shouts.

"I know what you need."

"What do I need?"

"This dick."

"You are so—"

Before Celeste can say anything Red has her dress lifted her panties ripped. He quickly unbuckles his pants and presses his body against Celeste. "Get on your fucking knees."

Celeste tries to hide her excitement when she slowly drops to her knees and she's eye to eye with his hardening dick, staring at the eye that's begging to be sucked.

"Don't just look at it. Put that dick in your fucking mouth."

"Jackson, shut up," Celeste says.

"Wh—"

"Before Red can react Celeste takes his whole dick into her mouth as far as she can and grabs his balls."

"Shit," Red says.

Celeste inhales his scent as she works her head from side to side sucking him in and as he expands in her mouth. When he's fully hard she swirls her tongue around his head before she takes his entire shaft into her mouth.

"Shit, swallow that whole dick. Just like that."

The more Red grunts, the wetter she gets. She moans as she takes his balls into her mouth and strokes his dick with her hand. His pleasure pushes her to give him her all. His dick is so hard and beautiful. It should be appreciated, and she plans to worship it. She teases the tip with her mouth sucking as she runs her hand down, loving the feeling of his silky skin. She pulls his pants down and they fall to his ankles. He grabs the back of her head and guides it along his shaft as she sucks him like a popsicle. She spits on his dick and grabs his behind pulling him deeper into her mouth. He grabs her hair as the head sinks into her throat. His hips thrust into her face. He watches his dick slide in and out of her mouth while she looks at him.

"That's a good mate," his hips move at a steady rhythm.

Celeste is so wet she might leave a puddle on the floor. Fueled by his pleasure she twists her head as she works up and down, faster, savoring his taste, his hardness, and his enjoyment. She wants him to lose control, but he pulls out of her mouth and pushes her against the wall. He removes her dress and places her hands over her head and holds them there with one hand as he pulls her hips out with the other. He lifts her leg with his, but he has no idea what Celeste's body is capable of. She lifts her leg along the wall, holding at a ninety-degree angle as he impales her with his dick. He growls when she cries out and he's buried deep inside her.

She lowers her leg as he pounds her over and over. The side of her face is pressed into the wall and the sound of his body slapping against hers echos through the room. He holds on to her hips as she screams his name. Her hands try to grab the wall. He lifts her slightly. She frantically moves her hands and legs up the wall.

"Where are you going?" Red asks in that deep, sexy voice. "Don't run from this dick."

Celeste extends her legs backward and wraps them around Red. He thrusts his body into her depths as her head bangs into the wall.

"Fuck me, Jackson," she shouts, and he does just that.

He pulls her from the wall and she bends over. Her hands are flat on the floor and her legs at his sides. His fingers sink into her skin as he holds on to her hips and thighs. He loses count of how many times she cums but he makes sure to wear that pussy out.

He pulls out stroking his dick and Celeste drops to her knees in front of him. She can see he's about to erupt. She opens her mouth.

He pulls her hair with one hand and strokes furiously with the other until cum streams out, dripping into Celeste's mouth. She flicks his tip with her tongue and sucks. His hips thrust and she grabs his behind, pushing him into her mouth as she swallows his cream.

"Fuck," he shouts as she sucks him. His body jerks and she stays attached until he's calm. "That was good," he says. "Shit."

Celeste is satisfied and ready to eat. She looks at herself in his bathroom mirror as she rinses her mouth. Her eyes focus on the pointe shoe necklace she cherishes. The effect that Red has on her can't be denied. Her desire for him can't be denied. She wonders what she's going to do, and if she manages to get away from him, how is she going to live without his touch? She tousles her hair and she and Red head to the dining room.

"I want to show you something before we eat," Red says. He leads her down the hallway to the gym.

As he turns the doorknob Celeste is angered by the reminder of the way he treated her. "Now the door magically works," she says. "I tried to get in here and it was locked."

"Can you be quiet?"

"No. I don't know why you'd bring me here. Did you want to rub it in that you can stop me from doing anything you want anytime? I just used the room to dance. I don't know why you would lock me out."

Celeste is so busy seething that she doesn't notice Red has opened the door. He leans against the door frame until she stops talking.

"Why are you standing there looking at me like that?" she asks.

He points his head inside the room and Celeste takes a look.

"You did this for me?" she asks.

"I sure as hell didn't do it for me."

"Jackson, I can't believe it."

"The floor has to settle for twenty-four hours so you'll have to wait until tomorrow to use it."

"How did you do all this? Why did you do this?"

"You love to dance and I wanted you to have everything you needed. There's a ballet barre and a yoga mat and blocks, resistance bands, some kind of spinning disc, and if you look over there," Red points to the center of the room.

"My pointe shoes."

"I was going to get some new ones, but I learned that they're personal and you'd probably prefer ones you already have."

"That's true. I can't believe it. You must've done your research."

"It was nothing."

"It's not nothing. I didn't think you could be so sweet. Thank you."

"You're welcome," he says.

"You're doing that thing again," she says.

"What thing?"

"You're smiling." She hugs him and squeezes tight until he wraps her in his arms and returns her embrace.

Something about the hug for Red seems more intimate than anything they'd done up to that point. He'd be lying if he said it didn't make him feel like a king being responsible for making his mate so happy.

"I guess you like it," he says.

"I love it. It's perfect." She tiptoes and gifts him with a kiss on the lips to his surprise.

"Are you ready for breakfast?"

"Yes, please," Celeste says with a smile on her face. Without realizing it she grabs his hand, intertwining her fingers with his as they head to the dining room.

Red pulls out a corner chair for Celeste and sits next to her at the head of the table. Celeste inadvertently grabs his hand again. Her face is glowing. She looks beautiful in her pink dress and Red fights with himself internally. Mating has done a number on him. Making love, hugging, and holding hands are things he'd never done. He was worried that he was losing himself, worried that he was falling.

"Good morning, Harrison," Celeste gushes bringing Red back to the moment.

"Good morning, Miss Celeste. Look at you. Somebody put a big smile on that pretty face."

Celeste squeezes Red's hand. "Jackson made me a dance studio. It's beautiful."

"Did he now?" Harrison looks at Red. "Good morning, Mr. Red."

"Good morning," Red says.

"Looks like you did something right," Harrison says.

"He did," Celeste says.

"That's what I like to see, young people in love."

The room grows quiet. Celeste's smile starts to fade. Red's grip loosens on her hand. They both freeze.

Harrison notices the shift in the room. "Now y'all stop that acting like you don't love one another. Anyone with eyes can see it. Now, you're having a beautiful morning. Mr. Red did something nice for you. Life is too short to be around here pretending. You're going to wish you had more moments like this. I'll be right back with your breakfast."

"Don't mind him. I don't know why he can't be quiet sometimes," Red says when Harrison leaves the room.

"He doesn't bother me. I love Harrison. I mean, I like him. He's a good man."

"He's a pain in my ass. He doesn't listen."

"But you haven't fired him so you must like him too."

"I tolerate him."

"Sure, you do. He was right about one thing though."

Red's heart pounds. "What?"

"This is a beautiful day and you did do something really sweet. Can we just enjoy it?"

"Yeah, we can do that. I did want to tell you something."

"What?"

"I want to take you to a pack meeting tonight."

"You do? Why?"

"They want to congratulate us."

"Oh."

It's obvious to Red that Celeste doesn't know what to say. He can feel her hesitance.

"It's not every day their alpha finds a mate. They're excited."

"I take it mating is a big deal."

"It is."

"Are they going to be okay with me?"

"Yes, they'll embrace you."

"Will I be safe?"

"I wouldn't let anything happen to you."

"Okay."

"Don't be nervous. My pack knows how to have a good time."

Harrison brings two plates and two glasses of orange juice for Celeste and Red.

"This is too much," Celeste looks at all the food Harrison prepared.

"I know you didn't eat supper last night. You need to start the day off right." Harrison walks out of the room.

"You're right. He doesn't listen." Celeste laughs.

"I told you."

Celeste takes a bite of her eggs and closes her eyes. "How can someone make eggs so good?" She takes a sip of orange juice.

"You have something on your lip." Red brushes a piece of pulp away and gets caught staring into his mate's eyes.

"Thank you," Celeste says staring back at him.

Red's hand still rests on her face. Warmth spreads through his body.

"Don't read anything into this," Celeste says. She leans in and pauses. Red leans in and their lips touch. Without thinking they're swept up in passion and the room fades.

"I need to talk to you," Olivia stands in the dining room looking down at Red and Celeste.

Celeste freezes.

"I'm busy," Red says.

"I see that. You're so busy you didn't even hear me come in."

"Good morning, Olivia," Celeste says.

"Why are you talking to me, Tinkerbell?" Olivia snaps.

Celeste looks at Red in disbelief.

"Olivia, if you're rude to me or my mate again I'll rip your fucking tongue out."

"I'm sorry Red. I just need to talk to you."

"Don't come into my home and disrespect me or Celeste. You must've lost your fucking mind."

"Seriously, Red?"

"Apologize to Celeste."

"Red, come on," Olivia pleads.

"Don't make me repeat myself."

"I apologize," Olivia says.

Red stands. "Like you mean it."

"My behavior was out of line. I'm sorry, Celeste."

"Now get the fuck out of here. We're having breakfast. Wait for me in the backyard."

Olivia starts to question him, but she doesn't want to make him angrier so she leaves the room and paces the backyard.

"Don't pay her any attention," Red says to Celeste as he sits.

Celeste could only think about the way Red handled the situation and he was growing on her. "Thank you for defending me."

"I'm not going to let anybody treat my mate that way, okay."

"Okay."

Once they're done with breakfast Red meets Olivia in the backyard.

"What's up with you, Red?" Olivia asks.

"I want to know why the fuck Celeste was in the woods alone. Why was she out there at all?"

"She walked out there. I don't know why."

"You know I told you to do something and you fucked up. How many fuck ups do I allow?"

"None," Olivia says quietly.

"My mate could've been killed. Tell me why I shouldn't snap your neck."

"Because it wasn't my fault."

"Are you sure that's your answer? If security hadn't called

130

me I don't know what would've happened to her. I trusted you and you failed me."

"With all due respect, this is not my fault. You once again kept me in the dark. What's with you?"

"Anything that's between me and my mate is none of your fucking business, and I'm not going to tell you that again."

"When you hide shit, especially from me, this kind of shit happens. You're as much to blame."

"You had one job. Watch Celeste."

"You didn't give me all the details. I didn't know you were locking her in the house. If I had known the circumstances I would've acted accordingly. You didn't tell me she was going to try to run away."

"I told you to watch her. That's all you needed to know."

"I learned a lot last night when you forgot I was there."

"Tread carefully, Olivia."

"You need to be careful around her."

"What do you think she's going to do to me?"

"Great men have fallen victim to the wiles of crafty women. You're losing focus. You need to be at your best right now. These moments are crucial, and you need to stop thinking with your dick and get your head in the game."

"I know what I have to do."

"I ride hard for you. I don't understand why you would keep things from me. I was here before her, and I'll always be here."

"Are you done?"

"You don't have anything to say to me?"

Red stands directly in front of Olivia looking down at her sour face with his shoulders squared and his chest poked out.

Olivia looks up at Red. He has that violent look in his eyes. She bows her head and takes a step back.

"We're old friends. It's true, but I don't know what made you think you could question my authority. I will see you at the gathering tonight, and you will treat Celeste with the utmost respect as will everyone else."

"Alpha Red," Olivia begins.

131

"Don't talk. You should've welcomed my mate and respected my choice as I would've done for you. I won't tolerate another second of your insolence. If she wants you to feed her grapes, you'll do it with a fucking smile, and if I get a whiff of disrespect or attitude from you I will remove you as beta permanently. Do you have a problem with that?"

"No, alpha."

"There aren't too many alphas who would allow a female beta. They think women are too emotional. I put a lot of faith in you. Whatever your issue is I suggest you get over it quickly. You need to get your shit straight. Don't ever disappoint me again."

"Understood."

"Get the fuck out of my house."

Red goes to his office while Celeste sits in the kitchen talking to Harrison.

"He wants to take me to a pack meeting," Celeste says.

"That sounds promising," Harrison says.

"I've never been around shifters like that before."

"Don't fret. They're people just like me and you."

"But they're different."

"The things that matter are still the same."

"Is there anything I should know?"

"They're big on respect. That's the main thing. You have to respect their traditions and their way of life."

"How do I do that?"

"Everyone in the pack earns their place. It starts at the top with the alpha, the highest-ranking member of the pack."

"Jackson is the alpha."

"That's right. He's the one in charge, their leader, and the strongest wolf in the pack. Everyone in the pack depends on him and they have high expectations of him. They look to him for wisdom, instruction, and protection. The balance of the pack is all on his shoulders, and for that, he's respected and honored. Alphas are used to being obeyed. No one questions their authority, and if they do there are consequences.

"I had no idea."

"This is not a game young lady. Next is the beta. That's the second-highest rank."

"That's what Olivia is."

"That's right. The beta is second in command. They're responsible for keeping order in the pack and in the alpha's absence they're looked to for guidance as well."

"Why is Olivia his beta?"

"She's strong and smart. She wouldn't be appointed without proving herself."

"Is there something between her and Red?"

"I've never seen that man more taken with anyone than he is with you. You have nothing to worry about. As far as I know, they're friends who grew up together. That's all."

"Do you trust her?"

"That, my dear, is something you'll have to judge for yourself. Now deltas are third in command. They're strong as well and usually train pack members to fight."

"Got it."

"Those are the most important positions. The pack is also made up of warriors, hunters, and healers."

"I didn't know how deep this was."

"Like I said, it's important. Finally, there are the omegas. They're the lowest in rank besides the pup and are treated as such. They are the weakest and for that, they get no respect."

"Why would anyone want to do that?"

"That's the way it is. It's survival of the fittest at its finest. You may think being an omega isn't ideal, and it's not, but they're also necessary. They're the heart of the pack and without them, the pack wouldn't survive."

"How do I fit in?"

"You, my dear, are the alpha's mate?"

"Do I even deserve such a title?"

"You do if the alpha says so."

"What if they don't respect me?"

"You make them respect you. They smell fear and they prey on it. Never forget you have the power of the alpha behind you. He wouldn't dare let anyone disrespect his mate.

Don't let them wolves run all over you, and don't back down. You walk in there with your head held high. Do you hear me?"

"I hear you."

"Now you're important too because the alpha needs you. You complete him. Their kind don't play around about their mates. They understand how important the mate is, and if the alpha is happy, the pack is happy."

"How do you know all this, Harrison?"

"I been around a long time, and I'm a firm believer that you should always know who you're dealing with."

Chapter 12

"I like this outfit," Red says.

"Thank you. I wanted to honor the alpha," Celeste says.

Red swells with pride as he takes his mate by the waist and leads her through the woods.

Celeste dons a red camisole slightly cropped at the waist with a black stripe down the sides and matching red pants. Her outfit is complete with black shoes and her silver necklace. Red wears a black polo shirt and khaki pants.

The sun has set and bonfires burn in the heart of the forest. Lanterns light the way to the evening's gathering. The Bayou City Pack stands at attention along the dirt path. Olivia stands at the front of the line.

"Good evening, alpha. Good evening Celeste," Olivia smiles.

"Good evening, Olivia," Celeste says noting that Olivia seems to be much nicer than her usual scowling self.

Red says nothing to his friend.

Olivia's heart sinks. It's unclear whether things will ever be the same between her and Red. "Celeste, we would like to welcome you to the family. We are pleased that our alpha has found such a beautiful mate, and we are honored to have you as part of the Bayou City Pack."

"Thank you, Olivia," Celeste says.

Olivia gets down on one knee and bows. Red leads Celeste past Olivia down the path. As they walk, the members of the pack on both sides bow in the same manner. Celeste is in awe of the display of respect. She walks with her head held high as the pack welcomes her.

The other members of the pack wait in the common area and bow until Red and Celeste reach the head table that sits on a stage facing everyone. Tables sit before them surrounded by bonfires. Harrison has a staff that mans a line of barbecue pits. Celeste nods at Harrison and he nods back assuring her that she's doing well.

Celeste looks into the crowd and sees shifter eyes in an array of colors. They seem to glow in the night.

A woman prepares plates for Celeste and Red.

"Is everything to your liking?" Red asks Celeste.

"Yeah," Celeste says.

"Are you sure?"

"I don't like baked beans, but it's okay."

"No, it's not." Red hands the plate to the woman. "Make her another plate."

"I apologize. I'll get you another right away," the woman says with a smile.

"Oh," Celeste says. "Okay."

The woman brings Celeste another plate.

"Thank you. This smells so good." Celeste inhales the smoky scent of Texas barbecue.

Celeste spots Olivia at one of the tables, and when their eyes meet Olivia smiles.

"Olivia is suddenly being nice to me," Celeste says.

"She never should've mistreated you, and she won't again."

"Jackson, that's—"

"Necessary," he says.

Once Red and Celeste are served their drinks the rest of the pack gets their food in order of rank. They operate like a well-oiled machine.

Music blasts through large black speakers placed around the area and the pack starts to cheer. A group of four women rushes the area in front of the stage naked as the pack howls and barks. Celeste tries not to react, but she notices the pack goes wild as the women begin a tribal dance smearing their bodies with mud and clay.

"What's going on?" Celeste asks.

"They are praying for a blessed union. They talk with their bodies, and they bring us good fortune, protection, and fertility," Red explains.

Celeste cheers along with the pack and they feed off of her energy and begin to chant her name. Red howls at the pack, and they all howl back in unison using the same patterns. The women complete their dance and Red leads Celeste to the stage. The dancers walk by them one by one. They each bow standing. Red holds out his left hand and motions Celeste to do the same, and they each kiss Red and Celeste's hands, and they each offer blessings.

When they're gone Red bows to Celeste. "I pledge my life to my mate, the one fated to me by the heavens. You and I are one from this day forward." He kisses her hand.

Celeste, in turn, bows to Red." I pledge my life to my mate, the one fated to me by the heavens. You and I are one from this day forward." She kisses his hand.

The pack howls and Red howls back. They bark in a steady rhythm, and Red pulls Celeste in for a kiss. Everyone cheers.

Olivia has never put on such a performance in her life, pretending to be happy for Red and Celeste makes her stomach churn. It's all too real at this point. Celeste is bound to Red and their union is blessed. There's sorrow and anger hidden behind her smile, and she doesn't know how long she can keep it up.

Drinks are flowing, and the night is young. The tables are pushed back. The pack is happy, dancing, and celebrating. The energy and the love can be felt in the air. A line has formed in front of Red and Celeste at the head table. Pack members stop by and offer them gifts.

Celeste becomes alert when a woman approaches them wearing a short skirt and low-cut top showcasing her big thighs and supple breasts as she saunters to the table and stands in front of Red. She looks over his muscular body, teasing him with her eyes and her smile. Celeste notices how Red is almost smiling. She jerks her head back and nods. This woman isn't fooling anyone. She quickly glances at Celeste with a fake smile and then back at Red.

"We are very happy for you. Blessings on your mating. Please accept this gift. She places her neatly wrapped gift on the table and her hand on top of Red's hand.

Red nods and a woman grabs the gift and places it on a table behind the couple.

Olivia stands to the side smirking at Tasha. She never cared for Red's little fuck buddy, but she's pleased that Celeste has to witness her throwing herself at Red.

"Thank you," Red says.

"Yes, thank you," Celeste says.

Tasha maintains eye contact with Red. "My pleasure," she says as she bites her lip and flips her hair.

"You're so beautiful. What was your name again?" Celeste asks.

"Thank you. My name is Tasha."

Celeste places a hand on top of Tasha's hand. "Tasha, what a lovely name. We're so glad you came. She picks up Tasha's hand and places it on the table in front of her.

Tasha's eyes widen. "I'm happy to be here." She takes her hand back.

"Oh, no, please leave your hand where I put it," Celeste says with a threatening smile and an eerily pleasant voice. "Let me get a good look at your pretty nails."

Tasha looks at Red for clarification. Red isn't sure what Celeste is doing, but he can feel her anger rising.

"Don't look at him. I said put your hand back on the table," Celeste says.

Tasha reluctantly places her hand on the table.

Celeste turns to the woman behind her. "Can you bring me

a knife?"

She smiles as she brings a knife.

"Bigger," Celeste says with a smile.

The woman gets a butcher knife from Harrison and brings it to Celeste.

Celeste holds the knife in the air and studies it. She nods her approval and runs her index finger along the blade.

Tasha is shaken. "Ma'am I—"

"You're what, Tasha?" Celeste says.

"I'm sorry."

"Are you, Tasha? You didn't seem sorry when you were ignoring me and addressing my man."

The pack watches, looking around wondering what's happening. The music has stopped and everyone hangs on to Celeste's every word.

"I'm sorry. Alpha Red, please do something."

"Don't talk to him," Celeste says. She slams the knife onto the table without looking.

Tasha gasps. The tip of the knife sinks into the wood. The silver blade glistens as it sits up an angle perfectly positioned between Tasha's fingers.

"This is my mate, and if you ever disrespect me again," Celeste removes the knife and slams it between Tasha's fingers without looking. "I will cut off your fucking fingers one by one. Do I make myself clear?"

"Yes ma'am," Tasha says.

"Good. You can remove your hand." Celeste looks into the shocked faces of the pack. "Keep the party going," she says.

The music resumes.

"Tasha," Celeste calls as Tasha walks away.

Tasha turns around. "Yes," she says sheepishly.

"It was nice to meet you."

Tasha nods. "May I say something?" she asks.

Celeste nods.

"You're my type too," she says to Celeste with a wink.

Celeste smiles. "You can go."

Red is shocked. He looks at Tasha, then at Celeste.

"Don't even think about it," Celeste says to Red.

Red holds up his hand and the next person in line waits. "What the fuck was that?" Red asks Celeste.

"She thinks she can just walk up here and put her hands on you. Hell no," Celeste says.

"That was some gangster shit. I didn't know you got down like that."

"I come from the cut-throat worlds of ballet and rich mean girls. I've been preparing for this moment my whole life."

Red whispers in Celeste's ear. "You're all territorial and shit, got my dick hard and shit." He growls as he rubs his hands down Celeste's back and leg.

"We have guests," Celeste says.

"They can scent how much you want me to bend you over this table right now." Red grabs her hair and pulls her in for a kiss as the crowd cheers.

When they pull apart Celeste has a smile on her face, and she waves over the next person in line.

Once everyone has paid their respects Red and Celeste move to the dance floor. Red watches Celeste as she moves her body to the hip hop music blasting over the speakers.

"What are you doing?" Red asks Celeste.

"I'm dancing," she says.

"I can't believe this. You can't dance," Red steps back in shock.

"What? I'm a professional dancer."

"But, baby, you can't dance. You don't have any rhythm."

"I've been dancing since I could walk."

"This isn't the same."

"I've never had any complaints before," Celeste says.

"Don't get angry. You're a beautiful ballet dancer, but when it comes to this here you have to use those sexy hips. You need to loosen up."

Celeste crosses her arms in offense.

"Look at her." Red points to a woman next to them. "You see how she moves with the music." He grabs her hands and turns her around so her back is to him. "I know you know

140

how to work that ass. I've seen you do it." He pulls her body against his. "Ride the beat like you're riding my dick."

Celeste looks at the other women dancing, studying the way they move, the way they bounce, and the way their hips and bodies work. She bounces her head to the beat. "I can do that," she says.

She uses her legs to work her ass against Red as he dances to the beat.

"That's it. You got it."

Celeste concentrates on the rhythm and how her body moves.

Red grinds against her. "Now stop trying to choreograph and just let go."

She does, and she steps away from Red into the center of the crowd dancing, dropping, picking it up, bouncing her ass, until everyone stops to watch. They bounce their hands in the air up and down.

"Aye, aye, aye, aye," the pack cheers her on to the beat.

Red joins her again and smacks her on the behind. "That's what I'm talking about," he says.

While Celeste is enjoying the vibe, she feels a tap on her leg. She looks down. There's a cute little brown girl that has a ponytail in her hair with a pink ribbon tied around it. She looks to be about five years old.

"Hi there," Celeste says bending down.

"Are you the ballerina?" The little girl asks.

"I am," Celeste says. "My name is Miss Celeste. What's your name?"

"Adriana," the girl says with her finger in her mouth.

"Can you, can you," Adriana twists her body from side to side.

"What is it, Adriana?"

"Can you show me and my sister?"

"Where's your sister?"

Adriana points to a young girl, maybe a year or two older. Her sister is dressed just like her and she gives Celeste a shy wave.

"Of course, I can," Celeste says.

"I'll be right back," she says to Red.

He instinctively holds her back.

"I promise," she says.

He releases her hips and she kisses him on the cheek.

"Over here," Adriana takes Celeste's hand and runs to her sister. "Alexis, she's a, she's a ballerina."

"Hi Alexis," Celeste says.

"Hi," Alexis says quietly.

"You both look so pretty in your pink dresses."

"Thank you," they say in unison.

"Do you like ballet?"

Alexis smiles and nods.

"Would you like me to show you something?" Celeste asks.

"Yes," the girls say.

"Okay." Celeste stands back and does a sauté arabesque where she jumps high and her leg is extended behind her.

The girls clap and some of their friends come and watch.

"Can you turn around and around and around?" Adriana asks.

"I can."

"Do it, do it," Adriana chants.

"Okay," Celeste says but it's kind of hard in the grass. She looks around and has an idea. She kicks off her shoes and climbs on top of a plastic table nearby. "Ready," she says.

"Yes," the kids say in unison.

"I'll show you pirouettes."

She extends her arms, extends one leg out and in, then up. She lifts her foot and spins in one spot without stopping as her arms move up and down until she lands her foot behind her and takes a bow. She gets down from the table to applause. The girls and their friends grab her hands and jump up and down around her. She's overwhelmed by the questions and the tugging, but she tells them she took years and years of ballet classes and worked really hard.

"Children, come on. Let's leave Miss Celeste alone. She's busy." An omega shoos the children away. "Sorry ma'am," she says.

"It's fine," Celeste says as she waves goodbye to the kids. She stands and realizes there's a piece of paper in her hand. She opens it and drops it to the ground. Three words stare back at her, written in pencil. Three words that shake Celeste to the core. CHARLES IS ALIVE. She holds her breath. Her head spins. Everything becomes blurry. Music fades into the background, and she stands still.

Red grabs her from behind. "That was good."

Celeste can't form words.

"What's wrong baby?"

She shakes her head and panics. "Nothing." She discreetly picks up the paper between her toes and stuffs it in her shoe, hoping that Red doesn't notice. Her heart is pounding. She looks around to see who's watching her. Someone slipped that note in her hand, or they used one of the children to do it, but who?

"You seem rattled," Red says.

"No, I think I need some water." She turns to Red and puts her arm around his waist leading him away."

"Get Celeste some water," Red says.

When they get back to their table the woman who's been doting on them brings Celeste a bottle of water and a cup of ice.

"Would you like it on ice?"

"Please," Celeste says.

Celeste finds it hard to drink. She stares at the cup for a moment thinking about that piece of paper. What does it mean? Where did it come from? And why did she get it? She closes her eyes tight. That note is a distraction and she can't focus on it now. She needs to put it out of her head and focus on Red before he gets suspicious. She shakes it off and takes long sips of the cold water. She chews some ice and takes another long sip.

"You good?" Red asks.

"I worked up a little sweat," she says.

"Don't tire yourself out, because you're going to work up

another sweat tonight."

"You're a bad wolf," she teases.

"You love it," he says.

"I'm having a good time," Celeste says as she looks into the crowd.

Everyone seems happy. They're like a family. They love and support one another. Everything about them seems genuine.

"They love you," Red says.

"Do you think so?"

"I know."

Celeste smiles. "They're good people," she says.

"You're one of us," Red says. "These are your people, our people, okay."

"Okay," Celeste says looking around. Over the bonfires, in the tall trees, a shadowy figure sits. Celeste squints her eyes and it becomes clear. She trembles. Everyone around her seems to be oblivious, and the man seems to be unaware that she spotted him. He has a gun and it's pointed at Red. Celeste surprises him with a kiss. While his hands roam her body, she stands and straddles his lap then sits. In his excitement, Red doesn't question her.

"Let's get out of here," she says out loud. She kisses his face whispering to him between pecks. "There's a man behind me in the trees."

"Yeah let's go," Red moans.

"Can you reach your gun?" She whispers kissing his neck.

No sooner than the words leave her mouth Red pulls the gun from his pants. He points and fires two shots into the trees then dives underneath the table covering Celeste with his body. Red howls, signaling his pack that they are under attack.

Everyone is on high alert, some of the pack has shifted into their wolves. The kids' cries can be heard throughout the forest. There's a loud thud.

Olivia rushes to check out the noise. The warriors have already shifted and gone into the forest. "Hunters back them up, Olivia commands. If you find anyone who doesn't belong and bring them back here."

"Are you okay?" Red pulls Celeste to her feet and holds her close.

"I'm fine." Celeste looks around panicked. She grabs Red's arm. She fumbles over her words as adrenaline pumps through her body. "There's kids. Who would do that? Families. I, I." Celeste clenches Red's arm.

"I got him," Red says.

Celeste nods. She looks past Red and a body lies on the ground next to an automatic rifle.

Red runs to the body. He pulls the man's arm when she notices a bird tattoo. "He's a falcon," Red says.

"What's a falcon?" Celeste asks.

"A hired killer," Red says. "Falcon shifters are rare, and they work for hire. Looks like they planned to take as many of us as they could, starting with me. You saved us," Red says. "I have to go. Wait here. Big Don will watch you and Harrison. I'll be back."

Red shifts into his red wolf in front of Celeste's eyes. She watches in amazement as he leaps into the air and runs into the woods.

"Jackson, be careful," she shouts, but he's gone.

Harrison sits next to Celeste and gives her a comforting pat on the shoulder. "Well, I'll be damned," he says.

Olivia shifts into her white wolf and takes off behind Red. Howling can be heard in the distance. The pack is signaling one another, and then the woods get eerily silent.

"What's happening?" Celeste asks Don.

"They're hunting," Don says.

Some have stayed back and patrol the grounds.

"Where are the kids?" Celeste asks.

"The omegas are keeping them safe," Don says.

"Are you sure?" Celeste asks.

"They're safe. Don't worry."

Celeste waits patiently for Red to return. Her leg bounces up and down. The thought of not knowing what awaits him worries her.

Red stalks through the woods. Falcons usually work alone, but he wants to make sure any threat is eliminated. There's a faint rustle in the trees. It could be a bird. It could be the wind. Red inhales the scent of pepper and takes off in the opposite direction. He shifts and climbs a nearby tree. Once he's high enough he looks out into the distance. A falcon sits perched on a branch searching for him. Red quietly climbs down and creeps through the forest following the scent and his memory to the tree where the man sits waiting. He climbs into the tree next to the falcon and jumps through the air, grabbing the man by the throat, he pulls him off the branch and crashes on top of the man on the ground.

"Who hired you?" Red asks calmly.

The man winces in pain.

Red pulls his arm behind his back and snaps it out of the socket. "Who hired you?" Red asks.

"Please," he shouts.

Red takes the man's gun and points it at foot. "I'm a gentle man, but my wolf wants to tear you apart limb by limb and feast on your flesh. Don't make me ask you again."

"I don't know. I got a message through the dark web. I don't know. You have to believe me."

"Stop crying. I believe you." Red drags the man back to the gathering spot by his broken arm. His cries of agony can be heard in the night.

Celeste runs to Red. He takes her by the waist and howls. His pack howls as they make their way back. The warriors have found another falcon, and they push him next to the man Red has lying on the ground.

Red walks to the body of the man he shot. He wipes his thumb across the wound in his head and looks at the man's blood on his thumb. He stands in front of Celeste. She cringes at the sight. Her body quakes as Red holds his thumb to her forehead.

"Be still, " he says.

He presses his thumb into Celeste's forehead and smears

the blood. Celeste is horrified but presses her lips together to keep from screaming.

"Bayou City Pack," Red shouts.

"This woman saved my life and yours. Bow to your alpha female."

Celeste's mouth drops open. The Bayou City Pack shifts before her. There must be hundreds of them all around. They bow to Celeste and howl in unison. Red holds Celeste's hand in the air as the pack jumps up and down on their hind legs barking and howling.

Red drops to his knees and kisses her hand as Celeste holds her head high.

"This is what power feels like," Celeste says.

"This is just a taste," Red says. He turns his head and shouts. "Falcons, get the fuck out of my woods."

The falcons sit to the side watching in disbelief that they're being let go. They scramble to get on their feet and take off into the woods.

Red turns to his pack. "Hunt," he says.

The wolves take off after the falcons. Second later cries of agony can be heard as the pack rips the falcons apart.

Olivia stands back, no longer with a smile on her face. She's in disbelief. Her world has been tainted, taken over, and torn apart. Everything she's known is ruined. She's worked hard, served faithfully, proven herself, and now this. Celeste gets lucky one time and gets a title.

Olivia is outranked by a ballerina.

Chapter 13

Charles lies in a bed at Ben Taub Hospital staring at the ceiling of a dimly lit room. His jaw is wired shut. His body is weak and bruised with a broken rib and fractured leg, and he doesn't have Celeste. The pain in his heart aches more than his body as he wonders night after night what happened to the woman he loves. He doesn't care about the pain. He can only think about how he failed to protect Celeste.

His mother sits at his bedside holding his hand reading scriptures about healing to her beloved son. A hand touches the woman's shoulder. She jumps as she turns around.

"I don't mean to startle you, Ms. Robinson. I'm a friend of Charles's and I wanted to see him."

"God bless you," she says. "They still don't know who did this to my baby. I keep calling the detective and he can't tell me anything. This just ain't right," she cries.

"What happened is terrible. I'm just glad to see he's still alive. God saved him."

"Yes, he did. Bless his name."

"You must be tired. Why don't you go home and rest? I'll sit with him until you get back."

"I need to stay with my baby."

"He's in good hands. I promise. I want to pray with him

and spend some time with him. It's the least I can do."

Charles turns his head and makes noises, trying to say no.

"See he wants me to sit with him. I'll call you if anything happens I promise."

"Well, I guess he does. He hasn't made a sound since he's been here." Ms. Robinson grabs a pen from her purse. "I'll leave my number right here on the table, and I'll be back first thing in the morning." She squeezes Charles's hand. "Mama will be right back, okay. I'll let your friend visit with you."

Charles mumbles.

"What was your name again?" Ms. Robinson asks on her way out.

"Olivia."

Ms. Robinson grabs Olivia's hand. "God bless you, Olivia."

Charles wiggles his body the best he can and grunts as Olivia closes the door to the room.

"Charles, Charles, Charles. I've heard a lot about you." She hovers over him.

He squirms and his eye darts to the red call button.

Olivia snatches the remote away. "Relax, I'm not going to hurt you. The thing is Charles, I need your help, and you need mine."

Charles struggles to talk.

Olivia taps his cheek. "Don't try to talk. You'll only hurt yourself."

Charles yells in pain.

I know exactly what you want, a certain ballerina."

Charles stops moving.

"I got your attention. I looked into you, and I know who you are and what you do. You're more than just an earnest mechanic, aren't you? You're a member of the Anti-Shifter Movement."

Charles's eyes widen.

"You didn't think anyone knew about your little after-school club. Not the case. You're hardly a threat. No one cares."

Charles radiates anger.

"Don't get upset with me Charles. I'm here to help. I can get you out of this bed so you can get your little girlfriend back. How does that sound? Let's be honest, even on your best day you're too weak to take Red on your own. It was honorable, but it was foolish of you to try. I can help you get Celeste, but you have to trust me. If you want to walk out of here tonight and get your woman back, blink twice. If not, I walk out of here and you'll never see me again. She'll continue fucking Red Paw for the rest of her life, and you can live with the humiliation. Is that what you want for her?"

Charles's breath becomes ragged.

"I saw those two in action, and let me tell you, it was hot. She kept begging him for more and he couldn't get enough of that ballerina pussy."

Charles pounds his fist on the bed.

"Don't get me wrong you're a nice-looking guy. She loves you, but Red is a big, powerful, sexy beast. I don't know what it is about that girl. Red can't keep his hands off of her. She tried to get away from him, but she can't. He's got her Charles. He's got your girl, and she's falling for him. What's it going to be?" Olivia stares at Charles.

He blinks. She waits. He struggles. There's a pause. He blinks again.

"You've made the right choice." Olivia whistles.

The door opens. A tall, lean, slightly older man dressed in blue scrubs enters the room with a wheelchair. He has caramel skin and matching eyes. He appears to be a nurse or a doctor, but Charles recognizes him. He's not a medical professional. He's Tate Washington. He's a wolf shifter, and he's no better than Red Paw.

"Keep your mouth closed," Olivia says. "Oh wait, never mind."

Tate picks Charles up from the bed with no regard for his injuries. Charles cries out in pain.

"Don't worry. It won't hurt for long," Tate says as he sits Charles in the wheelchair.

His side is killing him, and sweat beads across his forehead.

Tate pushes Charles past the nurses' station with ease. Two women are talking and neither is paying attention to their surroundings. They make it to the elevator without any problem, and Tate swipes a badge that gives him access to the roof.

Charle's eyes are filled with fear as Tate pushes him to the edge.

"This is your lucky day. I want you to remember that a shifter gave you your life back," Olivia says.

Tate sinks his canines into his arm and grabs Charles's hand. He sinks his canines into Charles's right arm.

Charles tries to scream. Heat courses through his body. He jerks side to side and back and forth. He convulses as if he's having a seizure and then slumps in his chair. His body is still, and his eyes are closed.

"What's happening?" Olivia asks.

"I don't know. I've never done this before."

"Wake him up," Olivia says.

"Just wait," Tate says.

Charles opens his eyes and looks around. He jumps out of the chair and lunges at Tate until he realizes the pain is gone. He touches his sides. His body is whole. He can walk. He can jump, and he's sure he can talk. He's been dying to get rid of the wires. Charles screams through the pain as he forces his mouth open. Blood runs down his face. He pulls the wires from his mouth and grabs Tates arm. He sinks his canines into the spot where Tate bit himself and swallows a taste of his blood.

They both feel a burst of energy.

Charles falls back and quickly jumps to his feet feeling power and strength like he's never felt before "What have you done to me?" he shouts.

"Welcome to my world," Olivia says.

"What?"

"The only way to beat the monster is to become one," Olivia says.

"You're one of us, Charles," Tate says.

"I need to go. You got it from here?" Olivia asks Tate.

"I got it," Tate says.

"Forget that you ever saw me." Olivia walks to the back of the building and jumps off.

Charles runs behind her and looks over the edge. "What the fuck?" he asks.

Olivia takes off running like it's nothing.

"You're a wolf now?" Tate says.

Charles shakes his head. "No," he says.

"It's too late to cry about it. You're sired to me."

"Why? I didn't ask for this."

"No need to thank me."

"I don't want to thank you. I want to kill you. I don't want to be one of you. I hate shifters."

"You're going to have to get over that. You and I have a common enemy, and his name is Jackson Redding. You can stay on this roof and cry, or you can take back what's yours. What's it going to be?"

"What do I need to do?"

"You need to come with me. I'll show you, but you have to trust me."

"I will never trust you."

"Fine, trust yourself. I have no beef with you. I could've killed you if I wanted to. I didn't have to come here tonight, but I took a chance that you might hate Red as much as I do. We have to move quickly. Are you in or out?"

"Fuck," Charles shouts. "I'm in."

"You have wolf instincts and I don't have time to break you in slowly. Someone's going to have to teach you, and you have the best teacher you could want right in front of you. I need you to do as I say."

"Fine."

"Shift," Tate says as he picks Charles up and throws him off the roof.

"Charles screams until he can't make a sound. He's paralyzed by a sharp, tormenting pain. Instead of dropping to the ground, he soars through the air, but the ground is close.

He scrambles, sure that the impact of the concrete will take his life, but he lands on his feet with ease. Charles looks down. It's not his feet that hold him up, it's his paws. He turns and looks around. He sees a tail following him.

Tate lands next to Charles. "You're a grey wolf," he says. "When I make a command, you'll do as I say. Now shift."

Charles opens his mouth but all that comes out is a howl.

"Picture yourself as human and your body will follow."

Charles shifts into his naked human form. He looks around. "Why me?"

"You need to get your girl back, and I need to get to Red Paw. He'll see me coming from a mile away, but you Charles, he'll never suspect."

Chapter 14

"Who hired the falcons?" Red asks Olivia.

They sit at a round table in a conference room at his warehouse along with Bryan, the lead warrior, Torrey, the omega, and Celeste.

"We're still trying to figure that out," Olivia says.

"Try harder," Red says.

"I'll stay on top of it. I promise. Nothing is more important to me than this."

"Those motherfuckers were in my territory. That's unacceptable."

"We've made some enemies lately," Torrey says.

"The Southside Pack couldn't do this. They don't have the resources and they don't have a leader. Their pack no longer exists," Olivia says.

"How many of their members have tried to join our pack?" Red asks

"So far, twenty," Bryan says.

"I think it's one of two options," Olivia says.

"Who?" Red asks.

"One is Tate Washington, and the other maybe we should talk about later," Olivia says.

"We'll talk about it now," Red says.

"Are you sure you want Celeste here for this?" Olivia asks.

"Yes. Who?"

"The other is Douglas Emerson."

Celeste's heart quickens at the sound of his name. "My father?" she asks.

"You could've spooked Tate with your recent acquisitions. The only logical choice is that you're coming for him next. Maybe he wants to stop you before you get him," Olivia says.

"Why would Tate hire someone outside his pack?" Torrey asks.

"Element of surprise, I don't know, but I told you we should've struck sooner," he says.

"I want Tate to sweat. I want him to wonder when it's coming. All this started with Tate, and it's going to end with him. His will be the sweetest conquest, but also the most difficult," Red says.

"I understand, but you can't be moved by revenge. We have to be strategic," Torrey says.

"We're being strategic. We have to take down Tate's whole operation if we're going to take the Northeast. We have to cripple him and take the Port of Houston. Then we can take him down.

"I still think it's Emerson," Olivia says.

Celeste is scared to speak. She doesn't want to be kicked out of the room. She wants to hear everything they're saying.

"Why's that?" Red asks.

"It seems like the falcon that you shot wasn't interested in Celeste. He could've gotten both of you, but why didn't he? Was he instructed to leave Celeste alive? And if that's the case, the only person who would spare her life is her father."

Celeste wonders if she ruined her chance to get away. Were the falcons there to save her? This theory didn't make sense to her. "My father is not a murderer."

"Douglas doesn't have the resources to hire them," Red says.

"What do you mean?" Celeste asks.

"Maybe he rallied some of his rich friends," Olivia says.

"That's highly unlikely," Red says.

"The Guardians may want to retaliate. There's also the matter of his disappearance."

"What are you talking about?" Celeste asks.

"It's all over the news," Torrey says. "I thought you knew. Your parents are missing. The police are looking for them, but so far nothing. Their home was burned down, and no one has seen them."

Celeste feels like the wind is knocked out of her. "My mom," Celeste says.

"I'm sorry," Torrey says. The good thing is they could still be out there."

"Emerson isn't a threat," Red says.

"Maybe, but we have to be certain," Olivia says.

"I'm certain," Red says.

Celeste looks at Red. Disappointment and sadness are in her eyes.

"Do you have information that we don't?" Bryan asks.

"Look into Tate," Red says.

"I'll take care of it," Olivia says.

"Coordinate with Bryan," Red says.

"I can handle it."

"That wasn't a suggestion."

"Understood," Olivia says.

"Leave," Red says.

Once the leaders have left the room Celeste addresses Red.

"What were they talking about?"

"There's an article in the Houston Chronicle."

"Let me see it," Celeste says.

"Torrey told you the details."

"Let me see it," Celeste shouts.

"That's not a good idea."

"I think I've been accommodating, Jackson. Things can be a lot worse."

"Don't you ever threaten me," Red says.

"I'm not backing down. We're talking about my parents. I deserve to know."

Red pulls out his phone and pulls up an article. He hands the phone to Celeste.

"Thank you." Celeste scrolls down the screen, reading every word carefully.

"How are they missing?" Celeste asks out loud. She keeps reading. "Houston Ballet Soloist, Celeste Emerson, daughter of Douglas and Regina Emerson who was recently engaged to local businessman Jackson Redding was unavailable for comment. Redding issued the following statement. Celeste and myself are saddened by the news of the disappearance of her parents. The police department is hopeful that they are still alive. We are using every available resource to locate Douglas and Regina and pray for their safe return. Please keep us in your prayers during this trying time." Celeste looks at Red. "Why didn't you tell me?"

"I didn't want you to worry."

Celeste scrolls up the screen. "This was published two days after the gala."

"I know."

"You were just going to keep me in the dark this whole time."

"That's not what I was doing."

"You're making statements on my behalf."

"It was for the best."

"The best for who? You wanted to take suspicion away from yourself. Is that it?"

"No."

Celeste takes a deep breath. "Did you kill my parents, Jackson?" Celeste asks.

"No."

A tear falls from her eye. "I don't believe you."

"Celeste I would never do something like that."

"You're always talking about what you'd never do. Do you expect me to believe you're some kind of man of honor? I've seen the things you do. I'm not stupid, Red Paw. You're telling me killing is something you'd never do. What other lies do you expect me to believe? You want me to believe you're not the biggest racketeering boss in this city. You want me to think this warehouse isn't where you keep your drugs."

"Is that all you think of me? I thought you were getting to know me."

"I thought I was too."

"Baby, I've never pretended to be an angel, but I'm not the devil. I haven't lied to you, and who the fuck told you there were drugs in here."

"I know you all think I'm naive, but I'm not."

"No, you're not, but you're making assumptions about me that aren't true. I don't sell drugs nor does anyone in my pack."

"So how do you make all your money?"

"This warehouse is a distribution center."

"I know."

"For my chain of grocery stores not for my drug cartel. I'm not some stereotype. My businesses are legit. I own properties all over the city. I have employees with W-2s and 401ks and medical benefits and shit. I take care of my pack, and I wouldn't kill the parents of the woman I—"

"You what?"

"I wouldn't do that to you."

"I don't know what you'd do."

"Take my hands," Red says.

"No."

His voice is gentle and calm. "Just take my hands." He holds his hands, palms facing up in front of Celeste.

Celeste places her palms in his. "What is this?"

"Look into my eyes."

Celeste looks into Red's eyes. A wave of calm washes over her. "Are you hypnotizing me?"

"No, I'm being honest with you. Close your eyes."

Celeste closes her eyes.

"Take a deep breath. Feel my heartbeat. Breathe in and out with me. Now open your eyes."

Celeste looks at Red. He looks sincere. There's sadness is in his eyes. She hates that he does this to her. She knows she shouldn't feel sorry for him or sympathize with him, but she can't help it.

"Do you believe me when I tell you that I didn't kill your parents?"

"I believe you."

Red is overwhelmed with relief. "Do you believe that despite the things I've done, that I care about you?"

"Yes."

"Come with me." Red takes Celeste by the hand to his office. He opens a locked box inside his desk and pulls out a folder.

Celeste sits in a chair across from Red.

He hands her the folder. "Open it."

Celeste opens the folder and the first thing she sees is a photograph of a man and woman wearing baseball caps and dark clothes. "What is this?" She studies the photo. "This looks like my parents." She flips to the next page. There's a photo of the man and woman sitting on a porch at a house Celeste has never seen before. This photo is clear. "These are my parents. What is this? Where'd you get it?"

"Your parents fled the city for the Cayman Island. They have a home there. I kept tabs on them, but I haven't bothered them and I haven't killed them."

"I don't get it. Are they on vacation, or what are they doing?"

"When they lost their territory a lot of people had questions that your parents were not prepared to answer, and rather than deal with the fallout, they left."

"They left me." Celeste hangs her head.

"I don't know what their long-term plans are."

"Have they reached out to you? Have they tried to contact me?"

"No."

"I guess I shouldn't be surprised. Would you tell me if they did contact you?"

"If I'm being honest. I don't know. I may have waited until you asked about them. It depends I guess, but I promise you if they contact me I'll let you know. I never have and still have no reason to keep you away from them."

"My father is something else, isn't he? Just throw me to the wolves why don't you. And my mother is so fucking weak?" Celeste seethes with anger.

"That's her husband."

"So what?"

"She loves him."

"I thought she loved me too."

"She does love you. That's your mother. She'll always love you. Give them some time. They have a lot to figure out. They wouldn't forget someone as special as you."

"Thank you. I guess. Tell me the truth. What business did you have with my father? He says you came in and told him that you were taking over or killing everyone. Is that what happened?"

"No."

"Your father has many secrets. Everybody kisses his ass. The whole city thinks he's a hero, but it's all an act. You've heard of Jason Blaze."

"He's the former chief of the Southwest."

"He and your father are in business with Tate Washington."

"What kind of business?"

"Drugs, weapons, human trafficking, you name it."

"You're lying."

"I haven't lied to you and I'm not lying now. Tate controls the Northeast so he controls the Ship Channel and the Port of Houston. Your father and his Guardian friends allow Tate to handle their illegal operations so they never got their hands dirty. Jason worked for your father. Your father called the shots and cleaned the money. They've all made a killing, but your father has a bad gambling addiction."

"No, he doesn't. There would be signs if that were true."

"Your father stole money from Tate and Jason. He stole money from his charities. He was spiraling."

"Red, this doesn't make sense. My father has money."

"Your father started selling off assets trying to cover his habit. Donations to his charities were going to his pockets. He owes a lot of money to some dangerous people, and he couldn't go to Tate or Jason, because they would've realized he took money from them too. He had it bad, but he knows how to keep up appearances."

"And everybody is involved in this but you. You expect me to believe that."

"I don't work for anybody, and I never will."

"So, you're going to be the boss. You want to take over the whole operation."

"Six months ago your father came to me begging for a loan. That's not something I do, but I made an exception."

"And when he couldn't pay you back you took his territory."

"And his remaining assets. I did the same thing to Jason Blaze. When I came to collect at the gala, your father, the bullshitter that he is, said he would sign over his assets and give up control, and he offered to give me you. I was only there for the territory. It was his idea to say we were engaged so people would assume he was handing things over while keeping it in the family."

"That motherfucker. He lied to me. What about us?"

"Like I said. You're my mate. What your father did regarding you wasn't a factor."

"What about Tate?"

"What about him?"

"Why is it important that you make him suffer?"

"Tate killed my parents."

"I'm sorry. Was he the one they trusted?"

"There was a time when all the territories were involved in illegal activity. My parents once controlled the whole North. They were running shit. Tate was the beta of our pack. We were close. I called him Uncle Tate. He was fun and well-liked. He and my parents made a lot of money. He told them that he had a new hook up, and he set up a meeting with a new supplier. It turned out to be an ambush. My parents were killed and with them gone, that meant I was alpha. I went to The Guardians and demanded justice, but they told me I had no proof. Tate left the pack and took half of our members with him. Those that were loyal to my parents stayed with me. Those who were loyal to the streets went with Tate. Our packs went to war, and damn near destroyed the city. I was still young and looked to stupid advisors that didn't know shit. Innocent people were getting hurt, and we had to regroup and restructure. I decided to run the pack my way and handle business my way. To keep peace in the city, The Guardians created more territories. The North was divided into two territories. Tate got the Northeast. I got the Northwest. Jason Blaze got the Southeast and your father the Southwest. It became clear that the three of them had been working together. My parents shut out your father and he didn't like that. Suddenly he was working with Tate and Jason. That's when I realized they'd planned the whole thing."

"You've been plotting revenge this whole time."

"I was young then, but I'm not a boy anymore. I planned to make sure everyone involved got what was coming to them."

"Including my father?"

"Yes."

"When the two territories became four. I was surrounded by enemies."

"How did you survive?"

"Let's just say I made my mark. I couldn't let them think they could walk all over me. While they hid, I made sure the people in this city knew my name. My pack became powerful. I flexed on the other packs whenever I had the chance, and word got around that nobody crosses Red Paw."

"Why didn't you just kill them all?"

"I didn't just want them dead. I wanted them to suffer."

"Why is now the time?"

"They were all on top, and things are falling apart as planned. I wanted the whole city to see, and now that I have you it's time to end this. I want this city to be better for our future."

"Can we go home?" Celeste asks.

"Yeah," Red says.

Red spends the rest of the day alone in his office while Celeste thinks about everything she's learned.

Chapter 15

"What are we doing here?" Celeste asks Red.

"I thought I'd bring you somewhere to take your mind off of things," Red says.

"I could use a distraction, but this hardly seems like your scene."

"I thought you might like it. Was I wrong?"

"I love Kemah. I haven't been here in so long,"

"Good." Red leaves his car with the valet and grabs Celeste's hand.

Celeste looks around at the Kemah Boardwalk. They're surrounded by restaurants, shops, rides, and games, and it's a weekday so it's not too crowded. "You've been thoughtful lately," Celeste says.

"I'm trying," Red says.

A young girl asks if they want to take a picture.

"No, that's okay," Celeste says.

"We can take one," Red says.

"Okay." She puts her arm around his waist and he puts his arm around her shoulder. She holds on to his fingers with her free hand and smiles as he looks down at her.

The young girl gives them a piece of paper with a number on it and tells them where they can get their picture.

"Are you going to get on the rides?" Celeste asks Red.

"We can do whatever you want."

"This is going to be so much fun. I can't wait to hear you scream like a little girl."

"That's never going to happen."

"We'll see," Celeste says.

"Remember when Astroworld was in Houston," Red says.

"Oh yeah. That was the place to be," Celeste says.

"Then they closed it down."

"Now the city is seriously lacking. How is it possible that Houston doesn't have a theme park?"

"Our kids won't have a place like that to play. When I was little the kids in the pack used to save Coke cans so we could get discounted season passes. I bet your parents used to close down the park for you."

"Ha, ha," Celeste says hoping Red didn't notice how she froze when he mentioned their kids. What was your favorite ride?" she asks Red.

"Texas Cyclone," Red says.

"Good choice, but I'm going to go with Batman's Escape."

"That's weak," Red says.

Celeste hits his arm. "No, it's not. You rode it standing up. That's not weak."

"That stand-up thing was a gimmick. The Cyclone had everything."

"Please. The Cyclone is basic," Celeste says.

Red laughs. "What do you want to do first?"

Celeste points to the big wooden rollercoaster ahead.

"The Bullet. You didn't come to play, did you?"

They walk to the back to find the line for The Bullet. People can be heard screaming as the rollercoaster whips past them on the tall, creaky, wooden structure.

"I think we just passed the line," Red says.

"I know. I just want to look at the water for a moment."

They walk to the wooden deck and lean against the rails looking at the water. Red stands behind Celeste with his arms around her waist and his head rested on her shoulder. The water is still and relaxing. There are boats in the water and a couple of jet skis. Celeste remembers that her parents have a boat in the marina next to the boardwalk. Her father named it after her mother, Regina. She wonders if it's still there. There isn't any reason it shouldn't be there.

"What are you thinking about?" Red asks interrupting her thoughts.

Celeste turns around. "Standing here with this strong sexy man with his arms around me. It feels good."

"Are you trying to get fucked on this pier?"

Celeste's body tingles. "That wouldn't be appropriate."

"I don't give a fuck."

"Last night and this morning weren't enough."

"Nah. It wasn't enough for you either," Red says.

"You can't blame me when I have all this lying next to me." She places her hand between his legs.

"Excuse me, Celeste. I have so much to offer. I'm more than just a big hard dick."

Celeste laughs then stops.

"What's wrong?" Red asks.

"Am I just here for your sexual pleasure?" she asks.

"Have I treated you that way?"

"I don't know."

"If I just wanted sexual pleasure, as you call it, I could get that anywhere, anytime, anyplace. I do enjoy your body, but I don't want a sex slave unless you're into that. I made you a part of my pack. You're my alpha female. Do you know what an honor that is?"

"I do."

"I told you what I wanted that night in the woods."

"My heart," Celeste says. "I almost forgot about that."

"I haven't, and I meant it."

"How does this work, Jackson? What does our future look like?"

"Babies and our pack and anything else you want."

"I want to dance. I lost everything. It's all I have left. I need to dance."

"I know."

"We're on break now, but I have a contract with the company. What about my career?"

"I won't keep you from dancing or from The Houston Ballet."

"You can't sit in on rehearsals and scowl at everyone."

"Trust me I have no intention of doing that. I have businesses to run. We have a pack, and as much as I love watching you dance, I don't want to watch ballet that damn much."

"Promise me. Promise me you won't keep me from dance."

"I promise. Promise me that you'll give this a chance."

Celeste turns around. "What do you mean?"

"Never mind."

"Jackson," Celeste says cupping his face.

He looks at her with those puppy dog eyes. The ones that make her heart melt.

"Let's go get on this rollercoaster," Celeste says.

Once they're strapped in and secured Celeste feels butterflies in her stomach. "I haven't ridden a rollercoaster in years," she says.

"Me either."

She grabs Red's hand and squeezes. The ride takes off and Celeste is filled with dread. She closes her eyes and screams to the top of her lungs. Her stomach drops as they're violently jerked back and forth and side to side. Red laughs at the ride. Celeste is terrified. As it rips through the tracks, around the curves, jerking her body. She covers her face with her hands begging for it to be over, but it's not. It seems to go on for an eternity. When the ride stops Red pulls Celeste up.

She's shaken and horrified. "Why would anyone want to ride that?" She clutches Red's arm as he laughs.

"That was what you wanted to do."

"Why didn't you stop me? That ride is psychotic. I don't remember it being like that before."

"What do you want to ride next?" he asks.

"Nothing. Let's get some drinks."

Red looks at his watch. "Okay, but let me win you a prize first." He stops in front of a basketball hoop and buys a shot.

"Just one?" Celeste asks.

"That's all I need."

"Cocky."

"You know it."

A boy hands Red a ball, and he sinks it in one shot.

"Never doubt me," he says. "Now which one do you want?" He points at the assortment of bears. "This one," Celeste picks a red bear.

They walk around and Red wins Celeste more prizes. "I don't know how we're going to carry all this," Celeste says.

"You can put all that shit in the trash for all I care," Red says.

"I'm not putting them in the trash. You won them for me. I'm going to keep them. They can sleep in the bed with us."

"Not in the bed."

"Yes, and I'm going to tell everybody in the pack that you sleep with stuffed animals."

"You wouldn't do me like that."

"I would, but I may change my mind if you give me something."

"Anything."

"A hug."

"You want a hug?"

"I do."

"I think I can do that." Red asks one of the employees for a bag. He takes Celeste's prizes and stuffs them in the bag and sits them on a nearby bench. Celeste snuggles into his open arms and welcomes his embrace. She closes her eyes and inhales his scent. His head rests on top of hers, and they hold one another for minutes. Neither of them wants to let go of the other.

Finally, Celeste looks up at Red.

"Are you happy now?" he asks.

"Yes."

"Are you glad we came?"

"I am. I'm having a good time with you."

"Thank you."

"And…" Celeste says.

"And what?"

"You're supposed to say you're having a good time with me too."

"Oh, is that what I'm supposed to say?"

"Only if it's true."

"Hmmm."

Celeste hits his shoulder. "Jackson."

"What?"

"Forget it." Celeste lets go of him and reaches for the bears. Red takes her hand and pulls her back in. "Don't act like that."

"I'm not acting like anything."

"You can't possibly be mad at me for not saying what those movies you watch tell you I'm supposed to say."

"Nope. I'm not mad. I told you I'm having a good time."

"Then why do you have that look on your face?"

"I don't know what you're talking about. This is my face. What do you want to do now?" she asks.

"I want another hug," Red says.

"I'm good on hugs," Celeste says.

"You are tripping."

"I'm not," Celeste says. She walks to the rail and looks at the water.

"Fucking women," Red says as he follows her. "What's wrong with you?"

"Nothing. I said I'm having a good time. Quit asking me," Celeste snaps.

"Who the fuck are you talking to?" Red asks.

Celeste rolls her eyes.

"Straighten your face."

"You are not my father."

"Damn right. This damn temper tantrum isn't going to work on me. You like those simple boys that do whatever the fuck you say."

"I never said that."

"You're spoiled."

"I'm not spoiled. I wanted to know if you were having fun. I'm out here feeling good, enjoying a moment, or so I thought. It's fine though. I guess it was just me."

"So if I don't say what you want when you want, then what? That makes me wrong in this situation."

"Yes."

"Do you hear how ridiculous you sound?" he asks.

"Nope." Celeste tries to fight a smile.

"Are you laughing at me?" Red asks. "This is what I get for trying to do something nice for you. I wanted you to have fun. That's the idea, but you can't just enjoy it."

"Did you yell at your girlfriends like this?"

"I never had girlfriends like that. I never did this shit before. I never gave a damn about nobody but you. I'm a fucking alpha, and I'm out here with you playing games and shit. I thought it was obvious I was having a good time with your ass. What the fuck?"

Celeste wraps her arms around his neck. "Jackson, that's so sweet."

"Woman, what is wrong with you?"

She shrugs.

"I didn't know you cared what I thought," he says.

"I guess I do."

"I want you to like me."

Celeste beams and she can't help but blush at his honesty. She bites her bottom lip and teases him, batting her eyelashes.

"What are you supposed to say right now?" he asks.

"I do like you."

"Let's go get you that drink," he says.

They walk to The Aquarium hand in hand, and Red tells the hostess he's meeting two people.

"Who are we meeting?" Celeste asks as they walk to their table.

"Celeste," a woman shouts across the room.

"Kierra," Celeste shouts. "Kierra, what are you doing

here?" She runs to her best friend hugging her tight.

"Red invited us."

"Us?" Celeste asks.

"You know I had to make sure you were okay."

"Chase," Celeste shouts hugging her friend.

"I can't believe you guys are here. I missed you so much. Give me one minute okay." Celeste turns around and walks to where Red is standing. She hugs him tight. "I can't believe you did this for me. Thank you so much, Jackson."

He kisses her on the forehead. "You're welcome."

She grabs his hand, but he stops her. "No, you go ahead. Spend some time with your friends. I got us a room at the Boardwalk Inn." He hands her a card slid in an envelope with the room number written on the front. "Just meet me when you're done." He's tempted to give her a speech about not fucking up, but he decides against it.

"Are you serious?" she asks.

He nods.

"Jackson, this means so much to me." She pulls him in for a kiss.

He smiles. "I'll see you later."

She watches him walk away thinking how sweet he is before she goes back to Kierra and Chase.

"Let's go to the bar."

"Yes, please," Kierra says.

"So I guess this thing between you and Red is real," Chase says after they order drinks.

"I wouldn't say that."

"What would you say?" Kierra asks. "I don't walk around kissing Chase like that."

"But you tried," Chase says.

"Shut up," Kierra says.

"You guys so much has happened."

"I can only imagine," Kierra says. "We've been calling you, trying to find you. We didn't know what to do."

"I lost my phone."

"How did this happen?" Chase asks.

"Something went down between Jackson and my father."

"Are you going to go through with this wedding?" Kierra asks.

"I don't know. He hasn't said anything about it, but there's something else."

"What?" Chase asks.

"I'm his mate."

"Oh shit," Kierra shouts.

"What about Charles?" Chase asks.

"I don't know. Have either of you seen him?"

"No," Chase says.

"Have either of you seen my parents?"

"Not since that night. No one's seen them. It's like they vanished, and then their house burned down. I don't know what to make of any of it," Kierra says.

"Neither do I," Celeste says.

"And I don't know what to make of you and Red Paw. You mated. You look like you're in love. Did he force you?" Kierra asks.

"Not exactly."

"So you wanted to?"

"It's complicated."

"Tell us something," Kierra says.

"I made some mistakes. I cheated on Charles."

"I can't believe it."

"Please don't judge me. I've never felt lust like that before. One minute I was disgusted by Jackson. The next I couldn't get enough of him. It was so strong, and we mated. I tried to leave town with Charles and he proposed to me. Then he and Jackson got into a fight. I thought Charles was dead, but I don't know now."

"It is complicated," Chase says.

"I need you two to do something for me."

"Anything," Kierra says.

"I need you to find Charles. I need you to see if he's alive and see if he's okay. If you find him tell him I'm sorry. Tell him I'm fine. Tell him not to look for me, and tell him thank you for standing up for me."

"We'll do it," Chase says.

"How are things with Red?" Kierra asks.

"At first it was awful, but it's gotten better, a lot better actually. There are times when I think I could really like him, and the rest of the time I wonder what's wrong with me."

"Are y'all fucking?" Kierra asks.

Celeste diverts her eyes and tries not to smile.

"See that shifter dick can make you crazy."

"Who do you want to be with? Charles or Red Paw? I really can't tell," Chase says.

"I want my life to go back to normal."

"Do you want to leave?" Kierra asks.

"We can go right now," Chase says.

"I can't."

"Yes, you can. We can just walk out of here. We'll be with you." Kierra says.

"Where will we go? Are you two prepared to leave your lives behind for me? Do you want to be on the run, looking over your shoulders? Red is powerful and resourceful. You guys are sweet, but I can't just leave my mate."

"Do you need help?" Chase asks.

"No, Jackson takes care of me."

"Celeste," Kierra gives her a sad look.

"I'm serious. Now let's talk about something else. What are you doing with your break?"

Celeste, Kierra, and Chase laugh and talk through the night. Anytime they asked her about Red she assures them that she's okay.

"Thank you so much for coming," Celeste says hugging her friends outside the restaurant.

"We love you," Kierra says.

"We're here for you," Chase says.

"I love you guys too," Celeste says. "Bye."

Celeste walks alone realizing she hasn't had freedom like this since she met Red. She looks around at the shops and realizes she can't buy anything because she doesn't have money. She doesn't have her purse, credit cards, or cash. She fooled herself into thinking things were better with Red, but she's still a prisoner. She stands in the middle of the boardwalk and looks around. She pulls the key card from her pocket.

She knows she has two choices. She looks at The Boardwalk Inn and she looks at the water. The water could carry her away to who knows where. It's the perfect escape. Red can't walk on water, but Red would be hurt, betrayed, and angry.

"What should I do?" she asks herself.

Chapter 16

There's no sign of Red, no sign of his pack. No one is watching. With her heart racing and her hands shaking Celeste puts the room key in her pocket and walks to the marina. She enters the code to the gate while trying to steady her hands. Afraid to look back she runs to her parent's boat, The Regina, and climbs on board.

She takes a moment to catch her breath. Freedom could be a step away. She goes below deck and looks in the drawer where her parents keep a spare key.

The key is gone. She pulls the drawer in and out.

"Where is it?" She shuffles some papers around and pulls everything out. "It has to be here." She opens another drawer. "Maybe I got the wrong one," she says as she shuffles through the junk inside. She gets on the floor searching through the mess she made.

"No," she says to herself. She has to think. She looks around the room. "It has to be somewhere."

"Looking for something."

Celeste turns around. Red stands at the entrance holding a keychain with a white sailor hat. "What are you doing here?"

"I own this boat," Red says.

"I know. I just came here to see if I could find something.

There's a photo album from times we took the boat out."
Celeste stands. "Since my parents are gone and my old house is gone I wanted something to keep with me, you know."

"Yeah," he says.

"I thought I was going to meet you back at the hotel."

"I thought so too, or at least I hoped."

"Do you want to look around with me?"

"You think I'm stupid, don't you?"

"What are you talking about, baby?"

"Don't baby me. I tried. Do you know that. I tried to be nice, understanding, supportive. I tried to be everything I'm not for you."

"I appreciate that."

"You don't appreciate shit. Let's go."

"That's fine. I didn't find anything. I'm ready to go to the hotel." Celeste wraps her arm around Red's waist.

He pushes her off. "Don't fucking touch me."

He takes Celeste to the car and opens her door. "Get in."

"Look I don't know what you think, but I promise you I was coming back."

"What did I tell you about lying to me?" Red asks.

"I mean it," Celeste replies.

"Fuck this shit," Red says. "I'm out here jumping through hoops for your ass. You got me out here looking like a pussy for your ass. That's alright though. I got something for your ass."

"Can you slow down?"

"Don't fucking talk to me," he says. "You think you can play me. Me. I'm motherfucking Red Paw. You must not know about me. That's alright you're about to find out."

They ride in silence for a while.

"Please," Celeste says. "It's not what you think."

"The disrespect is astounding," Red says.

"That's it. Fuck you," Celeste shouts.

"Fuck me?"

"What do you expect, you asshole?" Celeste says.

"I expect your ass to stop lying. I was real with you."

"I was real with you."

"You're full of shit."

"You are if you think I want to be controlled, held against my will, and kept away from the people I love. What's wrong with you?"

"Are you still on that shit?"

"What shit? Being held hostage? I don't lie to you about what we have, but I don't want to be a prisoner in your home. I don't care who you are."

"You want to be free."

"Yes," Celeste shouts.

"You wish you still had that pussy ass boy you were trying to run away with."

"Sure, at least he respected me."

"So you don't want me. You don't want this life. Is that what you're saying?"

"No. I don't want any of it. You happy?"

Red doesn't say anything. He just drives, seething, feeling like a fool. After a while, he picks up his phone.

"Meet me at my house," he says. Then he hangs up.

"Who was that?" Celeste asks.

"None of your fucking business. You don't give a fuck about me, remember."

"Oh, right. That's why I didn't want to see your brains splattered all over the table because I don't give a fuck."

When they reach the house and go inside. Red opens the door and Tasha is there waiting.

"Alpha Red, you asked me to meet you here. Is everything okay?" Tasha asks.

"Everything fine," Red says.

"What is she doing here?" Celeste asks.

"Tasha, wait for me in my bedroom, and take your clothes off."

"Are you sure?" Tasha asks.

"Yes, I'm sure."

Tasha looks at Celeste. Steam is coming out of her ears.

"Don't worry about her. Celeste doesn't want to be with

me. She doesn't appreciate anything I've done for her," Red says.

"Jackson, I swear," Celeste says.

Red walks over to Tasha and whispers in her ear. "Anything that happens here tonight is just between us. Got it."

Tasha nods.

"You appreciate me, don't you Tasha?" Red asks.

"Yes."

Red kisses Tasha. She's shaken and scared.

"Look at me. It's okay," Red says. He kisses Tasha again. This time she kisses him back. "I'll meet you in a minute."

Tasha walks away in some tight leggings and a shirt tied around her waist.

"What do you think you're doing?" Celeste asks.

"Look at all that ass," Red says licking his lips. "Since you don't want me I'm going to spend some time with someone who does."

"You know what I don't even care. You can do whatever you want."

"I will." Red removes his shirt. "Don't get me wrong. Your pussy is spectacular, but if you want to move on I can get pussy anywhere. I can have five different bitches rolling through here every damn day if I want."

"Good, then I won't have to deal with your ass."

Red removes the rest of his clothes. "Good to know. Come on."

"Come where?"

"You didn't think you were going to get away with what you did today."

"It looks like I didn't get away with anything."

"You know your actions have consequences, Celeste."

Celeste rolls her eyes. "If you want to fuck Tasha, I don't care. Fuck her, mate her, and let me get the hell out of here."

"Nah, I'm going to fuck Tasha, and you're going to watch."

"And if I don't?"

"You thought you were a prisoner before. You ain't seen

shit yet. Get your ass to the bedroom."

"If you're trying to prove a point you're going to look stupid. I don't care."

Red grabs Celeste by the throat and pushes her against the wall. "I won't tolerate any more of your mouth. Lock that shit down and get in this room. Understood."

Celeste nods and follows Red into the bedroom, and he closes the door.

"You stand right here and don't move," Red says. His dick is hard and he's angry. He needs to work out his frustration, and Tasha stands on the edge of his bed, waiting. Her clothes are in a pile on the floor.

Red sits on the edge of the bed next to Tasha. He licks his lips and grabs Tasha's ass, pulling her between his legs. He kisses her breasts and squeezes her body. His lips trail down her stomach. Celeste stands back with her arms folded. Tasha is excited to have Red's hands and mouth on her body again. She moans and runs her fingers through Red's hair.

Celeste watches in disbelief, looking to see if Red makes eye contact with her, but he ignores her. His attention is on Tasha. He touches her the same way he touches Celeste.

Red gets in the bed and lies with his head at the foot of the bed and Tasha climbs in behind him.

"You know what your alpha likes," Red says.

Tasha positions herself on her knees between Red's legs. "Are you sure?" she asks one final time. She glances at Celeste but doesn't want to make eye contact.

"Don't mind me," Celeste says.

"Don't pay attention to her," Red says. "Your alpha just wants to feel good. Can you do that, sexy?"

"You know I can."

"Thirsty bitch," Celeste says.

"She doesn't mean that, because she doesn't care."

Tasha climbs on top of Red and kisses his lips.

Red has no problem touching, caressing, and squeezing her voluptuous curves as she kisses his neck and his chest. She bites her way down his body and grabs his dick, stroking up and down his shaft. It doesn't take long for her to forget Celeste is there. Red has her dripping wet.

"May I suck your big alpha dick?" she asks teasing him with a sexy smirk.

"You may," Red replies.

Tasha opens her mouth and moans as she takes Red in her mouth.

"Just like that," Red says as his eyes roll back in his head.

"I don't care," Celeste says.

"Shut the fuck up," Red says as Tasha takes him further into her mouth. "Yeah, baby, suck that dick."

Tasha works him with her hand and mouth while Red moans his delight. He runs his fingers through Tasha's hair and guides her mouth down his length. Tasha opens her mouth and as his head reaches the back of her throat.

"Shit," Red says as his hips lift off the bed.

"You like that?" Tasha asks.

"Fuck yeah," Red says.

Rage builds in Celeste. The fact that Red would do this in front of her is unforgivable. She tells herself that he'll never touch her again. She's determined to get away from him the first chance she gets, and if anyone tries to shoot him again, she'll move out of the way.

Red sits up and pulls Tasha to him. He slips his fingers inside her. "You're so fucking wet," he says. Tasha's head rolls back as she sinks her nails into Red's shoulders.

"Fuck me, alpha," she says.

Red positions Tasha in front of himself with the both of them facing Celeste. He kisses her neck and her back. He squeezes her breasts and rubs her body. Celeste stares and ignores her rage. Red touches Tasha between her legs, massaging her clit, and playing with her wetness while he sucks her neck.

Celeste feels a tingle where he bit her neck. She balls her fists as Red bends Tasha over and grabs her hair.

"I know you love that rough shit," Red says.

She growls, ready for him to invade her. "Fuck this pussy,

Red," Tasha says.

Red whispers in her ear. "Tell me you want this alpha dick."

"I want it," Tasha says.

Red strokes his dick and grabs Tasha's hips.

Celeste charges to the bed like a raging bull. "Bitch, what the fuck did I tell you," she shouts at the top of her lungs.

She's possessed as she grabs Tasha's arm and pulls. Tasha falls flat on the bed. Celeste yanks her out of the bed and pushes her on the floor. Then she grabs her hair and slaps her across the face.

"Didn't I tell you not to touch my mate?"

Tasha screams.

Red jumps off the bed and pulls Celeste off of Tasha, holding her by the waist while Celeste kicks and screams.

Tasha scoots backward. "You're crazy," she shouts.

Celeste tries to break away from Red's grip. Her arms are flailing and her rage can't be contained.

Tasha isn't sure what to do. There could be serious consequences for attacking the alpha's mate.

"Tasha, you should leave. I'll call you," Red says.

Tasha grabs her clothes and scurries out of the room.

"Get the fuck out of my house, bitch," Celeste shouts trying to get away from Red. "Let me go," she shouts.

Red waits until Tasha is out of the house before he lets go. Celeste takes off running, but Red cuts her off at the bedroom door.

"What do you think you're doing?" Red asks.

Celeste jumps back when she realizes he jumped in front of her. "Get out of my way."

"She's gone. Stop acting like a lunatic," Red says.

Celeste punches Red in the face. "How could you do that to me?"

Red laughs.

"You think this shit is funny?"

Red walks away.

Celeste jumps on his back and hits him repeatedly. "I hate

you," she shouts over and over.

Red grabs her hands and flips her over his body, throwing her on the bed. "What's your problem?" he says calmly. He jumps over her and lands on top of her, pinning her arms and legs to the bed.

"My problem is you, you bastard." Celeste struggles to move. "You were going to fuck her in front of me."

"You don't care. You don't want to be here. You hate me. You can't wait to get away from me. Isn't that right?"

Celeste grits her teeth. "You disrespectful son of a bitch."

"I told you this shit was real. Don't tell me you don't want me. Don't tell me you don't want to be here. Even if you did leave you wouldn't get far, because something would bring you back where you belong, to your house, as you stated. Admit it."

"You're the lunatic. Let me go."

Red releases his hold on Celeste.

She throws her legs around his waist and pulls him on top of her.

He growls.

"You said you were mine," Celeste says.

"I am."

"Don't you ever do that to me again."

"Are you going to be a good mate?"

"Celeste growls."

"You're growling now."

Celeste nods. "I'm sorry, Jackson."

"You're not sorry. You just want some dick." Red sits up with his back against the headboard.

"I know I've been a bad mate. I will make it up to you."

"Don't worry about it." Red gets out of bed and puts on a robe.

"What are you doing?"

"I'm going to my office. Don't wait up."

Hours pass and Celeste showers and lies in bed naked and alone feeling the emptiness of missing her mate, wishing he'd come back to bed and hold her. She hurt his feelings and she can't shake the guilt or forget the somber look on his face when he walked out the door.

She finally gets out of bed and goes to the kitchen to look for a snack wearing one of Red's t-shirts. With the day she's had she settles on some Blue Bell Rocky Road ice cream. She grabs a spoon and digs in, closing her eyes as the rich, chocolate flavor bursts in her mouth, and as good as the ice cream is she can't help but think about Red.

She stands outside his office door and contemplates knocking. Red can hear Celeste pacing back and forth in front of his office. After a while, the back and forth starts driving him crazy.

"Celeste, what are you doing?"

Celeste opens the door slightly and pokes her head in.

"Can I come in?"

Red nods.

"What are you doing?" Celeste looks around the room as she walks to Red's desk.

"Reading," Red says.

"You read?"

He gives her a strange look.

"You know what I mean," she says.

Red points to a gigantic bookcase behind him filled with books. Celeste walks by the bookcase and touches the spines of the historical tomes and literary fiction. She looks at Red with shock and admiration.

"I just learned how to read last year so I thought I'd keep working at it," he says.

Celeste laughs. "Jackson, you made a joke."

"Don't get your ice cream all over my books." Red turns his attention back to his reading.

"Can I give you some?" Celeste asks.

"No."

Celeste walks closer to Red but tries to maintain distance while he deprives her of the attention she wants.

"What are you reading?"

"Why don't you just tell me what you want?"

"I want you to look at me." Celeste walks past the invisible barrier she created and stands next to his desk.

"I'm not in the mood for whatever this is right now."

"What are you in the mood for?"

"To be left alone."

"Jackson," Celeste purrs.

"What?"

Celeste touches his shoulder. "I find it hard to sleep without you next to me."

"I'll be up soon."

She turns his chair so he's facing her.

He looks up.

"Can I sit with you?" Celeste asks as she sits on his lap.

"You're going to get ice cream on all my shit."

"I won't."

Red takes a deep breath as Celeste sits on his lap and lays her head on his shoulder. "What are you doing?" he asks.

"I don't want you to be mad at me." Celeste scoops some ice cream and holds the spoon to Red's mouth.

"I'm not." He takes the ice cream in his mouth.

"What are you reading?"

He closes the book and shows Celeste the cover.

"The Tales Of Edgar Allen Poe. This is what you're reading?" Celeste feeds him some more ice cream.

"Yep."

"What's your favorite?"

"There's so many to choose from."

"Read one to me," she says.

"You can't come in here making demands."

"Hush now. Do as your alpha commands?"

Red laughs.

"I got you to laugh. I can't believe it. Record this day so we can remember it forever."

"Okay. I'm going to read you a short story, but you have to be quiet." Red opens the book and turns the pages.

"I will," she says.

He clears his throat. He reads slowly. "This is Spot. See

Spot r- ru-," he holds his finger over the word like he's trying to sound it out, "Run. Run Spot, run," he says.

Celeste bursts out laughing, spitting ice cream out of her mouth. She doubles over and Red has to hold her up to keep her from falling out of the chair. Her laugh is infectious. He tries to keep a straight face, but he can't help but laugh himself. It takes a while for them to settle down, and they can't help but look into one another's eyes before Red picks up the book. Celeste settles in his lap with her head on his chest as he opens the book and holds it so Celeste can see as well.

"The Cask of Amontillado," he begins.

"I have no idea what any of that means," Celeste says.

"You'll get it. Just listen." He begins. "The thousand injuries of Fortunato I had borne as I best could, but when he ventured upon insult, I vowed revenge."

"That sounds intense."

"It is." He keeps reading.

Celeste is enamored with the sound of his velvety voice and how he reads with passion and conviction. She holds on to him, feeding him ice cream, gripping his back as the story gets more and more intense.

Red smiles to himself feeling how enthralled in the story Celeste has become. She's full of questions and predictions as Red reads the words of Edgar Allen Poe until he reads the last line, 'In pace requiescat!'

"What does that mean?" she asks.

"It's Latin for may he rest in peace."

Celeste's face is contemplative. Her eyes are squinted. Her head shakes from side to side. She's speechless. Red awaits her reaction.

"That was amazing," she shouts. "I've never read anything like that."

"I was hoping you'd like it," he says.

"So we don't know exactly what this guy said that pushed him over the edge?"

"No."

"And the guy was just clueless."

"Basically."

"I mean, the story is so intricately designed. It's genius."

"I like how there were these clues that something was off but Fortunato ignored them and was so fooled that he basically—"

"He was begging for it," Celeste says.

"Yeah," Red says.

"The guy was so genius. He had Fortunato begging to be led to his death. He even offered over and over to turn around, and Fortunato just kept going deeper and deeper, and when he was dying he still thought it was part of a joke."

"That's fucked up. Ain't it?"

"That's an incredible story," Celeste says.

"Indeed."

"How do you feel about revenge?" she asks.

"I think you know."

"If you're going to do it, I mean this is the way to go. This guy was crafty and smart, like you."

"But," Red says.

"But I don't want you to live your life like this. Do you know what I mean?"

"I know what you mean. I don't plan to."

"I know you already have something cooking, things you're trying to do. Revenge will consume you. I want you to enjoy your life."

"You mean that?" Red asks.

"Yes. Don't you want to be happy?"

"I don't really think about happiness. I think about surviving."

"When you're old and gray, do you want to look back at your life and say I survived?"

"Amongst other things," Red says.

"What other things?"

"Like most people, I want to leave behind a legacy."

"Of destruction?"

"No, of greatness."

"I think you can do it. You can show a little compassion

every once in a while."

"Have you read the story about the compassionate alpha?" Red asks.

"No," Celeste says confused.

"Exactly. Compassion will get you killed."

"You've shown me compassion."

"That's because —,"

"Because what?"

"Because it's all in your head. Have you ever wanted revenge?" he asks.

"I don't know. I never thought about it. I mean in ballet there's so much competition. People do some twisted things to get ahead. This girl named Denise hates me. She reminds me of Olivia just hates me for no reason."

"She probably sees you as a threat."

"That's what Kierra says. Denise is always trying to get in my head, make me lose focus. One time when we were in the academy, she destroyed my costume right before a major performance. She never got caught, but I know it was her."

"What did you do?"

"There was nothing I could do, but improvise. I put something together backstage and just went on with the show."

"You should've beat her ass."

"That's what Kierra said."

"Kierra's right."

"I just decided to rise above it. She'll get what's coming to her."

"What's coming to her is an ass-whooping. You should've dragged her like you dragged Tasha."

Celeste covers her face. "Don't remind me."

"That shit was sexy. Don't let anybody put you down. That's what I want for you."

"Do you think there was a moment of regret in the story?" Celeste asks.

"No. I think Fortunato crossed a line that sealed his fate. The man said he gave him a thousand chances."

"I hope that's a hyperbole."

Red and Celeste stay up for hours talking about The Cask of Amontillado with Red answering her questions and shedding some light on the imagery and symbolism. Celeste was impressed, to say the least. There was a moment when Red looked at her and she looked at him, and she had that look on her face like he was her hero or some shit, and Red knew he was in trouble.

Celeste fell asleep in his arms as he read more Poe to her. When Red hears her snoring, he picks her up and throws away her pint of ice cream that left a ring on his desk. He carries her to bed and kisses her forehead as he lays next to her.

Chapter 17

"It says this is the place." Kierra studies her phone.

"Are you sure this is it? I don't see a sign," Chase says.

"Welcome to the hood. I knew Charles didn't have much, but I didn't think it was this bad," Kierra says.

"Stop being stuck up. After everything he and Celeste have been through, give him a break. This place isn't bad at all. It looks like they're changing the sign."

Kierra reluctantly turns into the parking lot of the auto shop. "I'm only doing this for Celeste."

She and Charles get out of her sports car and walk toward the building. A man wearing coveralls approaches them.

"Can I help you?" he asks.

"My phone said this was Mick's. Are we in the right place?"

"Right place. Wrong name. It's Robinson's now. Sorry about the confusion. We're under new management."

"No problem. Is there someone named Charles here?"

"There is. He's in the office. Just head inside."

"Thank you."

Kierra and Chase enter the building. The interior is nice and comfortable. There are couches and chairs and a TV that plays a court show. The room is nice and illuminated, and there are windows with views of the garage that's packed with cars. A woman sitting at the counter smiles politely. Chase approaches the desk.

"Good morning ma'am. We're looking for Charles."

"Just one moment," the woman says. She picks up the phone and alerts Charles that he has guests. "Okay," she says. "Just head down the hall. Last door on your right."

"Thank you," Chase says.

Kierra and Chase step into the office. Charles stands behind a desk. Kierra notices something is different about him right away. His presence is almost intimidating. He's wearing a crisp white shirt and tailored black slacks. He stands tall, and he looks buff, in a way that he didn't before.

"What are you two doing here?"

"We wanted to see you," Chase says.

"Why?"

"We were concerned about you," Kierra says.

"You expect me to believe that?"

"We came down here just to see you. Why wouldn't you believe it?"

"You think I never caught on to your snide comments, Kierra. I know what you think of me so I'll ask again. What are you doing here?"

Kierra wasn't used to Charles being so direct. She had to take a step back and think before she spoke again.

"We know you care about Celeste. We wanted to check in on you," Chase says.

"I'm fine. You can both leave now."

"Have we done something to offend you?" Kierra asks.

"Other than coming in here faking concern, pretending you want to check on me. I don't have time for your bored ballet girl games." Charles sits at his desk.

"We heard about what happened. We're genuinely here to check on you." Chase says.

"As you can see I'm doing well."

"We thought you were badly injured. How are you back at work so soon? You look better than ever," Kierra says.

190

"When you own the company, you don't get days off or have time for this shit. Thank you for stopping by." Charles turns his attention to some invoices on his desk.

"He owns the company," Kierra whispers to Chase.

Chase shrugs.

"Yes, he does," Charles says still looking at his papers.

"We'll get out of your hair," Chase says. "We saw Celeste."

Charles stiffens. He loses focus. The words in front of him become blurry. "Really," he says.

"She thought you were dead," Kierra says.

"She asked us to check on you. It's why we came."

Charles looks up from his papers. "When was this?"

"A little over a week ago," Chase says.

"What did she say? How is she?"

"She's dealing with a lot. She's trying to be brave."

"Was she with him?"

"Yes," Kierra says. "He arranged for us to meet with her."

"We're not sure what's going on. I don't know if you heard what happened at the gala."

"I heard. He took over their territory and announced he and Celeste were getting married," Charles says.

"I don't know where that came from. Everyone was shocked, including Celeste," Kierra says.

Charles remembers how frantic she was when she showed up at his apartment asking him to leave with her.

"Does she look okay? Does she look hurt?"

"She looks good, no signs of abuse, physically anyway," Kierra says.

Charles fights the impulse to get choked up. "Thank you for letting me know. You can leave now."

"She told us to tell you something," Chase says.

"What's that?"

"She says she's sorry. She said she's okay and not to look for her, and she said thank you for standing up for her," Kierra says.

"Thanks, guys."

"We'll see ourselves out," Chase says.

Charles nods.

Once Chase and Kierra are gone Charles thinks about all the things they told him. With everything Celeste told them to relay he couldn't help but focus on the one thing she didn't say, I love you.

The next day Charles stands on a rooftop looking down at Celeste and Red. They're standing in line at The Breakfast Klub. It's a Saturday so the line to get inside wraps around the side of the building and down the street.

"I can't risk doing this again so get a good look," Olivia says to Charles.

Thanks to his transformation he can see clearly from far away. He told Tate he wanted to see Celeste, and after some resistance, Tate forced Olivia to make it happen to keep Charles compliant.

"I think it's the least you can do," Charles says.

"You should want to be more careful. If he scents you everything could be ruined."

"I'm not worried."

"You should be. Everything hinges on the element of surprise. You just had to see her, didn't you?"

Charles watches Celeste and Red as they stand in line. Many of the patrons have let them skip ahead out of respect for Red, and Charles is disgusted at the display. The owner comes out to personally greet them. Photographers take their pictures. Red and Celeste converse like it's just a normal day for them. Celeste doesn't appear to give a second thought to Charles. Anger seeps from his pores.

"Stop that growling. He'll hear you."

"Fuck him," Charles says.

Celeste turns around and looks at her surroundings. Charles swears she's looking right at him. His heart skips a beat. Red slips his hands around her waist and she smiles and leans into his body. They look like a happy couple. Red can't seem to keep his hands or lips off of Celeste and she is soaking up the attention. She always did love being adored. Her white sundress showcases her long legs, and she looks radiant even in the sweltering Houston heat. Around her neck, she wears the pointe shoe necklace that Charles gave her. It's not the expensive jewelry that he knows she's used to, but it was more than he could afford when he bought it for her. He didn't even know what pointe shoes were until he met Celeste. He remembers the way her eyes lit up when she opened the box and the way she hugged him. She told him that she'd never let anything happen to the necklace and it was her favorite piece of jewelry.

Charles feels a glimpse of hope when Celeste tugs the necklace. Maybe she was thinking about him. Then something catches his eye, almost blinding him. Celeste is wearing a ring, not the ring he gave her, that he spent every dime he had on. She was wearing a huge diamond on a platinum band. It was elegant, sophisticated, and way more expensive than anything Charles could afford.

The wind is knocked out of him as he sinks to the floor of the rooftop.

"Get up," Olivia says.

"She's wearing his ring," Charles says.

"You asked for this. Now you see what I deal with every day."

Charles slams his fist into the ground.

"Be careful," Olivia warns him. You don't want the roof caving in. That'll give us away.

"I don't even care."

"Look you knew what was happening. I prepared you for this. You don't have time to sit around and cry if you want to get your girl back."

"I can't believe this. She looks happy. I can't tell you if she's ever looked at me the way she looks at him."

"Look those two are in lust. Don't get your panties in a bunch. Once they get tired of fucking that shit will go away."

"That's not what it looks like."

"He's forcing her to stay with him. She tried to escape."

"Yeah, she looks real disheveled right now."

"What do you expect her to do? This is a delicate situation.

What is it about Tinkerbell that has you all losing your damn minds?"

"Probably the same thing that has you so jealous."

"Please, I'm not jealous. I'm a fucking catch."

"Maybe if you smile every once in a while, someone would see that."

"Seriously. What the fuck? Why are men always telling women to smile? I have more to offer than a smile. Fuck all of y'all."

"Celeste is intelligent and funny. She's beautiful and kind. That's why I fell in love with her."

"Look she loves you too. I heard her say it. To Red. If you want her back this sulking and crying isn't going to work. She's been with an alpha. She needs a strong man."

"Don't you worry about me. I'm all the alpha she needs."

"Good so get off your ass and let's get out of here."

Charles stands and sees Celeste holding hands with Red as they enter the building. "Unbelievable," he says.

Olivia drives Charles to his place.

"Tate hooked you up with a nice spot."

"It's pretty decent," Charles says.

"Can I use your bathroom?" Olivia asks.

"Yeah."

They get out of the car and walk inside the four-bedroom house Charles is staying in. When the door closes Olivia pushes Charles against the wall.

"What are you doing?" he asks.

"I don't want to beat around the bush. Just fuck me," Olivia says.

"Quit playing," Charles says.

"You're a wolf now, an alpha wolf, go figure. You should live like one. Celeste is enjoying herself. You should too." She bites his lip and growls. "Show me the alpha," she says.

"This isn't right."

"I promise you it'll feel right." Olivia releases her hair from the ponytail and shakes out her long brown locks. She removes her shirt and bra.

"What you mean is it'll feel like you're sticking it to Celeste," Charles says as her blue eyes flash green.

"It'll feel fucking amazing." She unbuckles Charles's pants.

He struggles with himself internally as he watches her slide his jeans to the floor.

"You have a lot of aggression. Work it out on me."

She turns around and removes her pants. When she stands so does Charles's dick. She presses her ass against him. He touches her skin and runs his fingers through her silky hair. "Don't be a pussy. Fuck me like an alpha," she says.

He growls and yanks her head back, then pushes her down. "I'll show you a fucking alpha. Bend that ass over," he says.

Olivia bends all the way over and her ass is perfectly placed in front of Charles. He spits on his erect, rock-hard dick and strokes himself.

"What are you waiting for? Red is probably over there fucking your girl as we speak, and once you had a man like that you can't go back to a pussy like you. What are you going to do to get your girl back?" Olivia taunts him.

Charles unleashes the fury he's been holding. He roars as he slams his dick into Olivia's ass, showing no mercy as he pounds her relentlessly.

Olivia cries out as his body crashes into hers over and over again. She loves the pain and pleasure, and Charles goes hard.

"Is this what the fuck you want? You want everything Celeste has, don't you?"

She shouts.

"Fuck that. I can't understand that. You'd better scream my fucking name."

She moans.

He pulls out and sticks her again and again giving her all his anger and rage. "What did I say?"

"Charles," she cries out. He lifts her and pushes her against the wall. With his body pressed against hers and his breath on her skin, Olivia is pushed to the brink as she cums.

He squeezes her breasts and digs into her skin. "Say my name."

"Charles," she shouts as he bangs her into the wall.

"I'm more man than that motherfucker you want. Don't you ever talk that pussy shit to me again. You hear me, bitch?"

Her head bangs into the wall as Charles pounds her.

He slaps her on the ass.

"You better answer me."

"I hear you."

He sinks his claws into her side.

Olivia growls and moans. "I hear you," she cries out.

"You hear who?"

"Charles, Charles, Charles," she screams.

Charles has stamina like he never has before. Gratification courses through his body as he bites Olivia's back. He loses himself as he watches his dick invade her over and over. He fucks her all around the room in every position imaginable, using her body, channeling his pain into her, and she soaks it all in. When he's done, Olivia is on her knees. He stands over her stroking his dick in her face. She's exhausted and panting. He shoves his dick in her mouth and she sucks him until he's ready to erupt, and he pulls out. He howls as cum squirts from his dick all over Olivia's face. He coats his tip with his cum. "Open," he says, and she takes him in her mouth again.

Looking at what he's done, he feels like something possessed him. Olivia's body is bitten and bruised. Her peach skin is red and purple and he wonders how he could do something like that. As he scans her body the marks and bruises heal before his eyes. He watches in amazement as she's restored. He takes his shirt off and wipes her face.

"Get up," he says.

Olivia rises from her knees.

"That was good," she says.

"That's what you like?" he asks.

"Did you hear me complain?"

"In that case take your ass to the bedroom. I'm not finished with you."

Olivia happily complies. Their encounter was as beneficial for her as it was for Charles. She needed the release just as much as he needed to unleash.

Chapter 18

"You see this shit?" Charles wakes up early while Olivia sleeps in his bed.

"What time is it?" Olivia yawns as she rises.

Charles holds his phone to Olivia's face. "Do you see this?"

Olivia grabs the phone. It's a photo of Red and Celeste on the front page of The Houston Chronicle, *Businessman Jackson Redding and Houston Ballet Soloist Celeste Emerson Making A Difference.* Red and Celeste have been followed by photographers who have gotten photos of the couple out and about, volunteering, making a donation to the Houston Food Bank, and catching them at events around the city. "It's part of their image," Olivia says. He's using her to make himself look good."

In the main photo, Celeste is smiling. Her hand is rested on Red's shoulder showcasing the ring he bought her. Red is looking in her eyes and they look like they're in love.

Charles shakes his head. "This is some bullshit."

"It'll be over soon."

"You sure are calm about this for someone who's obviously in love with this Red bastard."

"I was like you. I got worked up over every little move they made, but then I decided to do something about it. I'm tired of trying to fight it. I'm tired of trying to talk sense into Red. I just can't do it anymore. I ended up being the one looking crazy, so I just ignore it."

"That's easier said than done."

"Just look at it as temporary. This will all blow over soon. Thanks to me everybody can get what they want."

"I'm pretty sure you're in love with this man, so why are you leading him to his death."

"I gave him a chance. He chose Celeste. He doesn't see my value."

"Are you're going to kill him for that?"

"I'm going to let Tate kill him."

"All because he's not in love with you."

"He doesn't know who he is anymore. He can't lead the pack like this, and he won't listen to reason. He's been fucking up ever since he mated Celeste, and since his decisions can't be trusted I'm doing what's best for the pack. They deserve a leader who is dedicated."

"So, he fucked you and lost interest."

"That's not what happened."

"Then what happened."

"He and I grew up together. We've been friends practically our whole lives. I was taller than everyone else and awkward. He was a loner. I was trying to fit in and some kids at school dared me to talk to him so I did. I thought he was going to bite my head off but we ended up talking about basketball all day and we played together after school. After that day we were inseparable."

"When did you fall in love with him?"

"I don't know. It's not like I was pining for him. I had goals. I wanted to be an alpha, not just an alpha female. Everyone knew I was that, but I wanted to be in charge. I wasn't thinking about him. I was working hard, learning to fight, be smart, and do everything the male alphas could do. He encouraged me. He supported me. Then one day he went crazy. He showed everyone what I already knew. He had been suppressing himself, observing his surroundings. He let everyone underestimate him. Things changed after that. There was no doubt who the next alpha would be. Girls were always throwing themselves at him. Guys wanted to hang out with him."

"Did you get jealous?"

"I don't know. Maybe. I quickly realized I would have to share him, but he was a loyal friend. He did his best to include me, and we remained close friends."

"When did things change?"

"After his parents were killed. He was angry, always ready to fight. He must've torn the city apart. I was there for him through it all. One night it just kind of happened. We were feeling good after a fight, getting drunk, and one thing led to another and we started fucking."

"Was it a one-time thing?"

"No, we were like friends with benefits I guess you can say, and it didn't interfere with our friendship. We were solid. It was the best of both worlds and I started feeling like we could be great together like his parents were. Then the city was divided into four territories. He felt betrayed. He was angry that he had been getting bad advice from his advisors. He told me he needed me. He got rid of the pack's beta."

"Got rid of?"

"Killed him. He said I was the only person he could trust and we needed to work together. He needed me by his side. I thought that he would mate me and we'd run the pack together, but he made me his beta, which is an honor, but—"

"Not what you had in mind."

"No, still I was grateful and I thought that if I showed him my worth he'd mate me and we'd be the most powerful couple this city's ever seen, but it was the opposite. After that, he stopped hooking up with me. It was like a switch went off in his head. Our relationship was strictly professional. One day I asked him flat out why we stopped. He said we didn't need to use one another anymore. We needed to focus on the pack."

"He wasn't wrong about that."

"Silly me. I didn't know we were using one another."

Charles looks at Olivia with pity.

"Don't feel sorry for me. I got past it. He was right. We did need to focus on the pack, and we've been successful ever since."

"And now?"

"Now after all my work and sacrifices he names Celeste alpha female, a title she hardly deserves. She has nothing to offer the pack. It's not right. So now I'm going to get what I always wanted. I'm going to be alpha, and I won't have to answer to anyone."

"Olivia, you need to think about what you're doing. You said yourself that he's been a good friend, and he believed in you."

"Are you defending him? What would your anti-shifter group think about that?"

"It's not about him. It's about you. You don't have to be defined by him. You can start your own pack."

"I want what I deserve. I helped build this pack. When everyone left I was one of the loyal few who stayed by his side. I did his dirt and had his back. He dismissed me without a second thought the minute Celeste came along."

"Just because he doesn't love you doesn't mean he's not a good friend. What you're doing is fucked up."

"I'm not doing it, Tate is."

"That doesn't make it better, but I don't care. All of you can kill each other. I just don't want Celeste around for it."

"That's why this works for everybody. You take Celeste off my hands. Tate takes care of Red, and I take care of the pack in their absence. Your people will be happy that Red Paw is dead. Isn't that what you want?"

"You need to think about what it is that you want."

"You just remember that with Red alive there is no you and Celeste."

Across town, Celeste sits in the kitchen talking to Harrison as he prepares dinner.

"Would you look at this?" Harrison says showing Celeste

the newspaper.

"Front page of the Sunday paper. Seriously?"

"Whether you like it or not the whole city is invested in you two."

"Why?"

"You're both big names. With your family name and his reputation, people are interested."

Celeste studies the photo and her eyes look to the huge diamond on her finger. Red gave it to her, and the whole fiancé thing suddenly seemed real. He told her she needed to wear it because they'd be making some public appearances. She had no idea they'd be front-page news.

"The woman in this picture looks happy," Harrison says.

"She does, doesn't she."

"I don't think you're that good at pretending."

"We have our moments," Celeste says.

"There's nothing wrong with being in love with that man if that's where your heart's at."

"I don't know. Sometimes I think he's amazing and sometimes I can't forget the things he's done."

"You don't know the things he's done. Only what you heard."

"And what I've seen."

"How does he treat you?"

"That's a complicated question."

"All I know is that man paid all my medical bills when I was laid up in the hospital from a stroke. He made sure I got the best care. He came to visit me regularly, and he made sure that my family was taken care of."

"I had no idea."

"I'm saying there's more to him."

"I wondered why you worked here."

"He was a regular at my restaurant for years and when it closed down he asked me to work for him. Given everything he did for me and mine, I accepted. People say all kinds of things about him. Hell, some of it's true, but I know he has a good heart, and the both of you deserve to be happy."

Celeste looks at the ring on her finger. "Maybe," she says as she tugs the point shoe necklace around her neck.

"Your supper's almost ready. Why don't you go put on something nice?"

"Why?"

"I'm supposed to tell you to meet Mr. Red on the terrace."

"Did he plan something?"

Harrison shrugs. "I don't know."

"Okay."

"Look at that smile on your face," Harrison says.

Celeste heads up the stairs and opens the door to the bedroom. There's a black satin dress on the bed, a bouquet of flowers, and a gift box. Inside the box, there's a gorgeous red and white diamond necklace with matching earrings. There's a greeting card in the bouquet of dark red roses. The front reads *For Someone Special*. The inside is handwritten.

The red diamond is the rarest in the world and with all its beauty it still can't compare to you. Nothing is more precious and rare than the woman who captivates me and makes me want to be a better man. I hope we will spend many nights together whether I'm reading to you while you lay against my chest or I'm writing my name on that pussy.

Celeste covers her mouth in disbelief. She runs to the bathroom and takes a quick shower. She fixes her hair and makeup and puts on the necklace and dress along with her come fuck me heels. The dress has spaghetti straps and reaches mid-thigh showcasing her long legs. The fabric dances against her skin making her feel sexier with every step she takes. She twirls in the mirror before she steps into the hallway where red rose petals are laid out before her. She follows their path to the back of the house where red stands on the terrace wearing a black suit with no tie and a crisp white shirt unbuttoned at the top.

The look on his face is serious, sexy, and sinful and the only thing Celeste can think about is jumping on his dick. The terrace is filled with rose petals. There's a bistro table with white taper candles, a bottle of wine, and some wine glasses.

"You look beautiful," he says.

Celeste walks to the rail of the terrace and stands next to Red. Her skin shivers when he brushes his finger against her arm. The full moon shines bright in the distance, but it looks close enough to touch. With the beauty of the backyard from the glowing of the pool and the forest in the background, it's a picture of perfection.

"Why are you so quiet?" he asks.

Celeste stares at the moon and scans the stars. They seem to shine brighter than she's ever seen.

"Did I fuck up?" he asks. Red tried to plan a perfect evening but is suddenly nervous that he made a fool of himself.

Celeste is overcome with emotion. She tries to hide the tears in her eyes and turns her back to Red.

"Did I upset you?" he asks. "Look at me. Why are you crying?" Celeste turns around. He leans over her with his hand on her shoulder, full of concern. "If this is too much we don't have to do it."

Harrison rolls a cart onto the terrace with dinner, and Red steps away from Celeste.

"Thank you, Harrison." He motions for Harrison to step inside the door with him.

"Everything looks good," Harrison says.

Red whispers. "There's something wrong with her."

"What's that?"

Red motions for him to keep his voice down. "I don't know. She hasn't said a word."

Harrison looks past Red. Celeste's back is to them and she looks into the distance.

"What do I do?" Red asks.

"Go on out there, son."

"I can't. She won't stop crying."

"She's crying?" Harrison asks.

"I just said that."

"Youngblood, she's crying because you did good. Now go on out there."

"I'm not so sure. I think it was too much."

"She's happy. That's a good thing. Just give her a minute. You'll see."

"Okay." Red takes a deep breath. "Just stick around for a minute in case she loses it."

Harrison nods and he removes dinner from the cart and places it on the table.

Red walks to Celeste carefully. He stoops so he's eye to eye with her. "Harrison made dinner. Do you want to eat?"

Celeste attacks him with a kiss. Her hands hold the sides of his face as she pulls him in. Harrison smiles and makes himself scarce after he's done setting the table. Red breathes a sigh of relief as he lifts Celeste off the ground.

When they pull apart she has a shy smile on her face.

"You scared the shit out of me," Red says.

"I'm sorry. I didn't know what to say. No one's ever done anything like this for me before."

"You deserve things like this," he says.

"I'm still a little shocked."

"I hope that's a good thing."

"Do you know what my favorite thing is?"

"The necklace?" He touches the piece of jewelry around her neck.

"No."

"The dress?" He feels the satin fabric that hugs her body perfectly.

"No."

"The earrings?" He touches the jewels in her ears.

"The card," she says. "You wrote those words for me."

Red tugs at his collar. His cheeks flush.

"Don't be embarrassed. I love it so much."

"Why don't we eat before the food gets cold?" He pulls out a chair for Celeste and pours her a glass of wine once she's seated.

"Thank you, mate," she says.

"You're welcome."

"You look handsome tonight."

"Thank you, mate."

"You look really every night."

"Oh yeah?"

"Yes."

"Are you flirting with me?"

"Maybe."

"You better eat your food. Keep on and I'm going to knock all this shit off the table and eat you for dinner."

Celeste crosses her legs. "Harrison would flip out."

"I know."

Celeste picks up her knife and fork and cuts into her filet mignon. "You wrote me a poem," she says as she eats.

"I don't know what you're talking about."

"Yes, you do."

"Eat," he says.

"I saw our picture in the paper on the front page."

"What did you think?" he asks.

"It was a nice picture. We look like the perfect couple."

"Do you see us that way?" he asks.

"It feels that way sometimes. It's a little confusing given the circumstances."

"It doesn't have to be. I don't want to feel like you're pretending with me."

"I don't feel like that, Jackson. My feelings for you are not pretend, but I have to admit some things make me uncomfortable."

"Like what?"

"All these articles that call me your fiancé. I know you announced it, and you gave me this ring, but you never talk about it."

"I know I don't. I feel like we're mates and that means more to me than anything, but I figure a woman like you might want to get married and all that shit, and I feel like I should earn that. I want to marry you, but I'll wait until you're ready."

"How will you know when I'm ready?"

"I hope you'll tell me, but I'm trying to spend time with

you and get to know you so I can ask you properly."

"This kind of shit is why I'm confused. You act like I'm not trapped like I chose to be here."

"I want you to choose to be here. I want you to see that I care about you. I consider you to be my woman. I don't want there to be any confusion about that. I know we didn't date or anything and that's my fault, but I want you to consider me to be your man and not just say it."

"I feel like I'm yours and you're mine, but I got robbed of the experience, the stage where we get to know one another and I get nervous when you come to pick me up and take me out and we're crazy about one another. That experience, those memories, are what make relationships special. I would've liked to have that."

"I'm trying to make up for that."

"You are. You've been attentive, considerate, romantic, and even vulnerable, and that's what makes it damn near impossible not to fall for you, Jackson."

"Will you give me a chance and allow me to date you?"

"I don't know. I'm a busy woman."

"And I'm a busy man, but if I can't make time for a pretty lady like you I don't deserve to live."

Celeste blushes.

"I'm not a perfect man, but I'll try if you give me a little of your time."

"I don't know."

"I have a good job, good credit, a big dick. I got my own house, my own car."

"Well, I'm sold."

"Let me be your man. I'll be good to you."

"I'll give you a chance."

"Come over here. Let me whisper in your ear."

Celeste walks around the table. "What do you want to say to me?"

Red stands. "Dance with me."

In his arms, Celeste feels safe as they sway from side to side. Without words, they speak to one another. Without words, they fall deeper. Without words, he is hers. Without words, Red presses Celeste against the banister. He lifts her dress and smacks her naked behind. Without words, he unzips his pants and bends her over. Without words, their bodies connect and he fills her need. Her moans escape into the night sky. Without words, he removes her dress and caresses her body, keeping his eyes on his mark on her back. Without words, she is his.

"Write your name on this pussy," she says as he takes her to ecstasy.

Chapter 19

Things have changed for Red. Taunting Tate is no longer a desire, and the thought of revenge seems unfulfilling. With his relationship with Celeste growing stronger, he feels the time has come to forget about his vendetta and focus on his mate.

Red watches Celeste as she sleeps. Her hair is in disarray and she snores with a smile on her face. The last thing he wants to do is leave her, but he knows that once Tate is gone he and Celeste can look forward to a bright future together. With that in mind, he made love to her and made sure she'd be too tired to move when he was done. From her, he pulled the resolve he needs to take care of Tate once and for all. He can't resist kissing her lips before he walks out of their bedroom.

"Are you going somewhere?" Celeste asks. She can't open her eyes, but she hears Red moving around. She yawns and stretches her legs.

"Yes, but I'll be right back. Go to sleep."

"Okay baby."

With that Red leaves the house. Olivia waits for him outside.

"Sup," Red says.

"Ready to do this," Olivia says.

"Do we have eyes on Tate?"

"It's confirmed he's with his leaders. They're at his warehouse. There are five guys. It should be simple, in and out."

"Then this will be over."

"It's you and me just like old times."

"Just like old times." Red opens the car door for Olivia.

"You always were a gentleman," she says.

"I guess," he says waiting for her to get in the car.

"Red," Olivia looks into his eyes.

Red sniffs Olivia.

"What are you doing?" she asks.

"Who have you been with?" he asks.

"Excuse me. Since when do you ask me that?"

"Since there's something strange about this scent. You got a man I don't know about?"

"I didn't know you cared."

"Come on. I know we haven't talked lately, but you're still my friend."

"Don't get your panties in a bunch. I was in the woods pre-gaming."

"What?"

"I went for a hunt. I wanted to relieve some stress."

"Oh."

"Get in," Red says.

"I wanted to ask you something."

"What's that?"

Olivia kisses Red without warning.

He pushes her away. "What are you doing?" He looks around.

"I was hoping this could all be like old times."

"Get in the car," Red says.

Olivia gets in the passenger seat, and Red closes the door.

"What the hell was that?" Red says.

"I don't know."

"You need to figure it out. I thought we agreed to leave that in the past."

"I guess we did." Olivia rolls her eyes.

"I have a mate now. We've moved on. Is this going to be an issue?"

"No. I just thought we could have some fun."

"I thought you understood we can't do that. Why are you doing this now?"

"I don't know just forget it happened."

"Look I know that you were a little jealous of Celeste, but I didn't think you would take it this far. Maybe we should call tonight off."

"We don't have to do that. Come on."

"Shit," Red shouts as he hits the dashboard."

"Red, come on. We can do this. I still have your back."

"Everything is riding on this. Do you understand that? You know how important this is to me."

"It's important to me too."

"I need you to have your fucking head in the game. You're fucking with my head right now. I can't deal with this shit."

"I'm good. We can take them. We can do it tonight. You and me. I'm not looking for anything here. Let's go. Let's get your territory."

Red starts the car and drives, but he can't fight the nagging feeling.

After driving for a while Olivia notices they're headed in a different direction. They're near her house.

"What are you doing?" she asks as they pull into her driveway.

"This is over," Red says.

"What's over?"

"We can't do this tonight. It's not going to work. Go home."

"Red, don't be stupid. The time is perfect."

"I'm not going to tell you again. Get out of the car."

"Is this because of Celeste?"

"This is because of you."

"I knew she was bad news. You've gone soft since you met her. Are you scared now? Is that it?"

"Get out of my fucking car."

"No, I want answers. You gave her my title. I should be the alpha female. I worked for it, and you never thought about me. You just gave it to her."

"I gave you something more important, but I see now that I was stupid."

"How is beta more important?"

"Alpha female is just a title. I make all decisions, and you were my second. You're the one who had the power."

"And she's the one at your side. She's the one you chose. I've been there all along and you picked her over me."

"You pick tonight of all nights to start this shit. You can't be my beta or anything else. You're out."

"I'm out. You have to be fucking kidding me you disloyal son of a bitch."

Red's phone rings. "Hello," he shouts.

"Tate and his crew are on the move."

"Let them go."

"Are you sure?"

"Yes. We're not prepared. We need to regroup. I still want the warehouses torched. Get in and out. Don't leave a trace. Got it."

"Yes, Alpha Red."

Red turns to Olivia. "I need to go. We'll discuss this later."

"Red, I'm sorry. Can't we just act like it didn't happen?"

"I don't know. Right now, I need to go and I'm about to get really angry if you don't get out."

Olivia climbs out of the car. Before she can say a word, Red takes off, leaving skid marks in her driveway.

Red drives home cursing Olivia and thinking about his mate. He immediately checks on Celeste once he's home. She's sound asleep in bed. He goes to wake her up but hesitates. His instincts tell him to get Celeste somewhere safe and then take care of Tate himself. His grand plans for Tate are no longer important. This needs to end now.

"Celeste," Red wakes her up.

Celeste groans.

"Come on, baby. Get up," he urges.

"Sleep," she says.

"I need you to get up. Come on." He grabs a bag and throws some of her clothes inside as well as some of her things from the bathroom. "Wake up," he shouts.

Celeste yawns. Her senses kick in when she feels Red's agitation. "What's going on?"

"I have to get you out of here."

"Why? What's wrong?"

"We will talk about it in the car. I have a safe house. You need to get dressed right now. Let's go."

Celeste is terrified, but she jumps up to throw on some sweats.

"I packed you a bag. Everything's going to be okay. You ready?"

"Yes."

Red grabs Celeste's hand and she squeezes tight as they walk out of the house. They step outside and head to the car. There's a loud crash. A big black truck rams into the front gate and a group of men jump out howling, barking, and growling. Red's house is surrounded and men are closing in from all sides.

Red takes in his surroundings. His main priority is protecting Celeste. She clutches his back.

"What's going on?" she asks.

"Looks like an ambush." Red is outnumbered. He counts twenty men. Celeste can't make it into the house. They're closing in. The guards at the gate are down. The house is empty save a few of the staff.

A black car drives over the gate and out walks Tate Washington. "Nice to see you old friend." He walks toward Red. "It's been a while."

Celeste digs her nails into Red's sides.

"We're not friends," Red says.

"This must be Celeste. You're more beautiful than I imagined. Don't be afraid, little one. I'm not here to hurt you. I'm here to save you."

Red puts his arm around Celeste. "It's going to be okay."

"Not for you it ain't. My warehouses are on fire as we speak. You wouldn't happen to know anything about that, would you friend?"

"It's a shame. That sounds like an expensive problem. Sounds like if I don't kill you, someone else will."

"The great Red Paw. Look around. There's no way you get out of this alive, and your pretty little mate will have to move on. That's enough talk. Attack."

Tate's pack moves in.

"Celeste get behind me." Red pulls out his gun.

"Now," Tate shouts.

Red pushes Celeste out of the way as he fires, killing four of Tate's men before his gun is knocked out of his hand.

Red looks for Celeste. She's ducked behind a car.

"Jackson," she shouts. She looks around her. There's a gun laying on the ground. She picks it up and fires, shooting one of Tate's men.

"That's not nice," Tate says. "I brought a gift for you and everything."

Celeste looks up, and someone is walking toward her. "Charles," Celeste shouts.

"Celeste," he walks to her dressed in all black. "I'm getting you out of here. Let's go."

"Is this real?"

"It's real, baby." Charles holds out his hand. "Let's go."

Celeste reaches for Charles, but then she looks around.

"Celeste," Red calls out to her as he fights off Tate's men. He's holding them off, pushing them away and tossing them as they attack, but he won't be able to keep them at bay much longer.

"Jackson, watch out," she shouts.

"We have to go now," Charles says.

"Don't leave me," Red shouts.

"Isn't that sweet?" Tate stands back watching, sure that Red will be defeated soon.

"Now," Charles shouts.

Celeste looks behind her and in front of her. She grabs

214

Charles's hand and they run.

"Celeste," Red shouts. His body crumbles, and he's punched in the face, then kicked. He struggles to fight off Tate's men. He's down on his knees and he feels like giving up.

Celeste stops with tears in her eyes. "Jackson, I'm sorry." She lifts the gun and shoots two more of Tate's men.

Tate knocks the gun out of Celeste's hand and growls. "Let's go," he says. Tate gets in the car and Charles pulls Celeste inside. They take off.

"I can't believe this," Celeste says.

"Me either," Charles says.

She touches Charles's face. "You're alive, and you're okay. I didn't know if it was true. She cries."

"I'm here now. I'm sorry I let him take you away. I didn't protect you."

"You did."

"Are you okay? Did he hurt you?"

"He didn't hurt me." Celeste can't help but think about Red. She wanted to be free, but she doesn't want him to die.

"Don't worry, little one, your mate is surely dead," Tate says.

Tears stream from Celeste's eyes.

"Everything will be okay," Charles says.

"Now that Red is dead and the city is mine, finally," Tate says.

"Wait," Celeste says. "Why are you here with him?"

"He helped me."

"How? Why?"

"So that I could help you."

"Aren't you the one who told me how dangerous he is? You can't trust this man?"

"That sounds like Red talking. Is that what he told you while he was fucking your brains out?"

Celeste turns red.

"Where are we going?" Celeste asks looking around. "Let us out."

"I have a spot nearby."

"No, I want to get out. Charles, tell him to let us out." Celeste gets a bad feeling in the pit of her stomach.

"It's okay Celeste."

"No, it's not okay. What reason does he have to be here? He has nothing to do with you or me. Where is he taking us?"

"I can answer that, Charles. I'm going to have a little fun with Red's mate. I hope you don't mind. See, he's been a thorn in my side for years and I need to take something of his. Killing him just isn't enough."

"What are you talking about? That's not part of the deal."

Tate ignores Charles. "I mean that must be some good pussy to bring a motherfucker like Red to his knees. I can't wait to taste his mate."

"If you're joking this isn't funny," Charles says.

"Have I ever joked with you before?"

"We have to get out of here," Celeste says. She tries to open the car door, but it's locked.

Tate laughs. "Damn child locks."

Charles breaks the rear window next to him with his fist. He lifts Celeste to push her out of the window.

"Not so fast, my boy. You didn't think it was going to be that easy, did you? You're sired to me.

"What do you mean?"

"I turned you. I control you."

"Bullshit."

"Sit Celeste in her chair and put her seatbelt on." Tate uses his sire mind control on Charles.

When Charles tries to resist his eardrums are invaded with a high-pitched screech and his body does whatever Tate commands of him.

Celeste squirms. The instant Charles thinks of resisting his head pounds and he covers his ears.

"Stop," Celeste shouts, but Charles can only do as he's told.

"What did you do to me?"

"I hope you're not naive enough to think what we did comes without repercussions. We're born this way. We're at

216

the top of the food chain. You can't just step into this life and reap the benefits."

"I didn't ask you for this."

"Didn't you?"

"What do you want from us? We have no beef with you."

"I want what belongs to Red, and to celebrate our victory, so does my pack."

"Over my dead body."

"You want to die for this girl again. This pussy I have to try. Don't worry. You'll get your turn too."

"Let me out of here."

"Hush now. We're almost there."

Chapter 20

Red is heartbroken and death seems like the only relief. His mate is gone and he's stopped fighting. He takes blows to the stomach and head from the shoes of the 713 Pack waiting for death's embrace. His wolf tugs at him, but Red ignores the animal. The wolf growls and wants to unleash. *MATE!* The animal urges. Images of Celeste flood his mind, her laugh, her smile, the way she moves, her touch, and her eyes, all the tears he caused her beautiful eyes. She shot some of Tate's men for him, but she still left. She left with the man she compared him to, and he realizes she's not only with Charles. She's with Tate, and that can't be good.

Red awakens. "Shit," he shouts. Celeste is in trouble and he has to protect his mate. He promised her he'd protect her, and if he hadn't given up he would've realized she's afraid. He can feel her.

"I'm coming," he says as the red wolf unleashes and jumps in the air. There are eight men left to take down. Red uses his hind legs to push one of the men behind him, and he falls to the ground. The man in front of him reaches for a gun. It's Tate's beta, Max. Red knocks the gun out of his hand with his head and growls. He sinks his teeth between Max's legs and latches on as Max cries. Red releases and pushes him to the ground, jumping on his chest and sinks his claws into his neck. He flips around and lands on the man lying on the ground. He bites his foot and rips until it's barely hanging on.

He whips around and jumps on another guy. He bites side and rips off a chunk of skin and jumps to another man and scratches his eyes out. He falls to the ground and Red sinks his claws into his stomach and drags.

He runs. Two of the guys have shifted, and two pull out guns. He circles the men with the guns whipping around them as they try to get a fix on his position, but he's too fast. The wolves chase him. He has an idea. He stops running and instantly jumps behind one of the wolves. Tate's men are so confused they shoot the wolves and miss Red.

Red jumps, taking both men to the ground and tears into their skin. He sinks his canines into one man's neck and his claws into the other's arm hitting major arteries in both. He jumps off and looks around.

He shifts and picks up a gun. One man is headed for a car. Red shoots him in the back of the head. The other is running out back, headed for the woods. Red takes off behind him. He doesn't want to leave anyone that can alert Tate that he's coming for him and for his mate.

The man leaps over the bushes and Red shoots him in the back of his head. Red heads inside the house to put on clothes and grab weapons and rushes out.

He finds his phone on the ground and jumps into one of Tate's trucks. He calls his lead warrior, Bryan, and tells him what happened and to have his yard cleaned up.

"Yes, sir. Where are you going? I can back you up."

"I don't know yet. I'll let you know when I find them."

"Do you want me to call Olivia?"

"No. Just handle it."

Red hangs up the phone wondering how he's going to find Celeste. His wolf is desperate to find his mate. It hasn't been long. He focuses on her scent and Tates as he drives in the direction they left going off his instincts. He slows down and lets down the window. He can still pick up her scent. He looks at the car's navigation system and presses buttons looking for a clue. He stops and looks up previous locations. There's a house that seems somewhat close and Celeste's scent still lingers. He presses the button to lead him to the house.

Tate has Charles and Celeste inside a modest two-bedroom cottage. Celeste has been stripped of her clothes by Charles and sits on a couch.

"You'll never get away with this," Celeste says.

Tate slaps her across the face. "I told you to shut up, or I will beat you to submission. Did Red let you get away with all this backtalk?"

"Fuck you," Celeste shouts.

Tate punches her in the stomach and she doubles over in pain. He seems to get some kind of thrill from her pain. Celeste is curious.

"You hit like a girl. Is that what it takes to get you off? You have to hit women?"

"Or just watch," Tate says. "Charles, slap your girlfriend for me."

Charles tries to resist, but can't. He slaps Celeste across the face.

The sting burns. Celeste winces, but she refuses to cry anymore.

"Wow, the alpha who can't get it up," Celeste says. "What exactly were you going to do to me? You can't even perform, limp dick. Are you sure you like women? Maybe Charles is more your type. Is that why you made him your boy toy, so you can fuck him whenever you want and order him to be quiet."

Tate grabs Celeste by the throat and squeezes. Her feet dangle and kick uncontrollably as she struggles to breathe. He drops her on the ground.

"You're about to find out."

"Hold her down Charles."

Charles stands over Celeste and holds her hands against the wooden floor. Celeste kicks her feet but it's no use. Tate gets on his knees and spreads her legs.

"Look at that. I'm about to tear this shit up." He unzips his pants and strokes his dick.

"Performance anxiety?" Celeste asks.

"Shut up bitch." Tate licks his hand and works at it again.

"You're no alpha," Celeste says.

"I'll show you an alpha."

"Sit her up," Tate commands.

Charles complies.

"Hold her hands."

Charles holds Celeste's hands behind her back. Tate pulls his pants down and stands in front of Celeste. His dick looks like a shriveled worm.

Celeste bursts out laughing. "What do you plan to do with that?"

"I'm going to let you suck, little one. Open your mouth."

Celeste seals her mouth shut. Tate pries her mouth with his fingers and she bites him. He slaps her again and squeezes her jaw. When her mouth opens a tiny bit he aims for the hole. Celeste squirms, moving her head from side to side.

The door slams open and bangs against the wall. Everything in the room shakes as Red charges into the room. Celeste head-butts Tate and he yells. Red grabs Tate by the back of his neck and slams his head through the front window. Glass shatters and Tate struggles to break free, kicking Red in the chest, but it has no impact on Red.

"Charles, kill Celeste," Tate says laughing.

Charles holds Celeste against the floor and chokes her. Celeste cries. She tries to loosen his grip, but Charles is powerful.

"What did you do?" Red shouts.

"He's sired to me," Tate says laughing.

"I know how to fix that."

Red slams Tate into the floor and picks him up by his legs. He slams his body from side to side in the window. Tate cries like a baby. A perfectly sharpened piece of glass sits along the bottom edge of the window. Red slams Tate down and the glass stabs him in the heart. Red takes his gun out of his pocket and shoots Tate in the back of the head.

Charles releases Celeste. He can feel something change in his body. He's no longer bound to Tate. "I'm sorry," he says to Celeste helping her off the floor. "I'm sorry. I couldn't resist."

Celeste coughs. "It's okay," she says.

Red growls. Charles got lucky before, and he came for his mate again. The wolf was not going to let him get away with it this time.

"You again," Red says.

Charles stands. "I'm not afraid of you."

"Guys, please don't," Celeste shouts.

"You haven't learned your lesson," Red says.

"I won't let you have her."

"She's mine. She belongs to me." Red growls. "Mine," he roars. His wolf is angry.

"She was never yours. She loves me." He looks at the pointe shoe necklace around Celeste's neck. "I'm not giving her up again."

"Fine by me. I don't have a problem killing you."

Red shifts. The wolf wants Charles's blood and his head.

Charles shifts.

The grey wolf and the red wolf circle one another. They're similar in size. Red is confident that with his experience he can lay Charles out in a minute.

"Stop it. Stop it right now." Celeste is frantic as she looks around the room.

Neither Red nor Charles is paying attention to her.

"Stop," she yells, not wanting either man to die.

Red and Charles lunge forward, their wolves scrapping, each ready to kill for the beauty.

Red knocks Charles across the face. Charles's head whips to the side and so does his body. The coffee table is knocked over. Charles jumps and gives Red a blow to the head. Barking and whimpers can be heard as they claw into one another. Red sinks his claws into Charle's flank.

Celeste spots Red's gun on the floor and fires a shot into the air. Charles and Red freeze, both turning their attention to her.

"I said stop," she shouts. She points the gun at her head. "I can't do this anymore. I won't watch either of you die."

Red and Charles shift.

"What are you doing?" Red shouts. "Put the gun down." He walks toward her.

"Celeste, it's okay," Charles says calmly.

"It's not okay. What's wrong with you two? Don't come any closer, or I'll shoot myself and you can fight over my dead body."

"You don't know what you're saying. You're confused," Charles says.

"I'm not confused. I'm tired. I can't lose anyone else. I have nothing," she shouts. "I can't shed any more tears."

"No, don't do that," Red says. "I'm sorry," he breaks down. "I'm so sorry. Please. This is my fault. Don't do it. Go," he says.

Celeste and Charles are both dumbfounded.

"Leave," Red shouts. "Be with him. I'm sorry. I never meant for any of this to happen to you. I won't try to stop you. I promise."

Celeste looks at Charles. He shrugs his shoulders. She drops the gun and runs to Red. He wraps his arms around her body and cries, apologizing and begging her for forgiveness. She lays her head on top of his and holds him.

"It's okay. I'm not going to do it. Okay." Tears stream from her eyes as she comforts him. "I won't do it."

Charles watches them, disturbed by their connection. His arms are folded.

Red stands and wipes his eyes as he turns to Charles. "I won't fight you."

"Me either."

Red holds out his hand to shake Charles's. Charles shakes his hand.

"I need you to come with me," Red says to Celeste. "I won't force you. Charles can come too."

Celeste is confused.

"I want to give you something."

Celeste looks at Charles and then at Red. "Okay," she says.

Chapter 21

Red sits at his dining room table across from Celeste and Charles. The sun is rising and it looks like it's going to be a beautiful day.

"What do you want?" Charles says.

"I want to talk."

"Go ahead," Charles says.

"I want to be clear that I want you to stay of your own free will. You can come and go on your own and have your life back, but if you want to leave, I'll understand. I hoped that after we spent some time together you'd get to know me, and you'd see that everything isn't what it seems."

"What do you mean?" Celeste asks.

"You need to know that this man isn't the choir boy you think he is either. He is, or was, part of the Anti-Shifter Movement. Maybe what the two of you have is real. I don't know, but his interest in you was to get close to your father. He wanted to get intel and their organization wanted to take down the whole system, Guardians and all."

"Is that true?" Celeste asks.

Charles closes his eyes before answering. "That was one of my objectives, but my feelings for you are real."

"You were trying to get to my father, this whole time?"

"It started that way, but in the end all I wanted was you. I meant it when I asked you to marry me. Nothing else mattered. I gave all that up for you."

"He may be telling the truth. I can certainly relate." Red looks at Celeste. "I know what you think of me." He looks at Charles. "I know what everyone thinks of me, but we're not that different."

"Yeah right," Charles says.

"I witnessed the destruction of this city firsthand. I even participated in it. I observed a lot when I was young. My parents weren't perfect. They lived the way they thought they were supposed to live. My goal was never to follow in their footsteps, but to clean up their mess. There's a lot of corruption in this city and someone had to do something, so I became the solution. I sacrificed myself. I became ruthless, respected, and feared so that I could fix things. I wasn't trying to destroy the city. I was trying to save it."

"What are you saying?" Celeste asks.

"The Guardians and the Territory Chiefs only cared about themselves and making money. I care about the people of this city." He looks at Charles. "Shifters and humans. I needed to take control from the Chiefs. I learned when I was that boy looking at the world around me if I wanted to take down the monster I had to become the monster. My goal was to cripple the Chiefs, take the territories, get rid of the crime and violence, and let the city blossom. I wanted to keep everyone safe, not just the rich and powerful."

"Jackson," Celeste says.

"It was almost time. Everything was falling into place, and then I met you, and I had to have you. You were not a part of my plan, but I didn't want to let you go, and with everything that was coming, I wanted to protect you, so I did what I had to do."

"You expect us to believe you," Charles says.

"I do," Celeste says.

"That's up to you, but I have no reason to lie," Red says.

"Thanks for sharing," Charles says. "Celeste, let's go."

"I'm not going with you," Celeste says.

"You have to get away from this man."

"I'm not staying here either."

"Celeste, you're not thinking clearly."

"I am. I'm seeing things very clearly for the first time in my life."

"I have something to give you, as I said. I'll be right back."

"What are you doing?" Charles asks.

"I've been through a lot. I've learned a lot, and I'm not the same woman I was before. You don't know me anymore, and I have a lot to learn about myself."

Red returns with a bag. All of your stuff is in here, your IDs, your phone, charger. I put some cash in there for you, and I have a bank account set up for you, in your name. I know you have your own accounts, but this is just in case you need it. There's a debit card in your wallet. My phone number is saved on your phone. If you ever need anything you call me." Red holds up a car key. "Take this. I won't try to stop you again."

Celeste searches through the bag in disbelief. "Jackson, thank you. I'm going to pack a bag. I'll be right back."

Celeste cries as she gathers a few things from the bedroom she shared with her mate. When she returns Red and Charles stand. Celeste runs to Charles and hugs him. "I know what we had is real. Thank you for rescuing me again."

"Anytime," Charles says.

She wraps her arms around Red. "I don't know what to say." She cries as he holds her. "I'll never forget you. You changed my life. You're my hero," she says.

"I thought I could make you happy," he says.

"You did, and our time together was special, but every step of the way you took away the one thing that mattered the most, my choice."

Red holds her as he walks her to the door. He whispers in her ear as he squeezes her one last time, rocking her from side to side.

"Me too," she says kissing him one last time.

She opens the door, and takes a step forward, embracing the sunlight. Free.

She hops into Red's black SUV and takes off thinking about the last words he said to her.

I've only been in love once.

Chapter 22

"She's gone," Red says.

"I'm sorry."

"Don't be. You were right. She never should've been here."

Red couldn't get out of bed for days after Celeste left, and even though his heart still hurt he knew he had to get up. The city was his, and he had to take responsibility for what he created and prepare his pack for the coming days.

"I never wanted to see you hurt," Olivia says.

"I know. You knew what was best all along, and I wouldn't listen."

"Don't say that. I spoke out of turn. I'm here for you, whatever you need. I'm still your friend so if you need to talk, I'm here."

"Do you mean that?"

"Of course."

"I was worried that I alienated you. I can't believe I was so stupid. Can you come over?"

"You don't even have to ask. I'll be right there."

Olivia jumps with excitement. She has butterflies in her stomach as she rushes to put on some tight pants and a crop top. She throws on nude lipstick with gloss and lets her hair down. Twenty minutes later she enters Red's home.

"You didn't have to rush," Red says.

"It's no problem. I was concerned about you."

"I'll be fine, Olivia. We're resilient."

"We are, and you'll be okay."

"I need to talk to you about some pack business and some personal business, I guess." Red has a shy look on his face, masking his sadness.

"What is it?"

"I know I have no right to ask this so if your answer is no, I'll understand completely. Just tell me."

"Okay," Olivia says.

"Celeste is gone. Our bond is severed. Things are about to change, and I need you."

"I'm here."

"I need you to… I don't know how to say this."

"Just say it. You're scaring me."

"I need you to be my mate, my alpha female."

"Are you serious?"

"You can say no, I understand. I put you through a lot, and I didn't appreciate what I had."

"Red, I don't know what to say."

"The pack needs solid leadership now more than ever and you put in the work, and I just thought that our connection could take us a long way. I know it's stupid."

"It's not stupid. It's smart."

"I don't know I thought you and I could be like my parents were back in the day, like Bonnie and Clyde or some shit."

"I can't believe this is happening."

"You can say no. It's what I deserve."

"What you deserve is a mate who appreciates you, who understands you, and who can bring out the best in you. I'll do it."

"Really?" Red's eyes widen with surprise.

"I told you I'm here for you."

"So should we?" Red reaches out to Olivia and they hug awkwardly.

"I'm sure we'll get the hang of it," Olivia says.

"We've done this before. You don't have to be shy." Red says. He grabs her hand and pulls her in for a kiss.

Olivia is thrilled and relieved as she savors the touch of Red's lips. He pulls her hips close to his so she can feel his erection against her leg. His kiss grows urgent as he grabs and squeezes her body. They pull apart panting.

"Better than I remember," Olivia says.

"We've both grown a lot," he says.

"Indeed."

"So, I know this is presumptuous of me, but I was hoping to do the mating ceremony sooner rather than later. In the hopes that you'd agree I called a meeting."

"You want to do it now?"

"Why not? I just want to get on with my life, our life."

"I agree."

"Let's go then."

Red sheds his clothes and Olivia licks her lips. She can't wait to have all of him once more, and forever. She sheds her clothes and they walk through the back yard and into the forest. As they reach the trail the pack is gathered on both sides and as Red and Olivia pass, they bow. Olivia has never smiled so much as she nods, acknowledging her pack. She's about to become the alpha female. She had given up hope, but it was happening.

Red holds Olivia's hand as they walk to the gathering spot. The pack gathers around them.

"Do you still like it rough?" he asks.

"Fuck yeah."

"Good. You're not like Celeste. I don't have to hold back."

"You never have to hold back with me. I can take it. I can take it all."

"I know you can."

Red howls and the pack howls back at him.

Olivia howls and everyone is silent.

"Over here," Red says. He guides Olivia, picks up a rope, and ties her hands together around a tree. "You ready?"

"Mate me," she says.

Red pops her behind.

She growls.

"It was the scent, you know."

"What?" Olivia asks, disappointed that Red hasn't entered her yet.

"The scent. I knew something was off about it, and it just kept nagging me. Then when I saw Charles I knew why. Were you fucking him?"

Olivia freezes.

"I asked you a question," Red shouts.

"I... I don't know what you're talking about."

"You found him somehow. You hooked him up with Tate. You plotted to kill me and get rid of my mate."

"Do you know how ridiculous you sound?"

"Why'd you do it?"

"I didn't."

"I saw Tate's phone. I know you called him when I left your house."

"Let me down and we can talk about this."

"I already know the truth. I want to hear you say it."

"You and Tate hired the falcons. Didn't you?"

"No."

"This betrayal is the worst. I never thought you'd do something like this to me. You stabbed me in the back." Red extends his claws and stabs Olivia in the back. "Why?"

She yells.

"Do you like that baby?" he asks.

"Yes."

"I got plenty more. This will heal, and if you tell me the truth I'll show you mercy. If you lie, you die." Red stabs her again.

Her body jerks back as she yells. This time Red drags his claws through her skin leaving deep, bloody gashes.

"Fine. I wasn't trying to kill you. I was just trying to get Celeste out of the picture. I knew Tate couldn't take you and I knew Charles couldn't take you. I was supposed to be by your side. We were going to take them out together, but everything fell apart."

"And the falcons?"

"I was supposed to spot them and stop them, but your bitch stole that from me too."

"You can't be this fucked up."

"I'm not. I love you."

"I thought you did, but you hurt me the most."

"Don't you see I believed in you? I believed that you'd win, and you did."

"Thank you for your honesty." Red walks away.

"Are you going to let me go?"

"No mercy," Red says as he leaves the woods.

The growls of the pack can be heard around the forest and so can Olivia's screams as she struggles to break free of ropes, but she's not quick enough. Someone stuffs a gag in her mouth.

The pack's members have their way with her and when they're done her body is bloody, ripped, limp, and unrecognizable. She no longer looks human. Red wants her body to stay as a reminder to anyone who thinks about crossing him again.

Chapter 23

The moment Celeste left Red's house she went to her childhood home where she last saw her parents. What they said was true. The home she grew up in was burned to the ground. She stepped out of the car and took in the once-glorious home that was stripped to nothing. Maybe it'll be rebuilt, but it'll never be the same.

Her next stop was IAH. She was leaving Houston behind knowing that if she fell, she was strong enough to get back up. Her flight was nine hours and thirty minutes and she landed in the city of light without a plan, without a crutch, and with no idea what her future held, but she was ready to strive for greatness.

Celeste took classes at the Paris Opera Ballet Academy. Their technique was impeccable and these classes were the toughest challenge she'd ever faced in ballet. She learned so much and was happy just to be there and take in the culture of Paris.

As fate would have it, after weeks of classes she ran into Marcel Creshnov who was delighted to see her.

"You dance for me," he said.

He took her to the auditorium and watched as she performed a solo.

"Your dancing has improved."

"Thank you."

"I see you have been through much."

Celeste nods. "I have," she said.

"This is good. You put it in dance."

Celeste smiles.

"You are Odette," he says.

"What?"

"You will dance Odette and Odile."

"You're joking."

"I do not joke. Rehearsal begins Monday."

Celeste had no idea she'd receive such an honor. To dance Swan Lake with the Paris Opera Ballet is a dream come true.

After the most intense rehearsals, blood, sweat, and tears, opening night arrives.

Celeste steps onto the stage as Odette and looks into the audience as the music swells. She can't help but scan the front row, unsure of what she's looking for. She focuses on the music and the movements and mesmerizes the audience. It seems like a dream.

The time has come for the third act. Celeste's big moment where Odile tricks the prince and gets him to confess his love. As Celeste stands backstage she can't help but remember her performance in Fate. She lost focus and missed her last two fouettés. The stakes are higher as she prepares herself mentally for thirty-two fouettés without stopping. In practice, she mostly performed flawlessly, but there were a few times when she stumbled.

As she stands in front of the audience, the prince dances around her. She focuses on her spot, a clock on the wall. She lifts her arms as she remembers the words Marcel Creshnov spoke to her.

This will be your moment, and you will excel. There is no room for doubt. Take everything, the hurt, the pain, the happiness, the sorrow, the tears, and the smiles, and release them in fouettés. Yes?

"Yes," Celeste says under her breath. It's time. Arms

extended, and up, lift, extend, spin. Up, lift, extend, spin. Let it go, focus on your spot, breathe, twelve, thirteen, fourteen. Spin, lift extend spin, twenty, twenty-one. Focus, breathe, let it go. Thirty-on, thirty-two. Celeste lands to thunderous applause from the audience. You did it. She keeps her composure as the Prince dances for her.

When the show is over, the audience is beside themselves. Celeste gets a standing ovation and high praise. She bows thinking of her mother and father who weren't perfect, but they raised her and gave her opportunity and options in life, her friends Kierra and Chase who loved her and supported her, Charles who loved her and cherished her, and Red who shaped her. The curtain closes.

Celeste politely greets the dancers and goes to her dressing room. There's a knock on the door.

"Come in," Celeste says as she removes her makeup.

The door opens.

"Mom? Dad? What are you doing here?"

"I couldn't let this day go by without seeing my baby," her mother says.

Tears stream from Celeste's eyes as she embraces her mother. "How did you know?" she asks.

"We kept tabs on you when you left Houston," her father says.

"I don't know what to say."

"Don't say anything. I'm the one who needs to speak. I'm sorry, baby," her father says. "I failed to protect you, and I hurt you. I ran away, and I'm sorry."

"Your father has a lot to make up for, and so do I. I should've said something, but I won't be silent again. Your performance was inspiring. I've never seen you dance like that before."

"Thank you. I put everything into that performance. I released it. I don't want to be angry anymore. I don't want to cry anymore. I just want to live." She hugs both her parents as they cry. "It's okay," she says.

They release with deep breaths. "What are you two doing

here? Are you staying?"

"We don't know. We just know we had to see you."

"Maybe we can take you out to dinner," her dad says.

"Of course. Call me, and we'll set up a date."

There's a knock on the door.

"Come in," Celeste says.

"Excuse me."

"Marcel Creshnov, these are my parents."

"Such a pleasure," Marcel says. "Beautiful tonight, beautiful. May I speak with you for a moment?"

Celeste looks at her parents.

"Of course," her mother says. "We'll call you."

Celeste looks at Marcel. "Thank you so much. You taught me so much."

"No, no. It was all you. It was all here." He places a hand over her chest.

"My heart," she says.

"Yes, now come. You have a gentleman here to see you."

"I do? Who?"

He waits for you on the stage. Celeste feels butterflies. "I'll be right there."

She removes the bun and tussles her hair. Excitement has her on edge as she checks herself in the mirror one last time.

She calms herself before she steps onto the stage. He stands with his back to her. She smiles.

"Isn't this poetic," she says.

He turns around. "Charles," Celeste says, her eyes widened. "What are you doing here?" Charles looks sexier than he's ever looked. He's wearing a tailored designer tux. His hair and beard are perfectly groomed. He's quite a bit more muscular, and he still has that beautiful smile.

"Opening night in Paris. Where else would I be?"

Celeste smiles.

"You were spectacular. I've never seen anything like that."

"Thank you."

"How have you been?" he asks.

"I've been keeping busy getting my ass kicked in

rehearsals."

"It paid off."

"I guess it did."

"I miss you," Charles says.

Celeste nods wanting to say the words, but she's so full of emotion.

"I know you had to do what you had to do, and now I have to do what I have to do. I couldn't just let you walk out of my life and not try."

"You always were persistent."

"You were always worth it."

He touches the pointe shoe necklace around Celeste's neck and holds her gaze. There's passion and fire in his eyes like she's never seen.

"Was that your whole speech?" Celeste asks.

"Not enough?" Charles asks.

"I think you can do better," Celeste says.

They laugh.

"Let me take you to dinner. I'm sure I can come up with something. I want to catch up with the international superstar." Charles holds out his hand.

Celeste grabs it. "I'd like that," she says.

They sit in a French restaurant sipping wine while their meals are being prepared.

"I'm just happy to be here with you," Charles says.

"This is nice."

"Give me another chance," Charles blurts out.

"Charles, I don't know about that."

"I still love you, and I'll do anything for you."

"It's not that simple Charles. I'm not the same woman you fell in love with."

"I know that. I like this woman too."

"You don't know that, Charles."

"I know you."

"No, you don't and before things go any further you need to listen to me."

"Go ahead."

238

"First of all, thank you. You defended me when no one else would, and it almost cost you your life. I felt a crippling amount of guilt thinking you died because of me."

"It's fine."

"It's not fine. I know you think Jackson captured me and tricked me and held me against my will and some of that is true, but it's not all black and white."

"I don't need to know."

"You do. I owe you the truth, and you owe it to yourself to listen. Any decision you make needs to be informed."

"Celeste, please, don't."

"I cheated on you, with Jackson."

"Charles's head drops."

"He didn't force me. I wanted it. I felt this strong desire and I didn't want to resist it any longer. It's not that I didn't care about you. I did. I just made a mistake, one that costed me dearly. I immediately regretted it and I tried to get away. That's when he told me I couldn't go anywhere. I convinced him to let me see my parents, and then I came running to you, and you were so kind and I didn't deserve you. You didn't deserve what I did."

Charles's nostrils flare, and his smile disappears. "Okay," he tries to come to terms with what Celeste says.

"While I lived with Jackson we had some turbulent moments and we had some good moments. He never forced himself on me, and though I was confused and conflicted I laid with him because I wanted to. He and I did have something."

"Why are you telling me this?"

"I need to be honest. I don't want it hanging over my head, and I don't want to lie to you."

"Alright."

"Is that all you have to say?" she asks.

Charles thinks for a moment. The waiter brings their food, and Celeste waits anxiously for the man to leave.

Charles takes a deep breath. "I understand. It doesn't change how I feel about you."

"Do you mean that?"

"Yes. Why don't we start over?"

"Why don't we take our time?" she says.

"All I need is a chance," Charles says.

Celeste holds up her glass. "To new beginnings."

Charles clinks his glass against hers. "To new beginnings."

Chapter 24

"Oh, my word. Where have you been?" Harrison is in the kitchen preparing dinner when Celeste surprises him.

"Harrison, it's so good to see you." Celeste greets her good friend with a warm embrace.

"You too, dear. Tell me how you've been. Sit on down."

"I've been great. I went to Paris."

"Well, look at you." Harrison makes a plate for Celeste and a glass of wine.

"It was amazing. It was more than I ever dreamed. I danced with The Paris Opera Ballet. I was the lead in Swan Lake."

"Wow."

Celeste tells Harrison all about her trip while she eats the hearty meal he prepared. She waits for Harrison to update her about Red, but he doesn't say anything.

"How is he?" she finally asks.

"He's surviving. He ain't been the same since you left. The boy couldn't get out of bed for three days."

"I know it was rough on him."

"You have no idea. He pretended to be sick, but it was bad."

"It was hard for me too."

"He's never known heartache like that before."

"I never wanted that for him."

"And you know Olivia's gone."

"She is? What happened?"

"She was behind all of it. She set you and Red up. She brought that Charles fellow around here."

"She did?" Charles hadn't mentioned that part to Celeste.

"It was quite the scandal, but you won't have to worry about her anymore."

"I never trusted her. I swear she was going to let that mountain lion eat me before Red came along. I just didn't say anything, because I didn't think he'd listen."

"Well, it looks like you were right about her. I'm just so glad you're okay."

"Harrison, I wouldn't be okay if it wasn't for you. You gave me hope when I didn't see a way," Celeste places her hand on top of his hand and tries to stop herself from crying.

"Now you quit it with all that nonsense. I didn't do anything. You did. You hear?"

Celeste nods.

"Is he here?" she asks.

Harrison nods.

"Do you think he'll want to see me?"

"He's proud."

"I know."

"He's wounded."

"I know."

"He won't be very receptive."

Celeste drops her head. "I know."

"So you make him listen."

Celeste smiles. "I will."

"He's up there in the study. Why don't you take him this?" Harrison hands Celeste Red's food and a glass of wine.

Celeste heads up the stairs and opens the office door.

"Don't you knock?" Red says as he's writing on some papers at his desk.

"I brought your dinner, Alpha Red."

Red looks up, dying to get a glimpse of Celeste, and then he turns his attention back to his work. "Just sit it on the table."

"I've been staying on top of the news. Crime is down, employment is up, and there's a new theme park coming to the city."

"Really," Red says.

"I think the city of Houston owes you more than they'll ever know."

"What are you doing here?"

"I went to Paris."

"I know."

"I conquered my fear."

"What fear? Falling?"

"No, greatness. I danced at the best ballet company in the world. I was the lead in Swan Lake, and I didn't fall, and I didn't hold back, and that's because of you."

"Congratulations."

"I was offered a contract."

"You didn't have to come here to tell me that."

"I turned it down."

Red finally looks up. "Celeste, what the fuck do you want?"

"Charles came to visit me opening night. He said he still loved me."

"You can leave now."

"We talked. I told him the truth, how I cheated on him because I wanted to."

"Good for you."

"He said it didn't matter, that he just wanted to be with me."

"I hope the two of you are very happy together. Now if you'll excuse me."

"We dated. I wanted to take things slowly, and he respected that."

"He always was a swell guy, but I have work to do."

"In the end, I left Paris when the show's run was over, but it was one of the best experiences of my life."

Red has heard enough. "That's great Celeste."

"Do you want to know what the best experience of my life was?"

"No. I want you to leave, but you never could listen."

"The best experience of my life was falling in love with you."

"Come again."

She stalks closer to him. "There's something here, but it scares you."

"Nothing scares me."

"Then you're lucky. I'm terrified standing in front of you right now because I tried to leave, but something made me come back."

Red's wolf is overjoyed and pushing him to reconcile with their mate. "I don't believe this shit."

"I realized that if things had been different, and you had pursued me even though I had a boyfriend, eventually you would've worn me down, and Charles and I would've probably broken up. And if you had asked me on a date I would've eventually said yes, and it wouldn't have taken me long to realize that I need you. I need my mate."

"What about Paris?"

"I turned them down."

"What about Charles?"

"I was honest with him. I told him I didn't love him the way he loved me."

"You think that you can just walk back in here like nothing happened, and I'm just going to take you back with open arms. This isn't a fucking fairytale."

"Isn't it? You told me you've only been in love once, and I pray you were talking about me because when I said me too, I was talking about you."

"That's enough, Celeste. I can't do this."

"I thought I was in love before but it was nothing like this thing between us. It can't be ignored."

Red looks at the water ring on his desk. "You're free of me, and I've come to terms with that."

"I don't want you to come to terms with that. I want to

come home, and I promise, I'll never leave you again. We can live like normal people. Go to work, come home, make love, have some pups, run the city, just you and me, and our pack, of course."

"Our pack?"

"I am alpha female, and I'm putting my foot down. I've been accepted into the pack, and you can't get rid of me. That's an order."

"Is that right?"

"You may address me as Alpha Celeste."

Red smiles. "Alpha Celeste, huh? How do I know you won't run out on me again?"

"Close your eyes. Take a deep breath. Listen to me breathe. Listen to my heart. Do you believe me?"

"Yes."

Celeste runs to Red. He stands and lifts her off the floor and spins her around. Their lips collide.

"I missed you so much, Jackson."

"Baby, you have no idea." Red holds Celeste tighter than he's ever held her before.

"There is one thing," Celeste says.

"What's that?"

"I've confessed my love for you twice now. Feel free to throw it out there whenever you're ready."

Red kisses his mate. "Is that what the movies say I'm supposed to do next?"

"It is."

"I love you, Celeste."

"I love you too."

He holds her hand up. "You're wearing my ring."

"Forever, mate."

"Take your clothes off," he says.

"First I demand a story," Celeste says.

"What are you in the mood for?"

Celeste picks a book from the bookshelf. "How about this one?"

"Greek mythology," Red says.

Celeste sits on his lap and lays her head on his chest. "Yes, please."

With his arms around her, Red opens the book and reads to his mate."

Epilogue

The room is pitch black except for seven spotlights that shine overhead. There are six chairs at a long table and one chair at a small table in the center.

"Thank you all for coming. We are gathered here today for a good reason. Thanks to the efforts of Jackson Redding, our city is thriving and is a safer place. We owe him a great deal but something must be done to maintain order. The Guardians have served the city faithfully, but not as much as you've served your own interests. You all have sinned, and you need to make it up to the people of this great city. I have the connections. I have the ears of the people, and I have the power. I will lead The Guardians into a brighter future and restore that which has been destroyed by you all and by my father."

"Excuse me."

"Yes, Judge Willis."

"Why should we listen to you?"

"Because I have the power of the alpha behind me." The spotlight over Celeste widens to reveal Jackson 'Red Paw' Redding standing behind his wife.

"Does anyone have a problem with that?" Celeste asks.

"No," they all say.

"I didn't think so. You may all leave. I'll be in touch," Celeste says.

Everyone looks around.

"Now," her voice is eerily calm and The Guardians rise and exit the underground room.

Jackson steps in front of his wife. "Principal dancer by day and most powerful woman in the city by night." He rubs Celeste's belly. "Did you see that baby boy? Your mommy is running shit."

Thank you for reading Stealing the Alpha's mate By Zoe Ray. Don't forget to leave a review and recommend this book on Amazon, Goodreads, and BookBub.

Follow Zoe Ray on social media: https://linktr.ee/zoeray

Website
http://www.sincerelyzoeray.com

BookBub
https://www.bookbub.com/profile/zoe-ray

Goodreads
https://www.goodreads.com/author/show/14773767.Zoe_Ray

Facebook
http://www.facebook.com/sincerelyzoeray

Instagram
http://www.instagram.com/sincerelyzoeray

Twitter
http://www.twitter.com/sincerelyzoeray

Amazon
https://www.amazon.com/author/zoeray

Other titles by Zoe Ray

Alpha Boss
Mark Of The Dragon
Alliance
Alpha Professor
Take Me: My Night With Preston (One Night Stand Series Book 1)

Teach Me: My Night With Wade (One Night Stand Series Book 2)

Bundles

The Alpha Boss Collection (4 book bundle)

Romantic Suspense
He's Mine Not Hers